The Apartment

DANIELLE STEEL

The Apartment

A Novel

RANDOM HOUSE
LARGE PRINT

All rights reserved.
Published in the United States of America by Random House Large Print in association with Delacorte Press, an imprint of Random House, a division of Penguin Random House LLC, New York.

Cover design by Lynn Andreozzi
Cover illustration by Stephen Youll

The Library of Congress has established a cataloging-in-publication record for this title.

ISBN: 978-0-7352-0999-2

www.randomhouse.com/largeprint

FIRST LARGE PRINT EDITION

Printed in the United States of America

10 9 8 7 6 5 4 3 2 1

This Large Print Edition published in accord with the standards of the N.A.V.H.

3361405972543 1

To my beloved children,
Beatrix, Trevor, Todd, Nick,
Sam, Victoria, Vanessa,
Maxx, and Zara,

My prayer for each of you
is a happy ending,
with the right people and partners.
May your lives be sweet,
and life be kind to you.

I wish you peace, happiness,
and love,
with all my heart and all my love,

Mom/DS

The Apartment

Chapter 1

Claire Kelly hurried up the stairs, as best she could, carrying two bags of groceries, to the fourth-floor apartment she had lived in for nine years, in Hell's Kitchen, in New York. She was wearing a short black cotton dress and sexy high-heeled sandals with ribbons that laced up to her knees. They were samples she had bought at a trade show in Italy the year before. It was a hot September day, the Tuesday after Labor Day, and it was her turn to buy the groceries for the three women she shared the apartment with. And whatever the weather, it was a hike up to the loft on the fourth floor. She had been living there since her second year at Parsons School of Design when she was nineteen, and it was home to four of them now.

Claire was a shoe designer for Arthur Adams, a line of ultraconservative classic shoes. They were well made but unexciting and stymied all her creative sense. Walter Adams, whose father had founded the company, staunchly believed that high-fashion shoes were a passing trend, and he discarded all her more innovative designs. As a result, Claire's workdays were a source of constant frustration. The business was hanging on but not growing, and Claire felt she could do so much more with it, if he'd let her. Walter resisted her every step of the way on every subject. She was sure that business, and their profits, would have improved if he listened to her, but Walter was seventy-two years old, believed in what they were doing, and did not believe in high-style shoes, no matter how fervently she begged him to try.

Claire had no choice but to do what he wanted her to, if she wanted to keep her job. Her dream was to design the kind of sexy, fashionable shoes she liked to wear, but there was no chance of that at Arthur Adams, Inc. Walter hated change, much to Claire's chagrin. And as long as she stayed there, she knew she would be designing sensible, classic shoes forever. Even their flats were too conservative for her. Walter let her add a touch of whimsy to their summer sandals sometimes for their clients who went to the Hamptons, Newport, Rhode Island, or Palm Beach. His mantra was that their customer was wealthy, conservative, and older and knew what to expect from the brand. And nothing Claire could say would change that. He didn't want to appeal to younger customers. He preferred to rely on their old ones. There was no arguing with Walter about it. And year after year, there were no surprises in the merchandise they shipped. She was frustrated, but at least she had a job, and had been there for four years. Before that, she had worked for an inexpensive line whose shoes were fun but cheaply made. And the business had folded after two years. Arthur Adams was all about quality and traditional design. And as long as she followed directions, the brand and her job were secure.

At twenty-eight, Claire would have loved to add at least a few exciting designs to the line, and try something new. Walter wouldn't hear of it, and scolded her sternly when she tried to push, which she still did. She had never given up trying to add some real style to what she did. He had hired her because she was a good, solid, well-trained designer who knew how to create shoes that were comfortable to wear and easy to produce. They had them made in Italy at the same factory Walter's father had used, in a small town called Parabiago, close to Milan. Claire went there three or four times a year to discuss production with them. They were one of the most reliable, respected factories in Italy, and they produced several more exciting lines than theirs. Claire looked at them longingly whenever she was at the factory, and wondered if she'd ever have a chance to design shoes she loved. It was a dream she refused to give up.

Her long, straight blond hair hung damply on her neck by the time she reached the fourth floor in high heels. After nine years, she was used to the climb, and claimed that it kept her legs in shape. She had found the apartment by accident, by walking around the neighborhood. She had been living in Parsons's freshman dorm at the time, on Eleventh Street, and had wandered uptown through Chelsea, and continued north into what had once been one of the worst areas of New York, but had slowly become gentrified. Since the nineteenth century, Hell's Kitchen had had a reputation for slums, tenements, gang fights, and murders among the Irish, Italian, and later Puerto Rican hoodlums who lived there, in a constant state of war. All of that was gone by the time Claire arrived from San Francisco to attend design school. It was the same school where her mother had studied interior design in her youth. It had been Claire's dream to attend Parsons and study fashion design. Despite their tight budget, her mother had saved every penny she could and made it possible for her to enroll and live in the dorm for her first year.

By second semester, Claire had been looking for an apartment for a while, and had heard of Hell's Kitchen, but never ventured there until a spring Saturday afternoon. Stretching from the upper Thirties to the Fifties, on the West Side, from Eighth Avenue to the Hudson River, Hell's Kitchen had become home to actors, playwrights, and dancers, for its proximity to the theater district, the famed Actors Studio, the Baryshnikov Arts Center, and the Alvin Ailey American Dance Theater. Many of the old buildings were still there, some of them warehouses and factories that had been turned into apartments. But in spite of its modest improvements, the neighborhood still had much of its original look, and many of the structures still looked run-down.

She had seen a small sign in a window, indicating an apartment for rent, and called the number listed on it that night. The owner said he had a loft available on the fourth floor. The building was an old factory that had been changed into living space fifteen years before, and he said it was rent stabilized, which sounded hopeful to her. When she went to see it the next day, she was stunned to find the space was vast. There was a huge loftlike living room with brick walls and a concrete floor painted a sandy color, four large storerooms that could be used as bedrooms, two clean, modern bathrooms, and a basic kitchen with the bare essentials from IKEA. It was far more space than Claire needed, but it was bright and sunny and in decent condition, the building had been modestly restored. The rent was exactly twice what she could afford, and she couldn't imagine living there alone. The halls of the building were a little dark, the neighborhood still had a slightly rough quality to it, and it was located on Thirty-ninth Street between Ninth and Tenth Avenues. The owner told her proudly that it had been one of the worst streets in Hell's Kitchen forty years before, but there was no evidence of it

now. The street just looked shabby and still somewhat industrial, but she was excited by the loft. All
she needed to do was find a roommate to live there
with her and pay half the rent. She didn't say anything about it to her mother, she didn't want to
panic her over the expense. Claire had figured out
that if she found someone to share the rent with
her, it might be cheaper than the dorms.

The following week she met a girl at a party, who
was a creative writing major at NYU. At twenty,
she was a year older than Claire, and had grown
up in L.A. Abby Williams was as small as Claire
was tall. She had dark, curly hair and almost black
eyes, in contrast to Claire's long straight blond
hair and blue eyes. She seemed like a nice person
and was passionate about her writing. She said she
wrote short stories and wanted to write a novel
when she graduated, and she mentioned casually
that her parents worked in TV. Claire later learned
that Abby's father was the well-known head of a
major network, and her mother had had a string of
hit TV shows as a writer/producer. Both Abby and
Claire were only children, and were dedicated to
their studies and ambitions, determined to justify
their parents' faith in them. They went to see the
apartment together, and Abby fell in love with it
too. They had no idea how they would furnish it
other than at garage sales over time, but they figured out that it was within their budgets, and two
months later, with their parents' cautious blessing

and signatures on the lease, they moved in, and had been there ever since, for the past nine years.

The two women had shared the apartment for four years, and after they graduated, in an effort to rely less on their parents, be more independent, and cut costs, they decided to take in two more roommates, to reduce their expenses even further.

Claire had met Morgan Shelby at a party she went to on the Upper East Side, given by a group of young stockbrokers someone had introduced her to. The party was boring, the men full of themselves, and she and Morgan had started to talk. Morgan was working on Wall Street, and had a roommate she hated in an apartment she couldn't afford and said she was looking for an apartment farther downtown that would be closer to where she worked. They exchanged phone numbers, and two days later, after talking to Abby, Claire called her and invited her to come and take a look at the apartment in Hell's Kitchen.

Claire's only hesitation was that she wondered if Morgan might be too old. She was twenty-eight at the time, five years older than Claire, and had a serious job in finance. Morgan was pretty with well-cut dark hair and long legs. Claire had been in her first job at the shoe company that later folded and was living on a tight budget, and Abby was waiting on tables at a restaurant and trying to write a novel, and they both wondered if Morgan was too "grown up," but she loved the loft the minute she saw it, and almost begged them to let her move in. The location was much more convenient for her job on Wall Street. They had dinner with her twice and liked her. She was intelligent and employed, she had a great sense of humor, her credit references were solid, and six weeks later she moved in. The rest was history, she had been there for five years, and now they were best friends.

Abby met Sasha Hartman through a friend of a friend from NYU, two months after Morgan moved in, and they were still looking for a fourth roommate. Sasha was in medical school at NYU, hoping to specialize in OB/GYN, and the location worked for her too. She liked all three women living in the loft and assured them that she'd never be around. She was either in class, at the hospital, or at the library studying for exams. She was a soft-spoken young woman from Atlanta and mentioned that she had a sister in New York too, living in Tribeca. She failed to mention that they were identical twins, which caused considerable consternation the day she moved in, when her sister suddenly appeared, with the same mane of blond hair, in the same T-shirt and jeans, and the three residents of the apartment thought they were seeing double. Valentina, Sasha's twin, enjoyed confusing them, and had done so regularly in the five years since. The two sisters were close, Valentina had a key to the apartment, and they were as different as night and day. Valentina was a successful model, involved in a high-powered world, and Sasha was a dedicated doctor, whose wardrobe consisted mainly of hospital scrubs, and was in her residency at NYU Langone Medical Center five years after she'd moved in.

They were like unusual and unexpected ingredients and component parts of a fabulous meal. For five years the four roommates had lived together, helped each other, loved one another, and become fast friends. Whatever the recipe was, as different as they were, and their lives were, it worked. They had become a family by choice, and the loft in Hell's Kitchen had become home to them. Their living arrangement suited all four women perfectly. They were busy, had full lives and demanding jobs, and they enjoyed the time they spent together. And all four still agreed, the apartment Claire had discovered nine years before was a rare find, and a gem. They loved living in Hell's Kitchen, for its history and still slightly seedy quality, and it was safe. People said it looked a lot the way Greenwich Village had fifty years before, and they could never have found three thousand square feet at that price anywhere else in the city. The area had none of the polish and pretension and astronomically high rents of SoHo, the Meatpacking District, the West Village, Tribeca, or even Chelsea. Hell's Kitchen had a reality to it that had been dulled or lost in other places. All four women loved their home, and had no desire to live anywhere else.

There were inconveniences to living in a walkup, but it didn't really bother them. They were a block away from one of the more illustrious firehouses in the city, Engine 34/Ladder 21, and on busy nights, they could hear the fire engines scream out of the station, but they'd gotten used to it. And they had all chipped in to purchase air-conditioning units that took a while to work in the vast space they used as a living room, but the place cooled down eventually, and the heat worked fairly decently in winter, and their bedrooms were small, cozy, and warm. They had all the comforts they wanted and needed.

When they moved in together, they brought their dreams, hopes, careers, and histories with them, and little by little, they discovered each other's fears and secrets.

Claire's career path was clear. She wanted to design fabulous shoes, and be famous in the fashion world for it someday. She knew that was never going to happen designing for Arthur Adams, but she couldn't take the risk of giving up a job she needed. Her work was sacred to her. She had learned a lesson from her mother, who had left a promising job at an important New York interior design firm to follow Claire's father to San Francisco when they got married, where he started a business that floundered for five years and then folded. He had never wanted Claire's mother to work again, and she had spent years taking small decorating jobs in secret, so as not to bruise his ego, but they needed the money, and her carefully hidden savings had made it possible for Claire to attend first private school and then Parsons.

Her father's second business had met the same fate as his first one, and it depressed Claire to hear her mother encourage him to try some new endeavor again after both failures, until he finally wound up selling real estate, which he hated, and he had become sullen, withdrawn, and resentful. She had watched her mother abandon her dreams for him, shelve her own career, pass up bigger opportunities, and hide her talents, in order to shore him up and protect him.

It had given Claire an iron determination never to compromise her career for a man, and she had said for years that she never wanted to get married. Claire had asked her mother if she regretted walking away from the career she could have had in New York, and Sarah Kelly said she didn't. She loved her husband and made the best of the hand she'd been dealt, which Claire found particularly sad. Their whole life had been spent making do, depriving themselves of luxuries and sometimes even vacations, so Claire could go to a good school, which her mother had always paid for from her secret fund. To Claire, marriage meant a life of sacrifice, self-denial, and deprivation, and she swore she would never let it happen to her. No man was ever going to interfere with her career, or steal her dreams from her.

And Morgan shared the same fear with Claire. Both of them had watched their mothers diminish their lives for the men they married, although Morgan's more dramatically than Claire's. Her parents' marriage had been a disaster. Her mother had walked away from a promising career with the Boston Ballet when she got pregnant with Morgan's brother, Oliver, and then with Morgan soon after. She had regretted giving up dancing all her life, developed a serious drinking problem, and basically drank herself to death when Morgan and her brother were in college, and their father had died in an accident soon after.

Morgan had put herself through college and business school, and had only recently finished paying off her student loans. And she was convinced that sacrificing her career as a dancer, to get married and have kids, had ruined her mother's life. She had no intention of letting that happen to her. Her parents' violent fights and her mother drinking until she passed out, or being drunk when they got home from school, were all Morgan remembered of her childhood.

Morgan's brother, Oliver, was two years older, and had moved to New York from Boston after college too, and worked in PR. The firm he worked for specialized in sports teams, and his partner was Greg Trudeau, the famed ice hockey goalie from Montreal who was the star of the New York Rangers. Morgan loved going to games with Oliver to cheer for Greg. She'd taken her roommates a few times, and they'd all enjoyed it, and the two men were frequent visitors to the apartment, and were beloved by all.

Sasha's family situation was more complicated. Her parents had had a bitter divorce, from which their mother had never recovered, after Sasha graduated from college and Valentina was already working as a model in New York. Their father had fallen in love with a young model in one of the department stores he owned, and married her a year later, and had two daughters by his new wife, which enraged the twins' mother even more, proving that hell hath no fury like a woman whose husband leaves her and marries a twenty-three-year-old model. But he seemed happy whenever the twins saw him, and he loved his three- and five-year-old daughters. Valentina had no interest in them and thought their father was ridiculous, but Sasha thought their half-sisters were sweet and had remained close to her father after the divorce.

Their mother was a divorce lawyer in Atlanta, and was known to be a shark in the courtroom, particularly since her own divorce. Sasha went back to Atlanta as seldom as possible, and dreaded speaking to her mother on the phone, who still made vicious comments about Sasha's father years after he remarried. Talking to her was exhausting.

Abby's parents were still married and got along, and their busy careers in television had kept them from being attentive to their daughter, but they were always supportive of Abby and her writing.

The four women's careers had gone forward at a steady pace in the five years they'd lived together, Claire at both shoe companies she'd worked for. She dreamed of working for a high-end shoe company one day, but she was making a decent salary, even if she wasn't proud of the shoes she was designing.

Morgan worked for George Lewis, one of the whizzes of Wall Street. At thirty-nine, George had built an empire for himself, in private investment management, and Morgan loved her work with him, consulting with clients on their investments and flying to exciting meetings in other cities on his plane. She admired her boss immensely and at thirty-three, she was meeting her goals.

Sasha was doing her residency in obstetrics, and wanted to pursue a double specialty of high-risk pregnancies and infertility, so she had years ahead of her at the same frenetic pace. And she loved coming home to her roommates for conversation and comfort when she finally got off duty and came back to the apartment to sleep and unwind.

The only one whose path had altered considerably was Abby, who had abandoned her novel halfway through it three years before, when she met and fell in love with Ivan Jones, an Off Off Broadway producer who had convinced her to write experimental plays for his theater. Her roommates, and parents, had preferred her fiction and prose to what she was writing for Ivan. He had assured her that what she was writing now was far more important, avant-garde, and likely to make a name for her than the "commercial drivel" she had written before, and she believed him. He had promised to produce her plays, but hadn't done so yet after three years, and only produced his own. Her roommates suspected he was a fraud, but Abby was convinced he was talented, sincere, and a genius. Ivan was forty-six years old, and Abby was working as his assistant, vacuuming the theater, painting scenery, and working the box office for him. For the past three years she had been his full-time slave. He had never been married, but had three children by two different women. He never saw his children, because he said the situations with their mothers were just too complicated and interfered with his artistic flow. And through all his weak excuses about why he never produced her plays, Abby was still convinced he would, and believed him to be a man of his word, despite evidence to the contrary. She was blind to his sins and faults, among them the promises he constantly broke. And much to her roommates' dismay, Abby was always willing to believe him and give him another chance. Ivan was like playing a slot machine that never paid off. The others had lost patience with him long since. They didn't find him charming, but Abby did. She was trusting and loving and hung on his every word. Her roommates no longer discussed it with her, because it upset them all. She was totally under Ivan's spell, and sacrificing her life, time, and writing to him, and getting nothing in return.

Her parents had asked her to come back to L.A., to work on her novel again, or to let them help her find work in feature films or TV. Ivan told her to do so would be to become a commercial sellout just like them, and he insisted that she was better and more talented than that, so she stayed with him, waiting for him to put on one of her plays. She wasn't stupid, but she was loyal, needy, and naïve, and he took full advantage of it at every turn. None of her roommates liked him, and hated what he did to her. But they no longer said it to Abby— there was no point. She believed everything he told her. And they knew he had borrowed money from her several times, and never paid her back. She was certain that he would when things were better for him. He didn't support his children either. Their mothers were both actresses who had become successful after their affairs with him, and he said they were far better able to provide for the children than he. He was a man who shirked responsibility at every turn. He had bewitched Abby, and they all hoped she would wake up soon. She hadn't in three years. There was no sign of her awakening from the nightmare of Ivan yet. Her roommates, however, were wide awake, and hated him for the way he used and lied to her.

And it wasn't the first inadequate relationship Abby had had. She was their resident collector of wounded birds. In the five years they'd all lived together, there had been an actor who was dead broke and could never get a job, even as a waiter, and had spent a month on their couch until the others complained. Abby had been in love with him, and he had been in love with a girl who was in rehab for six months. There had been writers, and other actors, and a down-on-his-luck though brilliant British aristocrat who had constantly borrowed money from her, and a series of losers, aspiring artists, and men who had disappointed her constantly until she gave up. And unfortunately she wasn't ready to give up on Ivan yet.

Claire had only had casual dates for the past several years. She worked so hard she rarely had time to date and didn't care. She worked late at night and on weekends. Her career as a designer meant more to her than any man. She was burning with the ambition her mother had never had. And nothing and no one was going to take that from her. Of that she was sure. She rarely had more than a few dates with any man. She had never had a serious love affair, except with the shoes she designed. Men were always surprised to discover how passionate she was about her work, and how unavailable she became once they got interested in her. She saw any serious romance as a threat to her career and emotional well-being. She kept a design table in the corner of the living room at the apartment, and often was still sitting there after the others had gone to bed.

And while in medical school, and now as a resident in OB/GYN, Sasha had no time to date. She had brief relationships from time to time, but she lived a life and a schedule that made any kind of personal life nearly impossible. She was either on duty, exhausted, or asleep. She was spectacular-looking, but she literally had no time for a man, and spent her life in hospital scrubs, unlike her equally beautiful twin, who partied all the time. Sasha liked the idea of marriage and a family in theory, but for her it was still years away. And in reality, she often thought that staying single would be simpler. And the men she went out with occasionally got tired of the demands on her within weeks.

Of the four roommates, only Morgan had a serious relationship, and fortunately they all liked him, since he frequently spent nights at the apartment. Max Murphy had an apartment of his own on the Upper West Side, but theirs was more convenient for him for work, since his restaurant was around the corner. They had all met him at the same time, one night a year after Morgan and Sasha moved in, when the four of them went to try out the brand-new restaurant, which had been an old broken-down neighborhood bar he had bought and transformed into a popular hangout with a lively bar and great food. He and Morgan had started dating three days later. In the four years since, the restaurant was booming and a major neighborhood success. "Max's" was keeping him busy day and night. He was there until two A.M. every night, and back at work by ten in the morning to get ready for lunch.

Max was a great guy and they all loved him. He was a sports nut, a great chef himself, and a hard worker. He was an all-around nice person from a large Irish family that was always fighting but basically loved each other. At thirty-five, he would have loved to get married and have kids, but Morgan had told him clearly right from the beginning that marriage and children were not in her plans. Max thought she might soften on the subject, but she hadn't in four years, and he didn't push her. She was thirty-three years old, he figured they had time, and he was busy with the restaurant, and hoping to open at least one more, which was expensive, so he was in no hurry either. But he had come to realize how adamant Morgan was about never getting married or having kids. Their relationship was warm and solid, but Morgan's career meant everything to her, and she had no intention of putting it at risk.

Claire changed into shorts and a T-shirt and flat sandals when she got home from work, and Abby walked in a little while later, wearing overalls over a torn tank top, covered in paint. She had some of the paint in her hair and a blue smudge on her face, as Claire glanced up from her drawing board and smiled at her. Morgan usually came home late from work after meeting with clients, often over a drink, and Sasha came home from the hospital at all hours, depending on her shift, and stumbled straight into bed.

"Hi," Claire said with a warm smile. "I can guess what you did today."

"I've been breathing paint fumes all day," Abby said with a tired groan as she collapsed on the couch, happy to be home. Ivan had a meeting with a potential backer that night, but had said he might call her later. He lived in a studio in the East Village barely bigger than a closet. It was rent-stabilized, a sixth-floor walkup, and he had sublet it furnished from a friend.

"There's some stuff in the fridge," Claire told her. "I bought groceries on the way home. There's sushi that looks pretty good." They took turns buying basic food for everyone, which worked better than trying to figure out who had eaten what. They were generous and good-natured, and never quibbled over money. They were respectful of one another, which was why their living arrangement worked so well.

"I'm too tired to eat," Abby said, and the paint had made her feel sick. Ivan had changed his mind about the color of the scenery four times. And he was playwright, director, and producer, so he had a right to dictate how the scenery should look. "I think I'm going to have a bath and go to bed. How was your day?" Abby inquired, as Claire thought, as she always did, that it was nice coming home to people who asked, and cared. At home, her parents never talked to each other and hadn't in years. It was easier that way.

"Long. A running battle," Claire answered, with a discouraged look. "Walter hated all my new designs and wants them 'modified' to suit their style. And I have a new intern, the daughter of a friend of his in Paris. She looks about twelve years old, and hates everything about the States. According to her, it's all better in Paris, and no one here knows what they're doing. Her father is a banker, and her mother works for Chanel. I think she's all of twenty-two and knows it all. Walter is doing her parents a favor, so I got stuck with her."

"Maybe she'd like to paint scenery," Abby said with a grin. "Or vacuum the theater. That would whip her into shape."

"She'd rather criticize my designs," Claire said, correcting something on her drawing board, as Morgan walked in. She was all legs and high heels in a navy linen suit with a short skirt. Her dark hair was fashionably cut to her shoulders, and she was carrying several takeout containers from Max's restaurant. She set them down on the industrial metal table Claire's mother had found for them at a terrific price online.

"Those stairs are going to kill me one of these days. Max gave us roast chicken and Caesar salad." He was always sending food for them, or cooking for them on Sunday nights, which they all enjoyed. "Have you guys eaten?" Morgan smiled at them, as she sat down next to Abby on the couch. "Looks like you've been painting scenery again," Morgan said matter-of-factly. They were used to seeing her covered in paint. She didn't look like a writer—she looked like a house painter most of the time. "You know, you could get a job painting for a contractor. At least you'd be union and get decent pay," she teased her, as she kicked off her high heels and stretched her legs. "The restaurant was jammed tonight," she commented.

"It always is," Claire answered. "Thanks for the food." She got up from her drawing table, lured by the delicious scent of what Max had given them. The chicken smelled delicious.

The three of them went to the kitchen, got out plates and cutlery, and Morgan opened a bottle of wine for them to share, as Abby went to get napkins and glasses, and a minute later they were seated at the table, laughing and talking, as Claire described her new intern to them. Nothing ever seemed as bad when they could laugh about it, or talk about a problem. Their exchanges were always good-humored, there was no jealousy between them, they were just good friends with no ax to grind, and they knew each other well, their weaknesses and their strengths. They were forgiving, tolerant of occasional bad moods, and were a strong support system in the challenges that they faced. All of them had demanding jobs that added stress to their lives.

They had just finished eating when Sasha walked in, her blond hair in a rubber band lumped on her head with two pens sticking through it and a stethoscope around her neck. She was wearing clogs, and the familiar scrubs that were the mainstay of her wardrobe. Claire couldn't remember the last time she'd seen her in a dress.

"I delivered triplets today," she announced to the three women sitting at the table, as she sat down next to Morgan.

"At least you did something useful," Claire said admiringly, and Sasha shook her head when Morgan offered her a glass of wine.

"I'm still on call. I may have to go back later. We almost lost one of the triplets, but there were three OBs in the room. They let me close the C-section, but it was pretty impressive. We had three pediatricians too. The mom was forty-six—they were IVF babies. They were two months premature, but it looks like they're going to be okay. I don't know why anyone would want triplets at her age. Her husband's in his sixties—he'll be in his eighties when they graduate from college. But they were ecstatic, first babies for both of them. They got married last year. Instant family. She's a big deal on Wall Street, and he's a CEO of something. Maybe that'll be us someday," Sasha said with a smile as she helped herself to some of the Caesar salad. She'd had a sandwich at the hospital, but she could never resist the food Max sent home with Morgan. It was always delicious.

"Don't count on me," Morgan said, finishing her wine, at the thought of having triplets in her forties. "I'd jump off a bridge first."

"I'd love to have a baby," Abby said softly, "just not yet."

"And hopefully not with Ivan," Morgan said honestly, "if you want him to support it. You need a guy with a job, if you want to have kids, and be involved with someone responsible," which Ivan wasn't. They knew that Abby's parents still helped her at twenty-nine, which she was embarrassed about. She wanted to be independent, but so far no one had bought her work.

Claire made a decent salary, and Morgan worked hard to make what she did working for George Lewis. Her parents had been dead broke, and she and her brother had had jobs since they were kids. They both knew what it had been like to grow up with too little money. Abby and Sasha had been born into wealthy families, or at least families who had money and were very "comfortable." But the different circumstances the four roommates had known as kids didn't separate them. They were open about their previous lives and histories and were well aware that no life, with or without money, was as easy as it appeared from the outside.

"I don't want kids for a long time," Abby said thoughtfully.

"You too can have a baby at forty-six," Sasha said with a grin, helping herself to a piece of chicken. They all looked pleased to be together, sharing a meal, and relaxing at the end of their day.

"That seems a little late," Abby said, looking pensive. She took everything literally, just as she believed Ivan's lies.

"No shit," Sasha said, and laughed. "Remind me not to have babies when I'm nearly fifty." But she couldn't imagine having kids anytime soon either. She still had years of studying ahead of her, with the specialty she'd chosen. "I don't know what the answer is. Life moves so damn fast, and then you wake up one day and suddenly you're old. I can't believe I'm already thirty-two. It feels like I was eighteen about two weeks ago." Sasha shook her head as she thought about it.

"Don't whine to me—I'm a year older than you are." Morgan spoke to her directly, and then looked at the other two women seriously. "And you guys are just babies." She was five years older than Claire, and four years older than Abby. "It all goes by too fast, and there's so much I still want to do, to get where I want to be." She had come a long, long way in the years since she'd graduated from business school, and by most people's standards she was very successful, but Morgan had always set the bar high for herself.

Sasha stood up from the table then with a yawn, and walked her plate into the kitchen to put it in the dishwasher. "I'd better get to bed in case they call me later," she said, and disappeared into her bedroom a moment later, after thanking Morgan for the dinner.

Abby went to take a shower after that, to try and get the paint off. And a little while later, Morgan went to bed with some reading to do for work, and Claire went back to the drawing board. It had been a nice evening. It was rare for all of them to be home for dinner together. It made the day seem gentler and the bumps in it less unpleasant. Claire smiled to herself, thinking of her roommates. They were all good women, and the people who meant the most to her, other than her mother. They each supported one another in their endeavors. It was exactly what a family should be, Claire thought, as she came up with a detail she really liked on one of her drawings. And the best part for all of them was that this was not the family that they had been born with, this was the family they had chosen. And it worked for all of them.

As Claire thought about it and continued drawing, she hoped they would live there together forever, or for a very, very long time. The apartment was quiet as she mused about it. The others were asleep by then. She was the night owl in the group, and she liked working late. It was after two in the morning when she turned the lights out and went to her bedroom. She brushed her teeth, put her nightgown on, and climbed into bed a few minutes later. She hadn't realized it would turn out this way, but this was the home and the family she had always wanted. No one was bitter, no one was angry, and they had never disappointed each other. No one had made sacrifices they would resent silently forever. And the apartment in Hell's Kitchen was the safe haven that each of them needed in order to pursue her dreams.

Chapter 2

On the subway on the way to work the next day, Morgan saw a mention of Max's restaurant on Page Six of the **New York Post,** and smiled to herself as she read it. The few lines devoted to it talked about the great food and atmosphere, and listed several of the actors, writers, dancers, and sports figures who hung out there. And of course, they always mentioned Greg. She read **The Wall Street Journal** and **The New York Times** every morning, after going to the gym religiously at six A.M., but she liked glancing through the **Post** and reading the gossip on Page Six for a little levity and spice, and she knew who must have given them the information about the restaurant. She called her brother as soon as she got off the train and was walking from the station to work. It was another hot day, and she was wearing a short black skirt, crisp white blouse, and high heels, and men noticed her as she walked past.

"Nice mention of the restaurant," Morgan com-

plimented him, when Oliver answered his cell. He
had been in PR since graduating from Boston University with a degree in communications twelve
years before, and was now a vice president at an
important New York firm, and had several well-
known clients, mostly in sports. But he liked Max
and did him a favor whenever he could. One of his
clients, a pitcher for the Yankees, was mentioned
on Page Six that morning too. "That was nice of
you to do." She got along well with her brother.
He was her only living relative, and they had been
very close ever since their parents' deaths when they
were both still young.

Oliver and his partner had a nice apartment on
the Upper East Side, and loved to tease her for living in Hell's Kitchen, but they enjoyed visiting
her at the loft, and liked her roommates a lot. Oliver had come out and told her he was gay after
their parents' deaths. He said he would never have
dared while their father was alive. Their father had
been a contractor, when he was working, and
had been openly critical of gays, maybe because he
suspected his son was. But Oliver was comfortable
with who he was. At thirty-five, he and Greg, his
partner, had been together for seven years.

Greg had had his own family issues. He was one
of five boys, from a simple Catholic family in Que-
bec. Four of them were professional hockey play-
ers, and his father had been heartbroken when he
told him he was gay. He said openly now that he

had known he was gay all his life, since he was nine or ten. He just liked boys, and his father had eventually adjusted, although he was sad about it. Greg and Oliver genuinely loved each other, and Max enjoyed spending time with them too. Morgan and Max went skiing with Oliver and Greg sometimes, when Max could get away. He teased them about their dogs, which made Oliver groan. It was one of his few disagreements with Greg. They had two Yorkies and a teacup Chihuahua Greg was crazy about and dressed in tiny Rangers uniforms someone had made for them.

"For heaven's sake, you weigh two hundred and sixty pounds and you're a goalie. Can't we get a decent-size dog, like a Lab or a golden retriever? They make us look **so** gay!" Oliver complained, and Greg laughed.

"We are!" he reminded Oliver, and grinned. Oliver groused about it good-naturedly and regularly threatened to get a Saint Bernard, but he loved the dogs too. And he and Greg never tried to hide what they were. Greg had been one of the biggest sports figures to admit openly that he was gay.

"Do you want to have dinner at the restaurant Saturday?" Morgan asked her brother as she got to her office building.

"I'll check with Greg. He said something about a birthday party in Miami. If we're in town, I'd love it. I'll let you know."

"Sounds good." She blew him a kiss and hung

up, and her thoughts turned instantly to work. She and George, her boss, had a meeting scheduled that morning with a new client who was looking to place a lot of money. George had been courting him for months. He had made some very profitable investments for one of the potential client's friends, and Morgan had done her homework for the meeting, and had discussed George's plans for him at length. She had contributed several additional suggestions that George liked and was planning to present too. They were a good team. And he always said she was a genius with numbers and could read a spreadsheet faster than their accountants and spot an error everyone else had missed.

George was a handsome, successful bachelor, but his relationship with Morgan had always been strictly business. He never played where he worked, which she respected about him. At thirty-nine, he was hotly pursued by every gold digger in New York, and some very nice women too, some of them with a great deal of money. They felt safe with George since he had his own. He had made a fortune in recent years, and Morgan respected him for that. He was brilliant at what he did, and deserved his success. She had learned a lot from him in the past three years. They never saw each other socially, but she enjoyed traveling with him. They went to some terrific places to see clients, or check on investments—Paris, London, Tokyo, Hong Kong, Dubai. Her work life was a dream.

She checked all her facts on her computer, organized the papers on her desk for the presentation,
and made some calls, and the new client came in
at ten. He was a well-known man in his fifties who
had made a fortune in the high-tech dot-com boom,
and was said to be a billionaire, and he was interested in everything George and Morgan had to say.
George had suggested several additions to his portfolio, some of them high risk, which didn't seem to
faze the client, and George had incorporated Morgan's suggestions, and even attributed them to her.
He was always fair. She thanked him as soon as the
client left, and George looked pleased. The client
had been very receptive to everything they'd said.

"We're in," George said with a grin. He was
smooth as silk, and Morgan loved watching him
handle their clients. He had it down to a fine art.

She went back to her own office then, and the day
flew by with meetings, and some research she had
to do after their meeting that morning. She always
did her homework and followed up meticulously.
George knew that he could count on her, and she
gave him the information at the end of the day.

She had a meeting with a stock analyst that evening for a drink. She wanted to discuss two new
IPOs with him, and hear what he had to say. She
had her doubts about one of them. Her dream was
to have her own select group of clients one day. She
wasn't as aggressive a risk taker as George, but she
had solid knowledge, used sound investment prac-

tices, and had six years of great experience since business school. She was well on her way, even if she never attained the stellar heights that George had achieved in his dazzling career, but who knew what could happen? She was on a definite career path. Her life was in a good place.

It was another stressful day for Claire, with arguments with Walter about the quantity of shoes they should produce for their spring line. He always wanted to play it safe, both with production quantity and design. She wished he would give her more leeway, but he never did. He never budged on anything. And Monique, the new French intern, irritated her all day. Claire felt like she was babysitting a petulant child and didn't have time to entertain her. By the time she got back to the apartment, Claire was seriously aggravated, and wished she had the guts to quit. But she needed the money, and didn't want to take a chance on being out of work while she looked, or risking the job she had if she started looking and Walter heard about it and fired her. He had her back to the wall, and all she wanted to do was design more exciting shoes.

As she dropped her keys onto the hall table, and glanced at her mail—all bills and ads, everything else came to her by e-mail or on Facebook—she noticed that Sasha was already home. She could see her lying on the couch, barefoot and in shorts, reading a magazine. Sasha glanced up at her and smiled, sipping a glass of wine, which meant she was off call, which was a relief for her. She hardly ever got time off, and Claire couldn't remember the last time she'd seen her read a magazine.

"They finally gave you a break?" She was happy for her.

"I'm not working this week," Sasha said vaguely, sipping her wine.

"Not since yesterday. That's hardly what I'd call a vacation." Sasha laughed at her then and sat up on the couch. "I had a shit day," Claire complained to her. "I may have to kill the little French girl, if I don't kill Walter first. I'm beginning to have fantasies about it. I'm sick of designing shoes for women with no imagination and no taste."

"Then quit," Sasha said bluntly. "Fuck them. Why be miserable in your job?"

"Hello, remember me? I need the money. I'm not an heiress, and what if I'm out of work for six months? That could happen." Claire looked worried as she said it.

"There's always prostitution," Sasha said, sounding flippant, and suddenly what she said didn't seem like her. Sasha was always sensitive about Claire's fears about her job and her future.

And then Claire took a closer look and narrowed her eyes as she stared hard at Sasha.

"Smile at me," she said cryptically to the exquisite woman on the couch. Sasha had a natural beauty that nothing could dim, even uncombed hair and hospital scrubs.

"Why?" she said in response.

"Never mind why—smile at me." Sasha did as she was told, and smiled broadly, showing off gorgeous, perfect teeth. She hadn't even had braces. She'd been naturally flawless from birth. And Claire laughed the moment she smiled. "Jesus, you two ought to be forced to wear a sign, or get a tattoo on your foreheads with your name." Only when they smiled could she detect the faintest dissimilarity in the twins. Although they looked the same, and were truly identical, there was an almost microscopic difference in their smiles. Claire had noticed it early on, but Valentina still fooled her a lot of the time, especially when she wanted to, which she did often. She was much more mischievous than her twin, and explained it by saying that Sasha was older, by three minutes, therefore more serious. Valentina considered herself the younger sister, and was lying on the couch drinking wine. "I thought you were Sasha," Claire explained, but Valentina already knew that and looked amused. She loved fooling them. In some ways, she behaved like a naughty child, in contrast to her more responsible sister.

"Sasha said she'd be here by now, but she just called to say she got stuck at work. Some woman is delivering. I don't know why she didn't pick a better specialty, like plastic surgery."

"Face-lifts sound even more disgusting than child-birth," Claire said honestly, and poured herself a glass of the wine. Valentina had blithely opened one of their best bottles of white wine, although most of the time she preferred champagne. She was spoiled by the men she went out with, all of whom had vast amounts of money, and most of whom were twice her age, and dazzled by her. It was hard not to be, and she had all the habits of a spoiled brat, which Sasha didn't. All the roommates loved Sasha, and put up with Valentina. Sometimes she was funny, but none of them would have wanted to live with her. Nor did Sasha. Valentina had driven her crazy while they were growing up, although they still had the close relationship typical of twins.

Valentina then wandered into Sasha's bedroom and came out a few minutes later, wearing a very pretty skirt Claire hadn't seen her roommate wear all year. Valentina helped herself to whatever she wanted, always, and never asked her sister's permission.

"She'll never have time to wear this," Valentina said to Claire as she sat down and poured herself another glass of wine. "It looks better on me anyway. She's losing weight from working too hard. Everything hangs on her." Claire could detect no difference in their weight, or anything else about them, except the smile.

They chatted for a little while, and then Valentina went back to reading **Vogue,** and half an hour later Sasha walked in, and was surprised to see her sister wearing her skirt. "What are you doing wearing that?" She didn't look happy about it, and Sasha seemed like she was in a hurry.

"You never wear it, I'll just borrow it for a few days." **And then forget to give it back,** Sasha thought to herself. Their father had sent it to her from one of his stores in Atlanta, it was by a well-known designer, and he knew she never had time to shop for clothes. Valentina had no problem buying clothes for herself, or taking what she wanted from her sister. And she got a lot of the clothes she modeled after the shoots.

"Dad sent it to me," Sasha told her, as though that made the skirt meaningful to her. Valentina shrugged. She didn't get along with their father and didn't like his second wife and made no secret of it. "I'm going out," Sasha said to her sister, as Valentina settled back onto the couch, wearing the borrowed skirt.

"Back to work?"

"I have a date," Sasha said, embarrassed. "I forgot. He just called to remind me."

"With who?" Valentina looked surprised, and so did Claire. Sasha hadn't had a date in months.

"Some guy I met last month. I think he thought I was you. He acted like he knew me, and then I realized he had us confused."

"And he still thinks so?" Valentina was amused, and Sasha annoyed.

"Of course not. I told him, but he asked me out anyway. He's an actor, and he models underwear for Calvin Klein."

"He must be cute," she said, glancing at her sister.

"Yeah, kind of. I wasn't going to go out with him, but he made a big fuss that I sounded like I'd forgotten, and I didn't want to admit I had. He's taking me to some art opening, and dinner afterward." It didn't sound like Sasha's kind of date, which were usually with other doctors, people she met at medical conferences, or related to her work. An actor/model wasn't her style, or even Valentina's. "I said I'd meet him in half an hour." And thinking about it, she was sorry Valentina had taken the skirt—she didn't know what to wear.

"Wear something hot," Valentina advised her, as Sasha disappeared into her room, pawed through the closet, and came up with a white cotton dress and threw it on the bed. Valentina came in a minute later and shook her head. "You'll look like you're going to the beach. There's a black pencil skirt at the back of your closet, and a silver tube top. Wear that." Sasha hesitated for a minute and then nodded. Valentina knew a lot more about fashion than she did. She jumped into the shower, and was dressed ten minutes later, her long blond hair still wet.

"Blow-dry your hair, put on makeup, and wear high heels," her twin advised her, as Sasha headed back to the bathroom and emerged ten minutes later, and actually looked like she was going on a date, except that she couldn't find heels in her closet. She walked into the living room barefoot, and Claire handed her a pair of high-heeled sandals. Conveniently, they wore the same size. Sasha looked terrific in the outfit her twin had chosen for her with her roommate's shoes.

"Now you look hot!" Valentina said, smiling at her. Sasha suddenly looked like Valentina, but she could hardly walk in Claire's towering high heels.

"Can't I wear sandals? I think he was short anyway. I can't remember."

"No, you can't," Valentina and Claire said in unison, and five minutes later Sasha clattered down the stairs, feeling like a fraud and hoping she wouldn't break her neck in the high heels. She felt like a poor imitation of her twin, which was what her date had probably wanted anyway, a date with Valentina, not with her. It had been the story of their early life. They were always trading places. Sasha wrote term papers and took exams for Valentina, and Valentina sometimes went on dates pretending to be Sasha.

Sasha hailed a cab on Tenth Avenue, and gave the driver the address of a gallery in Chelsea, where she was supposed to meet her date. She saw him as soon as she walked in, and he made a beeline for her.

"Wow! You look amazing." He had his cell phone in his hand and snapped a picture of her before she could stop him.

"Why did you do that?" Sasha felt out of place and ill at ease.

"I put everything I do on Instagram," Ryan Phillips said to her. The thought of it made her uncomfortable, and she followed him into the crowded gallery, where he seemed to know everyone.

Ryan was a handsome man about her age, and as women crowded around him, Sasha felt naked in the top her sister had told her to wear. It just wasn't her, and it was awkward being out of hospital scrubs. A number of men talked to her, and Ryan was attentive, but she still thought she looked like a poor imitation of Valentina, and she was exhausted by the time they left the gallery and took a cab to a restaurant in SoHo, which was mobbed and noisy, and everyone knew him there too. Conversation was nearly impossible once they were seated at the table, and he took another picture of her on his cell phone, which unnerved her even more. She wondered if he was letting people think he was on a date with famous supermodel Valentina, and not with her twin. She felt like an imposter with him, but had told herself it would do her good to get out for a change. No one had asked her on a date in months, and she was guilty about not making the effort to meet new people and go out. But now that she was here, it was all too strange. He was a good-looking guy, but they had nothing in common, and she doubted he would ask her out again.

"So what do you do?" he asked her, shouting over

the din of the noisy restaurant after they had ordered. She noticed that his muscles rippled under the black T-shirt he was wearing with black jeans. He was in fantastic shape, and it was easy to guess he worked out every day.

"I'm a doctor," she shouted back, "an obstetrician." He looked stunned by her response.

"I thought you were a model, like your sister." She shook her head with a broad grin.

"No, I'm an OB/GYN resident at NYU hospital. I deliver babies." What she told him left him momentarily speechless, and then he nodded.

"I guess that's cool." He had no idea what she did for a living when he asked her on a date. He just liked the way she looked, and had lusted after Valentina for months. Sasha didn't say it, but Ryan was too young and too poor for her sister, who only dated very rich, much older men. Ryan was no match for her. "Do you like being a doctor?" He didn't know what to say to her.

"Very much. Do you like being an actor?"

"Yeah, I'm up for a part in a movie in L.A. I'm waiting to hear. I auditioned for it last week. I've had a few parts on daytime soaps, and the Calvin Klein ads have been great." She nodded, and as their dinner arrived and the noise level rose around them, they were spared further conversation until they were back on the street. He put an arm around her when they left the restaurant, with an expectant look. "Do you want to come to my place? It's a few blocks from here." The geography wasn't an issue, but she didn't know him, and it was obvious that he expected to sleep with her in exchange for dinner. And handsome as he was, having sex with a stranger didn't appeal to her.

"I have to be at work at six tomorrow morning. I should get home," she said, not knowing what else to say. **Are you kidding?** would have seemed rude, and she didn't want to sound like a prude.

"Yeah, right. We'll have to do this again sometime," he said, sounding unconvincing. She could tell that he thought that if she wasn't going to sleep with him, there wasn't much point in seeing her again. He put her in a cab five minutes later and waved as it drove her away. She was feeling dazed, the evening had been noisy, boring, and unfulfilling, and she knew nothing more about him than she had when they met, except that he was being considered for a part in a movie in L.A. And she got the feeling that the object of dates like it, with men like him, was not to get to know each other, but just to get out, dress up, share a meal, network at the gallery party, and if possible get laid. Almost none of it appealed to her, and was so superficial that it made watching game shows on TV seem more intimate. She felt like she had wasted the entire evening, and her feet hurt from the ridiculously high heels she'd borrowed from Claire. None of it seemed worth it. And it felt humiliating and stupid to have participated at all.

She heard sirens in the distance as the cab approached her street, and she saw half a dozen fire trucks and a chief's car, parked helter-skelter, and several policemen blocking traffic from entering the street. The cabdriver stopped, looked at what was happening, and turned to tell her that he couldn't drive into her street.

"It's okay," she told him as she paid him and gave him a decent tip. "I can walk in from here." Although as she got out of the cab, she felt a tingle of fear race up her spine. There were fire engines and police cars, an ambulance, and two paramedic trucks jamming the entrance to the street, and a policeman stopped her as soon as she tried to walk in.

"You can't go in there, miss. Several of the buildings are on fire. It's too dangerous. You'll have to wait here." He indicated a police line she couldn't cross, and she craned her neck to see which buildings were on fire. The hub of activity appeared to be in the middle of the block, where men were running. Firefighters wearing heavy packs, helmets, and face masks were lumbering down the block at full speed. She could see ladders going up the front of two buildings, and then realized how close their building was to the fire. Her heart started to pound as she watched, wondering where her roommates were. They were all supposed to be home that night, and she wondered if they were on the other side of Thirty-ninth Street, waiting on Tenth Avenue, and took out her cell phone to call them and check. As she did, she could see that Engine 34, housed only a block away from them, had sent two trucks to the scene.

Sasha watched the frenetic activity up and down the street, and now she could see flames coming from both buildings. And there were firemen on the roof to make holes in it with axes to let out some of the heat, while others shot water into the blaze. The smoke emerging from the buildings was inky black, which she knew meant the fire was still raging. Once under control, the smoke would be white, but it wasn't yet.

"Holy shit!" Sasha said, sounding shocked and nervous when Claire answered her phone. "What happened? Why didn't one of you call me?"

"There was nothing you could do. We didn't want to spoil your date. We've been out here since half an hour after you left. It started in one building, and set fire to the one next to it about an hour ago. They can't seem to get it under control."

"Shit, and we're only two buildings away. Where are you guys?"

"On Tenth. Morgan went to Max's to get us some bottles of water. You can feel the heat all the way down here." And the smoke was heavy in the air. As Sasha watched, she could see two firemen with face masks come down the ladders carrying people wrapped in blankets. One of them wasn't moving, and the other was an old woman, who looked terrified as the firefighter made his way down the ladder with her. It was obvious, watching the smoke billowing from the building, that by now there must have been very little left intact inside. And what wasn't being devoured by the fire was being drowned with the high-powered blasts of water being hosed into the building. It looked like they could lose the apartment, but for some reason the fire headed west instead of toward her, and another building on the far side of them caught fire as everyone stood watching. She felt guilty that she was relieved when she saw it head away from their building, though sorry for the people who lived on their other side, in the building that exploded into flames.

"This is getting really ugly," Sasha said sadly. "They just brought an old lady out, put a mask on her, and put her in an ambulance, and now they're bringing out two more."

"Are you going to help?" Claire asked her, as Sasha watched them with wide eyes.

"They don't need me, unless one of those old ladies is having a baby. They've got three trucks of paramedics who know what to do better than I do." Two of the ambulances had just gone screaming past her with their sirens on.

She and Claire continued talking for the next hour, neither of them wanting to leave where they were standing and miss something important that might happen. And then finally, an hour later, the first sign of white smoke came through the holes in the three roofs and out the windows of the buildings. The fire was getting under control. And the ambulances had raced past her several times. Sasha had lost count how many, and she had noticed somberly two gurneys with lifeless forms on them, and blankets covering the bodies, and she had seen a firefighter carried to an ambulance when another firefighter had dragged him out of the building, injured. Trucks and engines had come from all over the city.

It was two in the morning by the time the frenzy started to die down, but firemen were coming out of all three buildings carrying bodies. Sasha overheard among the police talking around her that seven people had succumbed so far, five were injured, and the fireman she'd seen carried out. She talked to Claire again then, and Morgan and Abby were with her. Morgan suggested they meet at Max's restaurant, half a block from where they were standing, at the other end of the street. Their building was no longer at risk, but they'd been told it would be another hour or two before they would be allowed back into their home. Sasha was sure it would reek of smoke when they did. But they could easily have lost it that night if the wind had changed direction, and she thought about the people who had died, as she walked around the block to meet the others on Tenth Avenue. They were quiet on their way to Max's. He had closed half an hour before, and was counting the money while the kitchen staff and bus boys were cleaning up. Max had come out to see what was happening a couple of times, and brought them more water, and then had gone back to work. It was a busy night.

"That was quite a blaze," he commented as they arrived, all four of them looking tired, and Sasha still teetering on Claire's high heels. The others were all wearing T-shirts, shorts, and flats and looked as though they'd dressed in haste.

"Seven people died," Sasha said sadly. "I think they were mostly old people, from smoke inhalation." They didn't know any of them personally, but all of the residents of the loft recognized some of their neighbors by sight and waved at them occasionally. It was tragic to think of how their lives had ended. It was one of the risks of very old buildings. One of the firemen had told Morgan it started as an electrical fire, in a building that hadn't been renovated like theirs, and since it was rent-controlled, it had some of the original tenants in it.

They shared a bottle of wine at Max's, and finally at three-thirty, they were allowed to go back to their apartment. The building reeked of smoke, and they opened all the windows when they got home, and turned on their air-conditioning units for ventilation, but they assumed correctly that it would take days or longer for the smell of smoke to dissipate. The buildings only two doors away were still smoldering, and firemen were hosing them down both inside and out. None of the possessions inside would remain.

"Boy, that was close," Morgan said as she sat down on the couch with Max. "We could have lost everything." In their haste, they had taken nothing with them, except Abby, who had grabbed her laptop with her novel on it. And Claire had stuck some photographs of her parents into her purse. The rest had seemed unimportant, but they would have hated losing their home. They had installed smoke detectors in the loft years before, and had never had a fire in the neighborhood come as close as that. It was an eerie, depressing feeling, especially knowing people had died.

It was five in the morning before they all went to bed, and just before they did, Claire turned to Sasha.

"By the way, how was your date?" Sasha had already forgotten all about it, in the excitement of the fire.

"Ridiculous," she answered. "A total waste of time. I'd rather stay home with all of you, or work, or sleep," Sasha said with a yawn. "He was pretty to look at, but there was nothing to say."

"There are some good ones out there," Morgan reminded her, as Sasha looked skeptical and Claire shook her head.

"I think you got the last good one left," Claire commented, referring to Max with a smile, as he went to get ready for bed and let the girls discuss the date.

"What do you expect from an underwear model, for chrissake?" Morgan said to Sasha.

"He kept taking pictures of me to send to his Instagram followers," Sasha said. "He probably told them he was out with Valentina." Morgan and Claire suspected that was probably true. He wasn't likely to be impressed by Sasha's medical school credentials, and claiming he was out with Valentina would blow the minds of all his friends. Morgan groaned at the description of his sending Instagrams to his followers from their date.

"At least you tried," Morgan commended her as Sasha turned to Claire.

"And how the hell do you walk in those shoes? I was afraid I'd fall and break a hip."

"You can't go on a date in clogs or Crocs," Claire pointed out to her, and they laughed.

"Why not? I did with the last guy I went out with. He was a resident in orthopedics. We went out after work in scrubs, and we had a fairly decent time, until he admitted that he was engaged, but he wasn't sure if he was going to go through with it, so he was checking other people out to see how he really felt about his fiancée."

"Nice," Morgan commented.

"I guess I didn't do it for him. I hear he got married over the Fourth of July. She's an ICU nurse, and he thought maybe he should be with a doctor.

Maybe they're all crazy. Thank God I don't have time to date. I don't know why I bothered tonight." Except to keep her hand in, and she thought she should. Her sister always said she had no life. And Valentina wasn't wrong, but Sasha didn't mind.

"Two bad dates are not an excuse to live like a nun. And you have no excuse," Morgan said to Claire. "You guys can't stay alone forever. It takes some effort to find the right guy."

"And then what? You get married and hate each other for the rest of your life?" Claire said in a negative tone. Her parents didn't hate each other, but in her opinion, her father had ruined her mother's life. And her mother had let him, which was even worse.

"It doesn't always turn out that way," Morgan insisted, although it had for her parents, who never should have gotten married in the first place. But her own generation was more careful, and a lot more cautious about who they married and why. Or they just lived together, which made more sense to her. Their parents' reasons for getting married no longer applied. Giving up lives, careers, and cities for a man seemed like a bad idea to all of them, and led to miserable lives like those of Claire's and Morgan's parents.

"Well, I think I'll give the dating thing a rest for a while," Sasha said with relief.

"You haven't exactly been knocking yourself out

in that department," Morgan chided her. "You can't give up after one boring date. That's ridiculous."

"No, it's ridiculous going out with guys you don't have anything in common with." But Sasha was too tired to think about it now. She said goodnight to her roommates, and headed for her bedroom to lie down. She had to be at work at six A.M. to deliver babies. Her life was much too real to be bothered with men like Ryan, and she didn't need dinner that badly. As she lay down and closed her eyes for a minute, he slipped totally from her mind into oblivion, where he belonged. It had been a long night, and it had been frightening for those at risk of losing their homes, and tragic for those who had died, all of which made her date seem utterly inconsequential. She fell into a deep sleep, grateful for even half an hour, and particularly so that their home was safe.

Chapter 3

Abby was painting scenery at the theater again, and Ivan was having lunch with a theatrical agent, when a pretty girl walked in, looking slightly lost and very young. She had enormous breasts that were nearly falling out of a man's tank top and was wearing skin-tight jeans, and she had tousled, long blond hair that looked as though she had just climbed out of bed. Abby wondered if Ivan had scheduled auditions, but they had no part in their current play, or the next one, for a girl her age.

Abby stopped painting and looked at her. "Can I help you?"

"I . . . I have something I wanted to drop off for Ivan Jones. He told me I could leave it at the theater for him. Is he here?"

Abby shook her head, and noticed that the girl was holding a thick manila envelope against her chest.

"It's . . . it's a play I wrote, and he said he'd take a look at it. I'm at the Actors Studio. I'm an actress, but I've been working on the play for two years. I think I need some help with it, and he offered. My name is Daphne Blake." Something about what she said struck a chord of memory. Abby had come to the theater with an envelope just like it three years ago, when Ivan first convinced her to try her hand at writing a play instead of her novel, and then promised to produce it. Abby heard an alarm bell go off in her head, and sensed danger. "Are you a set designer?" the girl asked with interest.

"No, I'm a playwright too. We all pitch in with odd jobs here, painting sets, working the box office before performances, cleaning up the theater. Do you want to leave the envelope with me? I'll give it to him when he gets back," Abby said quietly, trying not to seem nervous or suspicious. There was no reason for her to worry, and Ivan had every right to read other people's plays. Although he only did his own very avant-garde plays, which never got good reviews, or even attracted the notice of the press. Ivan was particularly irate that every play he had produced and directed was ignored. Even the critics who covered Off Off Broadway said nothing about his work. It was the greatest insult of all. He had a small coterie of supporters who gave him just enough money to get by and believed in his work. But he had used none of the funds to produce one of Abby's plays.

"Do you mind if I wait?" the girl asked Abby, continuing to clutch the envelope to her bosom, as though someone would try to steal it from her. Abby used to feel that way about her work too. More so about her unfinished novel than the very experimental work that Ivan wanted her to write. Some of it still felt forced and unnatural to her. But she trusted him.

"Not at all, but he might be a while, maybe a long while," Abby said to the girl. "I think he was going to do some errands too." It was a little bit annoying to have her standing there, waiting for the messiah to come, or the oracle to speak. Abby felt that way about him too. His particular style of writing was ethereal and strange. But he was so knowledgeable about everything involving experimental theater that Abby considered him one of the unsung heroes of his time. And apparently this girl thought so too. She sat down in the second row of the theater and prepared to wait while Abby continued painting scenery with a shaking hand. She was painting a large devil for them to use in the second act, and she had red paint splashed all over her, which looked like drops of blood in her hair.

The girl sat for two hours without making a sound, reading a book she'd brought with her, and Abby almost forgot she was there, but not quite. And then Ivan sauntered in, and smiled up at Abby onstage as he approached.

"How's it coming?" he asked, referring to the devil she was painting. "Terrifying, I hope." He beamed at her, as their eyes met, and she felt her knees turn to rubber as they always did when he looked at her. He mesmerized her, and she would have done anything for him. And they both jumped when the girl spoke in a soft voice from the second row in the dimly lit theater. Abby had turned the house lights down, and had kept only the spotlights bright on the stage so she could see her work, and had forgotten she was there. Ivan wheeled at the sound of the voice and was startled when he noticed her gazing adoringly at him, which Abby saw and didn't like. The hint of something ominous was in the air.

"What are you doing here?" He was obviously surprised.

"You said I could drop my play off and you'd read it," she reminded him.

"Yes, I did," he said as though he'd forgotten and smiled at her. Morgan always compared him to Rasputin when he focused on women. Sasha thought he was just a creep. But Abby saw something in him that they didn't, and the young girl talking to him did too. "I'll read it on Sunday and Monday when the theater is dark, and let you know what I think." And then he was struck by an idea. "Would you like to go for a cup of coffee and tell me about it for a few minutes?" he offered. "As long as you waited for me, you can explain what you tried to accomplish, so I don't miss any of your intent." Abby knew as well as he did that the play shouldn't need an interpretation from the playwright, it should speak for itself. But she didn't say anything as she continued painting the scenery, and pretended not to listen.

The girl instantly accepted his offer, and they left the theater a few minutes later, deep in conversation about her play, as she explained its message to him. And for a minute, Abby felt sick. She had heard it all before. He had said it all to her in the past three years. And she had seen him flirt with other young girls, actresses they auditioned, or young directors seeking work. She never took it seriously, or felt threatened by it, but this time, for some unknown reason, she did. The girl looked so innocent but determined, and he was so intense when he talked to her.

He came back an hour later, without the girl, and explained the meeting to Abby, so she wouldn't worry. He didn't want her to be upset.

"Her father has a shitload of money, and is willing to back any play someone will put on for her. I'm sure she can't write to save her life, but we can use the money, and if her rich daddy is willing to help us out, I'll read damn near anything, to keep our theater on its feet. It can't hurt." At least it explained why he was willing to talk to her, and appeared so interested in her play. "Sometimes you have to prostitute yourself a little, for the common good. Not like your parents, for the masses, which is selling out in its lowest form, but angels come into our lives sometimes, and her father may give us just the kind of backing we need."

Abby sighed as she listened to him, wanting to believe that what he said about the reason for reading the play was true. She wasn't entirely certain of it, but she was willing to give him the benefit of the doubt. And he loved the devil she had painted that afternoon, although most of the red paint was on her shirt and in her hair. He asked her then if she would come to his place that night, after he had dinner with a friend who was having woman troubles he wanted to talk about. "Would midnight be too late?" he asked, caressing her neck, and letting his hand drift to her breast, as she melted at his touch.

"No, it's fine." She would be half asleep by then, but the prospect of curling up in his arms, sated by their lovemaking, was too tempting to resist. He was an artful lover who understood women's bodies well, and the sex they shared was like a drug, and would make her forget everything else, the long delay waiting for him to produce her play, and even the little rich girl who had waited in the theater for him all afternoon. "I'll come over at midnight," she said in a soft voice as he kissed her.

And then she remembered that some of her roommates were thinking of dropping by Max's restaurant on Saturday night and wondered if he wanted to join them after the performance. He never said that he didn't like her roommates, but she sensed it easily. And it was mutual. He avoided them whenever possible, and when she extended the invitation to him for Saturday, he looked vague.

"The performance will take too much out of me. I won't be up to a lot of people and a noisy restaurant. But thanks anyway. Another time?" She nodded, and didn't insist. She knew he gave a lot to the plays they put on. "You go with them, though, if you want to. I'll just go home and go to bed." The invitation had been casual for anyone with no plans. But their Sunday-night dinners at the loft were a weekly tradition, and everyone came.

"Do you want to have dinner at the apartment on Sunday night?" she asked him timidly. He was awkward with her friends and almost never participated in their regular Sunday-night family-style meals. He always had an excuse to miss them.

"I have to meet with the accountant," he said quickly. "And now I have to read the girl's play, so we can snag her father's money as a backer. We'll have a quiet dinner together next week," he promised. But he was always soft about plans, and never remembered the nights he had suggested to her. The only way to spend time with him was impromptu, when he was in the mood, and not too drained by his writing, or a performance. She wasn't surprised that he'd declined—she was used to it. He was a creative being to his core, and not easy to pin down, so she no longer tried.

She left him at the theater and went home to clean up, and try to get the paint off before meeting him at midnight at his studio. He didn't like the lack of privacy at her place, and preferred spending nights with her, when they did, at his own. It was small and disorderly, but they could be alone for the tantalizing things they did in bed.

He kissed her again before she left, and the girl seemed insignificant to Abby now. She was a means to an end, money for his theater, which Abby knew he needed desperately. Even his regular supporters had limited funds. And theater as avant-garde as his was not a big moneymaker. They often played to a half-empty house, since so few people understood his work. It was very oblique.

Ivan had asked her to lend him money a few times to help pay the rent at the theater, when he was particularly strapped, and she had, which had left her short of money for the next several weeks. And she never wanted to ask her parents for money for him, since he didn't approve of their work and was so outspoken about it. Whatever she gave him was money she had saved. And he was always annoyed that her parents weren't willing to back his theater, given how rich he thought they were. Abby never told him her father was convinced he was a fraud, writing nonsense that went nowhere and never would. He wished that Abby would start writing "normal" material again, not what he considered experimental "garbage." And Ivan liked them no better than they liked him.

Abby arrived at Ivan's studio at midnight, and he was sound asleep. His graying sandy hair was tousled when he opened the door and he seemed surprised to see her, and then pulled her into his arms. He had been naked when he opened the door and didn't seem to mind, since it was a warm night, and he had no air conditioning in the tiny studio. She was breathless after climbing seven flights of stairs, and even more so when he peeled her clothes away and began making love to her even before they got to his bed. They made love all night long, and fell asleep in each other's arms at dawn. It was nights like this that kept her tied to him and washed all her doubts and disappointments away. He was so good at sweeping her off her feet again, turning her head, and playing her body like a harp.

Sasha was on call on Saturday night but dropped by Max's restaurant for dinner. Morgan was already there, Claire had no plans so she walked over with Sasha, and Abby had said she might stop in on her way home from the theater. Their Saturday-night plans were always loose and impromptu, and Max kept a table for them just in case.

"Is Ivan coming?" Sasha asked the others, hoping he wasn't.

"No, Abby said he'd be 'too tired' after the performance, thank God," Claire answered her.

And Sasha was praying they wouldn't call her in, but just in case, she wouldn't drink. Oliver and Greg said they might drop by, and Sasha had invited Valentina, but she was in St. Bart's for the weekend with a new man. She said he was French and a terrific guy, sixty years old, a multimillionaire, and had just moved to New York. All of the men Valentina dated were old enough to be her father, so Sasha wasn't surprised. Having distanced herself from her father, Valentina seemed desperate to replace him in other ways.

While the three women chatted comfortably, Oliver and Greg showed up, looking tan and relaxed after spending the month of August in the Hamptons, sharing a house with friends. They were all happy to see each other.

They ordered wine, except for Sasha. Max sent over some starters, and the restaurant was busy that night while they caught up and talked about the recent fire on their block, which had scared them all. Claire complained about her French intern again, Morgan said she had a slew of new clients, Sasha was hoping to work at the infertility clinic in the coming months and was excited about it, and they had agreed to buy a new black leather couch for the apartment from one of Claire's mother's decorating resources. And Oliver announced that he and Greg wanted to do Thanksgiving dinner at their place this year for anyone not going home. They caught up on news and made plans for the fall season together, and Morgan suggested they rent a ski house for a weekend in Vermont, which everyone thought was a good idea. Max and Morgan were avid skiers, as were Oliver and Greg, and Sasha said she'd love it too, if she wasn't on call that weekend. Claire had never skied but said she might come up anyway, just to be with them, it sounded like so much fun, although they always talked about it but could never find a date that worked for everyone.

They ordered their favorite dishes for dinner, and tried a few new things Max had added to the menu and recommended, and no one was disappointed by the meal. And Sasha made them all laugh when she described her date with the underwear model. She didn't expect to hear from him again, and didn't care. And just as she finished the story, Abby came in looking slightly flustered, sorry to be late, and apologized also for Ivan, who she said was exhausted and had gone home to bed. He wasn't missed, but everyone was happy to see Abby. She said the performance had gone well, although no one cared. The waiter cleared their plates from the table while they ordered dessert and cappuccinos. Sasha got a text and frowned, and looked at her friends a moment later.

"I just turned into a pumpkin." She had worn jeans and a pink sweater, and could change into scrubs when she got to the hospital—she didn't need to go home. They were pulling her in for a set of twins. They had admitted the mother to the hospital a week before, to stop premature labor, but they couldn't hold it off anymore. The babies were a month early, and had had complications. The text said she was dilating rapidly, and they wanted Sasha in right away.

"Duty calls," she said as she stood up, and kissed each of them before she left. "See you tomorrow. I'm in for Thanksgiving, by the way, if I'm not working," she said to Oliver when she hugged him. "I can't deal with being pulled between my parents anymore. Someone always gets pissed off. I'm staying here for Thanksgiving, and I'll probably be on call or on duty that day anyway. If I'm not at the hospital, count me in. I'll tell Valentina, but she'll probably be in Gstaad or Dubai with a new guy by then." Valentina hadn't gone home for holidays for years, for all the reasons Sasha had just stated. It was too stressful for them, and without meaning to, their parents made it miserable for them. It was like playing tug-of-war, and Sasha felt like the rope, being pulled in opposite directions by parents who were still at war seven years after their divorce.

"We'll be happy to have you," Oliver assured her, and she knew that Thanksgiving would be warm and wonderful at their home. They had a beautiful apartment, and loved entertaining friends, which they did well, unlike Morgan, who had never been the homemaker her brother was, and she couldn't cook as well as Max, who had made Thanksgiving for them the year before.

Sasha left quickly after that, while the others made plans for the fall. She was still smiling about the evening she had spent with them during the cab ride to the hospital, and then flew through ER and down the back halls, into an elevator and up to labor and delivery, where she knew they were waiting for her to deliver the twins.

On the way up in the elevator, she found herself thinking of Valentina and wondering how she was with the man in St. Bart's. Her romances usually only lasted a few months. Neither she nor Sasha seemed to have the ability to attach to anyone for long. The obvious reason was their parents' bad marriage, which had been poisonous even long before the divorce. And Valentina was a little too fun-loving and indiscriminate about the men she went out with—all they had to be was rich and old. And Sasha was "too busy" to get seriously involved with anyone, and yet other doctors and even residents seemed to manage to have relationships and get married, but Sasha couldn't see herself doing that yet, or maybe ever. She was too scared that everything would go wrong.

She sailed out of the elevator as she thought about it, and crashed into a doctor wearing a white coat. He was headed in the direction of labor and delivery as she was, and she almost knocked him down, and herself, when she bumped into him going full speed.

"Sorry!" she gasped, as he steadied her, and she looked up into the face of someone she had seen before, but didn't know. She hurried around him then, went to scrub up and change her clothes, and she was in the labor room with the twins' mother a few minutes later. She was another older mother, although the man next to her looked a lot younger than she did. They saw all kinds of combinations these days, male and female, same sex, older, younger, and infertility patients who were having multiple births with donor eggs or their own. There were a multitude of options and possibilities, and they hardly ever saw identical twins like her and Valentina, since they could only be natural, and the hormones used for infertility caused fraternal twins, not identical, which were a gift of nature.

"Hi, I'm Dr. Hartman." She smiled calmly at the patient, who was having severe labor pains and hadn't had an epidural. They were talking about a C-section, but hadn't made the decision yet. The twins' mother had wanted a natural birth, but was changing her mind about it rapidly, faced with the pain of contractions. She was crying while the younger man with her stroked her head and held her hand and spoke to her soothingly.

"It's a lot worse than I thought it would be," she managed to choke out, as Sasha suggested an epidural. The woman agreed, and Sasha went to the nurses' station to get the anesthesiologist to her room. She was back in the room two minutes later, while the woman in labor experienced another severe contraction that made her scream.

"You're going to feel a lot better in a few minutes

when we get a line in," Sasha reassured her, as the anesthesiologist on duty walked into the room. By sheer luck, he had been just down the hall in another labor room. He prepped her for the epidural, as she continued to cry with the pains, and fifteen minutes later, which seemed like an eternity to her, she was smiling in relief. They could see the contractions on the monitor, but she felt none of them, and her younger husband looked relieved. He had seemed panicked when Sasha walked into the room. She had a wonderful way of calming her patients, and making them feel like everything was under control. She made solid, rapid, good decisions, and her bedside manner was excellent. All of the doctors she had trained with were impressed with her. Now she had to decide whether to do a cesarean section or let her deliver vaginally. The babies' heartbeats were strong although they were four weeks early, and there was a good argument for letting them come through the birth canal naturally in order to induce them to breathe.

She consulted the couple about their options, and they wanted to avoid a C-section if possible. The chief resident came in and endorsed the decision, and they rolled the gurney she was on down the hall to the delivery room, with the anesthesiologist following them, a labor nurse, the babies' father, and two other doctors who had appeared since they were twins. And once in the delivery room, there were two pediatricians waiting for them too, and Sasha noticed that one of them was the doctor she had nearly knocked down as she ran out of the elevator. She realized that he was a resident too, from neonatal ICU, since the twins were technically premature. But twins at thirty-six weeks were a fairly normal occurrence, and the fetal monitors attached to the mother's belly and internally told them that the babies were doing well.

They lightened up on the epidural so she could push effectively, and she started to scream again and said it was too much pain.

"Let's get those babies out then, and this will be all over," Sasha said easily as she kept a firm eye on what was going on. There was a sense of heightened tension and anticipation in the room, as she told the mother when to push, and all she should do was cry and scream. Sasha knew they were looking at a C-section if the delivery took too long, to avoid undue stress to the babies, and she got firm and strong in her commands to push, while offering sympathy for the pain, and then a head appeared between the woman's legs, and with a quick sure movement, Sasha delivered the shoulders and the body, and a little girl emerged crying loudly, as the mother laughed through her tears, and then started to scream again as the nurses took the first twin away and handed her to the pediatric resident, who checked her carefully, while Sasha delivered the second twin, who was bigger and harder to maneuver than the first. But a moment later, the boy was out too, both umbilical cords had been cut, and the babies appeared to be healthy and undamaged and were breathing well, although they would be closely watched and kept in an incubator for a few days. They were a good size at five pounds each, which was a healthy weight for twins born at thirty-six weeks.

Everything had gone well, and Sasha could feel the tension ease from the room as husband and wife kissed each other, looking thrilled and relieved. The mother was allowed to hold her babies and put them to her breast for a moment, before they were taken to the neonatal ICU, tested further, and put in an incubator together. Sasha congratulated the couple, and did some minor repair work to the mom after the babies left the room. They had given the mother something to sedate her, and she was shaking violently from what she'd just been through, which was normal too.

Sasha made easy conversation with her, as she did some stitches. "Did I tell you I'm a twin? I have an identical twin named Valentina. You're going to have a lot of fun with your babies." She went on chatting with her to distract her from what she was doing, and after they took her vital signs, they wheeled her to a recovery room to observe her, and then she would go back to her own room. Sasha left her with the nurses in the recovery room and said she would come to see her tomorrow, and congratulated her again.

Her husband was in the NICU with their babies, and the mother drifted off to sleep with the sedation. Sasha went to get a cup of coffee in the doctors' lounge, and was just taking a sip when the resident from the NICU walked in, also looking for coffee. They were both exhilarated by the successful birth. It was three o'clock in the morning, and the time had flown.

"How are they?" Sasha asked to follow up, since he had examined the babies more thoroughly than she had.

"Perfect." He smiled at her. "You did a good job. I thought for sure we were going to wind up with a C-section when she wouldn't push, but you finessed it nicely."

"Thank you. Sorry I almost knocked you down when I got here. I wasn't paying attention, and I wanted to get there before she delivered. It took a little longer than I thought it would. I didn't mean to send you flying."

"I don't think you could have." He laughed. He was solidly built with powerful shoulders and a lot taller than she was. "But you gave it a hell of a try," he teased her. "I played football in college."

"I'm glad it all went so nicely," she said, relaxed. They both knew that wasn't always the case, and it was heartbreaking when that happened. She had been at deliveries before where the baby died during the delivery, or was stillborn. It was the part of her work she hated. But tonight had been exciting and fun, with a good result. "We did triplets earlier this week. That was pretty scary. You missed that one," Sasha said easily.

"I heard about it. I was off. Once in a while that happens, but not often." She laughed, knowing exactly what he meant.

"I was on call tonight, having dinner with friends, when they told me to come in," she said, while he assumed she'd been on a date. A woman with her looks could have been out every night, he thought to himself.

"Lucky for me they did," he said honestly, smiling at her, as she headed for the lockers to change back into the clothes she'd worn to dinner. "I hope we get to work together again." She disappeared through the swinging doors to the lockers and he didn't see her before she left. He said something to one of the nurses on duty when he went to check on the twins. "That was some hot resident on the delivery tonight," he said with a grin, and the nurse laughed at him. She knew Sasha well.

"Don't get too excited," the nurse warned him.

"Married?" He was instantly disappointed, but it wouldn't have surprised him. Most of the doctors he worked with were married. Some lucky guy might have snatched her up.

"She doesn't date anyone here. She does her work, and she doesn't fool around. She's a serious woman. I've never even seen her chatting with the guys."

"Maybe she has a boyfriend," he said, looking dejected.

"I don't know what her story is, but whatever it is, she's not telling. She's great to work with, but she never gets personal with anyone."

"I'll keep an eye out for her," he said, suddenly feeling tired as the tensions of the evening melted away, and he realized he didn't know her name and asked the nurse.

"Sasha Hartman. Good luck," she said with a twinkle in her eye, and a moment later the resident from the NICU left the building too. His name was Alex Scott, and Sasha hadn't given him another thought as she got back to the loft and climbed into bed. Her only thought was that it had been a good night's work, and before that she had had fun at Max's restaurant with her friends. She didn't need or want more than that.

Chapter 4

As he had promised he would, Max cooked dinner at the loft on Sunday night. He brought all the ingredients from the restaurant, and made two kinds of pasta, a big salad, and steaks for everyone. He had brought several loaves of French bread, freshly baked focaccia, half a dozen different cheeses, and a chocolate cake that had been baked that afternoon. Everyone was in good spirits, and gathered around the kitchen while he cooked. Morgan and Claire set the table. Oliver opened the wine to let it breathe. Greg made dressing for the salad. Abby was there, but Ivan had his meeting with the accountant, and was planning to read Daphne Blake's play after that, so he didn't come. And Sasha came home from work right before they sat down, and joined them wearing the familiar blue scrubs. Greg had put some music on, and the atmosphere was festive as Max poured the wine, and Morgan set the plates down at each place piled with food. It was a feast, and the kind of Sunday evening they all loved. They laughed and talked a lot. It was a family gathering of good people, good feelings in the home they loved. Abby seemed a little tense at first without Ivan, but she relaxed after her second glass of wine, and since she wasn't on call that night, Sasha drank too.

"Where's Valentina?" someone called out from the other end of the table, and Sasha answered.

"She's still in St. Bart's with a new guy. He's French."

"And rich," Morgan added, and everybody laughed. She was sitting next to Max, and he put an arm around her as she thanked him for dinner. It was delicious, and they ate everything.

Claire made coffee for those who wanted it, and Abby served it. Everyone pitched in, it was a perfect evening, and at midnight, Oliver and Greg left. Greg had early practice the next day, and Oliver had to take an important client to **Good Morning America** at seven A.M. The others lingered for a while, and Claire and Sasha did the dishes, while everyone else sat and talked. No one wanted it to end. And after they all thanked Max for bringing the food and doing the cooking, he and Morgan went to bed. She had to be up early the next day too.

They disappeared into her room, and talked quietly, sitting on the bed. He loved spending nights with her there, although he teased her about it and said it was like sleeping in a girls' dorm, but he loved the warm, welcoming atmosphere. It felt like a home, not just an apartment shared by four women. It made him sorry sometimes that he and Morgan didn't live together, but he knew he could stay with her anytime he wanted to, and he usually did two or three times a week, but they both liked having time on their own too, and they both had busy lives, and jobs that demanded a lot of them.

He lay down on the bed and beckoned to her. "Come lie next to me." They hadn't been alone all night, and in the sanctuary of her room, he wanted to make love to her. She had the same thing in mind. After four years together, they often didn't have the opportunity during the week, or weren't in the mood if they got together late at night after he left the restaurant, but Sunday nights were special for them, when the stresses of their work week were forgotten, and they could just be two people who loved each other, and had the time to do something about it.

They lay in each other's arms afterward, and a few minutes later, he was sound asleep, as she smiled at him. He was such a good man. She didn't know how she'd been lucky enough to find him, but she knew it was a blessing that she had. She and Oliver had both been lucky with their partners, and they had created the kind of relationships they wanted, which were nothing like what they'd seen when they were growing up. Her life with Max was perfect just the way it was, and the loft in Hell's

Kitchen was her home, the women she lived with the sisters she'd never had. Max understood how much that meant to her, and he no longer tried to change it. He accepted her as she was, independent, hardworking, successful, kind to him, and phobic about marriage.

In the living room, Claire and Abby were sitting on the couch, and Abby had admitted to her that she was worried about Ivan, and told her about Daphne Blake and her play.

"I know he wouldn't cheat on me, but she's all over him, and she's so young, and she has a rich father who wants to back a play. What if she traps him somehow? You know how men are. They're so naïve." Claire thought Ivan was anything but naïve, but she didn't say it to Abby, and tried to reassure her as best she could, without saying what she thought of him again.

"You're not exactly old, for God's sake," Claire said, sounding frustrated at how unaware Abby was of her many virtues, and Ivan's equally numerous flaws, dishonesty being at the top of the list. She was sure that Ivan was lying to her about the girl, but she didn't want to upset Abby. "She's five years younger than you are, and who cares if she has a rich father? Ivan is in love with you."

"I hope you're right," Abby said, sounding calmer and more confident than she felt. They both went to bed a little while later, and Claire strongly suspected that Ivan was cheating on her friend, and had before, possibly many times. There were so many nights he didn't spend with her, with thinly veiled excuses, or just didn't show up, or wouldn't answer his cell when Abby called. But Abby always gave him the benefit of the doubt.

Sasha had already gone to bed long before, exhausted from work, and relaxed after the happy evening Max had provided for them.

Max left before the others got up the next morning, and whispered to Morgan that he had to go to the fish market in the Bronx, to get their fresh catch of the day. He liked to pick the fish, meat, and produce himself. Usually the cook went with him, and sometimes Max let him go on his own. He ran a tight ship at the restaurant, and everyone liked and respected him there too. He was loved by all.

Morgan was at her office before anyone else the next day. She wanted to get ready for her first meeting, and still had research she wanted to read, and to check some numbers on her computer. There was an investment that George wanted to make, and she had promised him her opinion before the meeting. She was looking through what she had on her computer, when something caught her eye. It was just a name, on the list of directors of the fledgling company they were looking into, and something about it rang a bell. She Googled the man's name, and

saw that he had been indicted by a grand jury five
years before, but the charges against him had been
dropped. He had been accused of insider trading
by the SEC, but he had been cleared and was never
prosecuted, but she had remembered the name. She
didn't like the fact that he was one of the directors
of the company, and mentioned it to George later
that morning, and he laughed.

"That was all a big mix-up, some crazy coinci-
dence when someone in his family bought and sold
some stock. Don't worry about it—he was cleared.
You get an A for doing your homework, though."
He smiled at her and looked pleased. "I'm proud of
you." But she still didn't like the idea of their in-
vesting in a company where one of its directors had
been accused of fraud, even if his name had been
cleared. She was a firm believer in the theory that
where there's smoke, there's fire, and she didn't like
the idea of having to explain it to their client. But
the subject never came up, and George had told her
before the meeting that it wasn't worth mention-
ing, although she disagreed with him. It was one
of the rare times when they didn't agree, but he
was her boss, and she followed his lead. The client
was enthusiastic about the company, and they were
supposed to go public in a year. It was the kind of
young high-tech company that could make them
all a lot of money if it took off.

She forgot about it after the meeting, and had
other files to attend to and research to do. She

didn't see George again all morning, and she had a call from Claire at noon.

"I'm sorry to bother you at work," she said apologetically.

"Something wrong?"

"No . . . yes . . . I've been fighting with my boss for the last month. It's so frustrating. I need some good sound business advice." She lowered her voice conspiratorially. "I don't know whether to stay and tough it out, or look for another job and quit. Do you want to have dinner tomorrow night and talk about it?"

"Sure." Morgan was flattered to be asked, and it was obvious that Claire was troubled, and scared of what the job market would be like if she left. "Max's at seven-thirty? I'll tell him we want a quiet table in the back."

"Thank you," Claire said, grateful and relieved. She was sure that Morgan would help her figure out the right thing to do. She had a better head for business than Abby or Sasha, although they would have been willing to listen too.

"Happy to do it," Morgan said, and then went back to work, as Claire went back to her drawings for the spring line, which she hated. And Walter seemed to be looking over her shoulder constantly, as though he didn't trust her. And the little twit from Paris was driving her insane.

Sasha didn't have to be at work until noon after their Sunday-night dinner, so she could sleep in, and still almost overslept anyway. She was rushing again as she got to the hospital. She was wearing black jeans and a white sweater, and grabbed her white doctor's coat with her name on it out of her locker. She was surprised to see the resident from the NICU hanging around the doctors' lounge again.

"You seem to spend a lot of time here. Business must be slow in NICU," she teased him, and he didn't want to admit that he'd checked the schedule and had been lying in wait for her.

"I never got to introduce myself the other night," he said, feeling awkward. She was so damn beautiful it took his breath away, and she looked calm and cool. "I'm Alex Scott."

"Sasha Hartman," she said simply as she hurried to the door. She already knew she had three women in labor, one of them almost ready to deliver. She was a surrogate giving birth to someone else's twins, and the parents of the twins were planning to be in the delivery room with her—it was going to be a zoo. The surrogate was married, in her thirties, and had three children. It was the second time she had lent her body for surrogacy. She thought it was a noble cause, and it was a good source of income for her. The twins' biological parents had been desperate to have a baby, and had been willing to pay almost anything.

"Can I take you to dinner sometime . . . or lunch?" he blurted out as Sasha started to hurry away. She turned to him with a look of surprise on her face. The thought of sharing a meal with him, or anything more than coffee in the doctors' lounge, hadn't even occurred to her. He just seemed like a friendly guy at work, and she thought of him as collegial and nothing else. She didn't have the vaguest idea that he was interested in her.

"Either one," she said, noncommittal and businesslike, thinking about the babies she was about to deliver and hand over to their legal parents.

"Tomorrow?" he said quickly, looking hopeful.

"Tomorrow what?" She was in a rush to leave, and he could see it.

"Tomorrow dinner?"

"Lunch. In the cafeteria. I'm on duty." He could sense that it was the best deal he was going to get for now.

"Sounds good. So am I. I'll check in with you at noon to see how your schedule is looking." She nodded, touched her forehead in a military salute, and flew out the door, and he almost let out a whoop as he threw away his empty coffee cup and went back to the NICU. It had already been a terrific day, and it was just minutes after noon. He could hardly wait for lunch the next day.

Sasha was already in the labor room, checking her patient, who was handling the contractions well. The parents were so excited they were already crying, and it wasn't even time to push. They could hardly wait to get their babies in their arms. But for now, the surrogate was her patient, and Sasha was focusing on her. The babies were lined up nicely, and the monitors looked good, and Alex Scott was the farthest thing from her mind.

The theater was dark on Monday nights, but Abby went in that afternoon anyway. She had more scenery to paint, and a little carpentry to do. She and a janitor did the heavy cleaning on Mondays, and she had been calling Ivan since that morning, but he didn't pick up, and hadn't returned her calls. He had been MIA since the day before, and by the time she got back to the apartment at six o'clock, she was panicked when she ran in to Claire in the hall. They came up the stairs together while Abby told her that she hadn't heard from him all day.

"He's probably just busy, or sleeping, or reading that girl's play. You know how he is. Sometimes he just disconnects for a couple of days." Claire tried to reassure her. He had done it before, but Abby had a bad feeling about it this time. She didn't like the adoring look of that girl. And why was he reading other people's plays when he still hadn't produced hers?

They were both breathless when they got to the fourth floor and unlocked the door to the apartment. The others hadn't come home yet. Claire knew that Morgan was meeting a client for a drink, and Sasha wouldn't be home for several hours since she had only started work at noon.

"Try not to worry about it," Claire told her soothingly, sorry for the state she was in. "He'll turn up. He always does." **Unfortunately,** she added silently. The best thing that could happen to Abby, she knew, would be if Ivan really did disappear, but she also knew how upsetting it would be for her.

Claire went to her bedroom and changed out of her work clothes, trying not to think about her problems with her boss. And her mother called her a little while later, just to see how she was. Claire tried to talk to her at least once a week, but sometimes she got too busy, or forgot, or the time difference was wrong.

Her mother told her that she had taken another small decorating job, but Claire's father didn't know. She didn't want to upset him, and it was just freshening up a living room and two bedrooms for a friend. She always belittled what she was doing, and made it sound like a favor, instead of work, which was how she portrayed it to her husband if he saw her with samples or found out. She had been treating her decorating work that way for years, although she did a beautiful job and her clients loved what she did. She usually came in under budget, and had a knack for finding good-looking accessories and furniture at reasonable prices. She and Claire had decorated the loft together nine years before, and added new pieces from time to time, to keep it up to date and interesting-looking. The others loved what Sarah did for them. She had a great eye for color, and had found great resources online. She was always sending Claire new Web sites to check out, or sometimes she just sent her things as a gift.

Claire and her mother had a close relationship, and now that she was older, she appreciated even more the education her mother had provided for her, with her small but steady informal decorating jobs, that she passed below her husband's radar so he didn't get upset. Claire thought her mother should have established her own interior design firm years before, openly, regardless of what her father thought, but that wasn't Sarah's style. Her entire marriage had been spent soothing his ego, bolstering his self-esteem, and encouraging him after he failed again. Her mother had never given up on him. She even helped him sell real estate by staging houses for him. Claire thought she was a saint.

Sarah loved hearing about New York from Claire. Thirty years after she'd left and moved to San Francisco with her husband, she still missed it, and the more interesting life she had led there. And their life in San Francisco had shrunk steadily over the years. Embarrassed over his many failures, Jim no longer wanted to travel or entertain, and Claire thought they led a sad life. He hated the opera, symphony, and ballet, which her mother loved, never went to the theater, and they had few friends. The only two bright spots in Sarah Kelly's life were her daughter and her work, which didn't seem like enough to Claire. She wished she could do more for her mother to repay her for everything she'd done for her growing up. But she seldom went to San Francisco, except for Thanksgiving and Christmas, and it always depressed her when she did. She wished that she could kidnap her mother and take her back to New York with her, and free her from the dreary life she led. She deserved so much better, but her mother insisted she was fine. Things hadn't turned out as she'd hoped, but she was an intrinsically cheerful person and never complained. And she was happy for Claire that she was living in New York, which was where she would have liked to be herself.

"When are you going back to Italy?" her mother asked her as they chatted. She lived vicariously through her, and loved knowing that Claire got to Europe for work.

"Not for a few months. Maybe after Christmas, when our spring line is in production. I'm still working on the designs." She didn't tell her mother how bored and unhappy she was at work. She didn't want her to worry about her. She had enough on her plate, listening to her husband complain. Claire didn't want to add to it.

They chatted for half an hour and then Claire

hung up, happy to have talked to her. And by then, Claire realized that Abby had reached Ivan, and was questioning him intensely, which Claire thought was a mistake. It was more attention than he deserved after disappearing and not returning her calls.

"Why didn't you call me back?" Abby asked him, sounding strident. "I left you six or seven messages yesterday, and five today, and I texted you too."

"You know I hate technology," he said. "And my cell phone died. I couldn't find the charger. I just found it under the bed."

"So what did you think of Daphne's play?" Abby got right to the point, and sounded jealous, which Ivan could hear clearly. Claire silently cringed when she heard the question.

"It's very good," he said, seriously. "Not as good as yours, but I can honestly tell her father she has talent. I'm going to call him tomorrow, but I wanted to call you first and make sure you were okay. I was worried about you." But not worried enough to call earlier, yet Abby was instantly snowed by what he said. All she heard was that he was worried, which was what she wanted to hear, that he cared about her. Her parents had been busy when she was growing up, and never there. They left her with a nanny, while they pursued their careers, and she had been starving for affection ever since. They loved her, but just didn't have enough time for her. Even now, she had to speak to assistants when she called them. Her father was always in a meeting, and her mother was on the set of a new TV series.

"What are you doing tonight?" Abby asked him in a gentler tone, hoping he'd suggest they get together.

"I have a meeting with another potential backer. We need money to pay the rent." And the theater wasn't profitable yet. It never had been. He borrowed from Peter to pay Paul, and was always begging money from ex-girlfriends or friends. He owed everyone a fortune. And he was right, they needed an angel very badly. Maybe Daphne's father would be it. "I'll see you at the theater tomorrow," he said in a loving tone, and a moment later he hung up.

"Where was he?" Claire asked her, trying not to sound as angry as she felt, on her friend's behalf. But Abby looked relieved to have heard from him, and seemed satisfied with what he'd said.

"His cell phone died, and he couldn't find the charger, so he didn't get my messages. He was reading Daphne's play, and he's meeting with a potential backer." It all sounded like gibberish and lame excuses to Claire. Ivan was the consummate bullshitter, but it always worked, because Abby wanted to believe him, and disappointment had become a way of life for her. It didn't even surprise her anymore.

"What did he think of her play?"

"He said it was good. And supposedly her father is willing to put up some money. Ivan really needs the help." Claire thought he needed a good swift kick in the ass instead, but she only nodded. There was nothing left she could say. They had said it all in recent years.

Abby told Ivan again how worried she had been when she saw him at the theater the next day.

"I was suddenly terrified you were with Daphne," she said, embarrassed to admit it, and he put his arms around her and held her tight and then looked into her eyes.

"She's just a kid. You know I love you." But Abby also knew that she was a kid with a great figure and a pretty face. And a rich father.

"I couldn't imagine where you were," she said softly.

"I was digesting Daphne's play. I had to read it several times, and I was thinking this morning, maybe we can get enough money from her father to produce your play too. I'll talk to him about it."

"When are you going to see him?" Abby asked gently, still nestled in his arms, which was like a drug to her.

"Probably sometime this weekend. I'm waiting to hear from him. He's a very busy man. I hope he realizes how talented his daughter is, and that she deserves his backing. But you know how these important men are, their priorities are always screwed up." It was a thinly veiled jab at Abby's father, who had made it clear he would never give Ivan money to produce his daughter's play. Her father had met him once and didn't like him. Ivan's credentials didn't impress him, and he thought he was arrogant, a pretentious phony, and her father wanted her to come back to L.A. and work on her novel. But he and Abby's mother felt she was old enough to make her own decisions, and mistakes. They weren't going to force her to come home by cutting her off financially. They just hoped she'd see the light one day.

Her Off Off Broadway career had gone nowhere with Ivan. He had a thousand explanations and excuses, and begged her not to give up and be a commercial hack like her parents. He had nothing but contempt for what Abby's mother wrote, no matter how successful she was. He felt that Abby had a much greater, purer talent, and he pleaded with her to hold out. So far she had. But at twenty-nine, she had nothing to show for it. And her parents felt sorry for her, and were sadly aware of how naïve she was.

Ivan left the theater early that night to meet with the partner of the backer he had met the night before. And Abby was relieved that there had been no sign of Daphne. Abby acted as house manager for him, and handled everything, as she always did. She got home at midnight, after everyone had gone to bed. The loft was quiet. And Ivan sent her a text message before she went to bed. He told her that he loved her. Everything seemed to be back on track with them again. Abby wasn't worried about Daphne—she was just the conduit to the money they needed for the theater. And Ivan loved her. Abby was enormously relieved. That was all that mattered. The rest would fall into place sooner or later. All she had to do was keep believing in herself, and trust him, just as he said.

Chapter 5

Alex Scott went looking for Sasha in labor and delivery shortly before noon on Tuesday. He asked for her at the nurses' station, and they told him she was finishing a C-section, and they estimated she'd be out in half an hour—she had already closed and the patient was going to recovery in a few minutes. He came back half an hour later and saw her heading for the nurses' desk with a satisfied expression. Everything had gone well. He met up with her just before she got to the desk.

"Busy morning?" he asked pleasantly. He was happy to see her, and his own caseload was light that day. They'd had no big emergencies so far, and several of their patients from the day before had been moved to the healthy baby nursery.

"It's been pretty civilized," Sasha said easily. She had no one in labor at that precise moment, only patients she had already delivered, and the ones from the day before. It was a momentary lull. She had two patients on bed rest for early labor, and they had sent several moms and babies home.

"Let's make a run for it then, before it gets crazy," Alex suggested, about their lunch date. "You still want to eat in the cafeteria? We could try one of the nearby delis if you want something edible."

"It would probably shock my system. I live on cafeteria food. And the minute we go anywhere decent, we'll both have an emergency as soon as we sit down. It always happens to me if I try to eat anywhere when I'm on duty." Usually she had no time to eat at all, except a PowerBar she kept in her pocket, and she looked it. She had a slim figure, and was no bigger than her model sister, who worked out every day and dieted ferociously.

They took the elevator to the cafeteria a minute later, making small talk about the food. She helped herself to yogurt, a salad, and a fruit plate, and then added a large chocolate chip cookie, while Alex got a hot meal. They found a quiet table near the window, so they could see the outside world. She noticed him looking at her intently as she set her plates on the table with the Diet Coke she'd picked up on the way.

"Are you on a diet?" he asked with curiosity.

"No, my sister always was, growing up. She trained me not to eat anything she liked so she wouldn't want it. It's pathetic, but I still eat that way. She hates fruit and vegetables and would live on doughnuts and cookies if she could," Sasha grinned at him, and he laughed. She had an easy way about her, and seemed comfortable in her own skin, at the hospital at least. "She's a model," Sasha added for good measure.

"You could be too," he said admiringly. She seemed to have no sense of her looks and wasn't stuck up the way most pretty women were. He'd been burned by his fondness for beauties over the years. Sasha was a whole different breed, a woman with a brain, who was brilliant at what she did.

"Not if I want to stay sane," Sasha said about being a model. "Although I guess what we do isn't so sane either, but at least we don't have to do it in a bikini standing in the snow, or a fur coat in summer, in seven-inch heels. Modeling isn't as easy as it looks and I get to wear flat shoes." She smiled at him across the table.

"Where are you from?" He could hear the faintest hint of an accent, but he wasn't sure what it was.

"Atlanta. I moved here to go to NYU, and stayed for medical school. I was lucky I got in. I like it here."

"Me too. I'm from Chicago. It's a nice city. I miss it." He didn't tell her he'd gone to Yale undergrad, and Harvard medical school. It always sounded like bragging to him. His father and brother had gone to Harvard too. "Chicago is a little gentler than New York."

"My mother is originally from here. She's a law-yer," Sasha said simply, and he nodded.

"So is mine—antitrust law. She loves it, but it never sounded like much fun to me. She wants to be a judge one day. She'd be good at it."

"Mine is a divorce lawyer," Sasha said quietly, not wanting to admit how difficult she was. "What made you go to medical school?" she asked him. She was enjoying talking to him. She almost never stopped for lunch, or had time for a social moment with her colleagues.

"My father is a cardiologist, and my brother is an orthopedic surgeon. It just seemed obvious to me. What about you?"

"I always wanted to be a doctor, even when I was a kid. I just didn't know what specialty. I think in-fertility and high-risk OB is it for me. Especially now, there's so much high risk with older moth-ers, and infertility seems like a very rewarding field, when it works. I love what I do."

"Me too. I think I'll go into straight pediatrics, though. Neonatal ICU is fascinating, but I'd rather deal with less high-risk kids." He asked her where she lived, and she told him about the loft in Hell's Kitchen.

"I've lived there for five years. I have three room-mates. They've kind of become my family, since I hardly ever get home, and my own family has been pretty disjointed since my parents' divorce when I was twenty-five. You think you're all grown up then, but it hit us pretty hard. My father is remarried and has two little girls, and my mom isn't. She lives for her work." He said he had a furnished studio apartment a block from the hospital that he used to sleep and nothing else. The apartment she had described in Hell's Kitchen sounded great to him, especially if it provided a community of people she cared about, which appeared to be the case. Her eyes lit up warmly when she talked about her roommates and their siblings and significant others. It sounded like just what she said, a family of choice.

His own biological family sounded more run-of-the-mill than hers. His parents were still married. He had a brother who was four years older than he, and was thirty-six and still single. They still all got together for vacations and holidays since neither son was married, and they enjoyed spending time together. He didn't get that sense from her, although she offered no details. But she looked tense when she spoke of her parents, particularly her mother, and she said she had no desire to go back to Atlanta for work, and wanted to stay in New York. She was happy here. Alex said he hadn't made his mind up, if he wanted to go back to Chicago to join a practice there, or stay in New York. Chicago was an easier city to live in, except for the weather, and he liked the idea of being close to his family, but Chicago was a short hop by plane if he stayed in New York. He went home for weekends whenever he could.

"Families like yours are pretty rare these days," she said after he told her about them. She was almost envious of him, listening to it, and watching the loving look on his face. "People live all over the country, far from their siblings and parents. My sister lives here now too, and we're close, but very different. I'm happy that she's here, though. She hangs around at the apartment too, when she's not in Tokyo, Paris, or Milan. She leads a pretty glamorous life compared to mine," Sasha said apologetically, but she wouldn't have wanted Valentina's life for anything in the world, or the choices she made in men. "Most people think that kind of life is exciting. I think it's kind of sad. The people are very superficial, everyone is trying to use you, and when your big moment is over, what do you do? It seems scary to me, it's all about flash and nothing real. I worry about her sometimes." In fact, all the time. The men she was attracted to always appeared unsavory to Sasha. They were the exact opposite of someone like Alex, whom Valentina wouldn't have given the time of day. Sasha loved how normal he sounded, as far as she could tell. He had a stable background, and a family he still liked to hang out with. And his stories about his older brother Ben reminded her a little of her early years with Valentina, before the divorce and it all fell apart.

Valentina had already been a supermodel by then, but there had been a kind of desperation to her life choices ever since.

Valentina had played with drugs for a while, which were common in that world. At thirty-two, she was saner now, and still a top model, but one day her career would be over, and Sasha couldn't imagine her sister leading a quiet life with a husband and kids. She needed the frenzy and glamour now, and the high life. She had become addicted to it, and unlike Sasha, she loved being in the limelight. Coming back down to earth one day would be rough. And getting older was a nightmare to Valentina, or losing her looks. Whenever they talked about it, there was panic in her eyes. She ran harder every year, trying to escape the future and the truth.

"So what do you do for fun?" he asked Sasha, and for a moment she looked blank.

"What was that again? Could you spell that for me?" They both laughed, since they got almost no time off, and hadn't in years. "Work, I guess. I love what I do." She had said it earlier, and he could see that she did, and gave herself to it to the fullest. It didn't leave her time for much else. "What about you?"

"I love to sail," he said immediately. "My brother has a small boat on the lake. We go out on it every chance we get. I used to play tennis, but I never get time to play here. I was a jock as a kid, but some of the moving parts aren't what they used to be."

He and Sasha were the same age, but he said he'd had a lot of injuries playing sports in college. "I like being outdoors. I wanted to be a professional baseball player as a kid, a firefighter or a forest ranger, anything outside."

"I wanted to be a doctor, a nurse, or a vet." She smiled. "My mother had a fit every time I said I wanted to be a nurse. She's an overachiever and a big-time feminist. She'd really have preferred it if I wanted to be president of the United States, but that sounds like a lousy job to me. Everybody hates you, criticizes what you do, and tries to make you look like shit. I think my mom would like to be president, but I don't think she'd get a lot of votes. She's pretty tough." Alex liked the fact that Sasha wasn't. He could tell that she was strong, but there was a gentleness to her, and he liked how open and straightforward she was.

"Could we have dinner sometime?" He finally got up the guts to ask her. She was so beautiful that he still felt intimidated by her. She didn't flirt with him, or act coy, and she treated him like a pal more than a date. He wasn't sure what that meant. Maybe she wasn't interested in him, or attracted to him. He hadn't figured that out yet, and Sasha looked surprised for a minute when he asked about dinner, as though that hadn't occurred to her. He couldn't tell if she wanted to or not. She had said nothing about a boyfriend or her personal life during lunch, only about her family and her work.

"You mean like a date?" She almost choked on the words.

"Yes, kind of like that," he said cautiously. "Any interest?" She hesitated before she answered.

"I don't have much free time," she said honestly, but he didn't either, and it didn't stop him from asking. He wanted to go out with her, however infrequent or disjointed it might be. His own dating life had been spotty and irregular all through medical school and his training. It was the nature of the life they both led.

"You have to eat," he pointed out to her, "and from what I can see, you'd be cheap to feed. You don't eat much." She hadn't finished the fruit plate or the salad—she was more interested in talking to him—although the big cookie had disappeared.

She laughed at what he said, and relaxed again. "Sure. Maybe. I guess. Why not?"

"I wouldn't call that a vastly enthusiastic response, but it'll do." He smiled at her.

"I just hesitate to go out with anyone right now. You know what our life is like. Every time I make a plan, I have to cancel. They change my schedule every five minutes, or I'm on call and they yank me in, and I have to leave before the food comes. It pisses normal people off. And it gets old pretty fast. And I live in scrubs and Crocs. How sexy is that?" Not very, they both knew, but she was a beautiful, intelligent woman, and he was determined to go out with her. He liked everything about her, and he had a crazy feeling that they were meant for each other. He had never met a woman he liked as much.

"I get it. I'm a doctor too. Our lives will be sane one day," he said hopefully.

"Maybe not," she said truthfully, "if I stay in OB."

"So you're going to take a vow of chastity?" She grinned at what he said.

"No. But I hate disappointing people, and I always do. And dating is so much work."

"Dinner is easy. We each get ten free passes to cancel for work. And you can come to dinner in scrubs and Crocs." He looked as though he meant it, and she smiled. He was making it easy for her, and hard to refuse. And she liked him too. She couldn't see into the future, but she liked the idea of having dinner with him, a lot more than her recent dinner with the actor/underwear model. At least they had medicine in common, and they both had crazy schedules.

"Okay," she agreed. "Dinner in scrubs and Crocs. It's a deal."

"How about Friday or Saturday? Someone screwed up the schedule and gave me the weekend off."

"Lucky you. I'm working Friday, and on call Saturday. We could give it a whirl, and hope I don't get called in."

"Perfect." They exchanged cell phone numbers, just as she got a text from L and D. One of their mothers on bed rest had gone into labor, and her water had just broken. They wanted her to take a look. The attending was in surgery. She glanced at Alex regretfully and told him she had to go, but they had had a nice reprieve for lunch. They had been there for over an hour, and had established a good basis for a friendship, or anything else that happened. It had been a pleasant exchange, and she felt surprisingly comfortable with him, more so than with most men. She just didn't like the games you had to play, and that most men seemed to expect on a "date." She wasn't flirtatious, and she always said what she meant, which frightened a lot of men. Alex didn't seem to mind it—on the contrary, he liked it. And she wondered how he and Valentina would get along. He wasn't her style, and she suspected her sister would find him boring, which Sasha didn't find him at all. Their conversation had been lively and thoughtful, and she liked that there was no artifice about him, and he didn't seem to have a big ego, which was something she didn't like about male doctors. A lot of them thought they walked on water and were full of themselves. And she liked that he seemed able to laugh at himself, and was fairly modest and respectful of her.

They left the cafeteria, and he walked her back to labor and delivery, where she thanked him for lunch, and he headed back to neonatal ICU on the same floor. They had just texted him too. They both had to get back to work.

"See you Saturday," he said more casually than he felt. "Don't forget to wear your scrubs," he teased her, and half meant it. "That way I can wear mine and don't have to find a clean shirt." She laughed at him.

"I'll try for jeans," she promised, and as he walked down the hall, there was a spring in his step and a smile on his face.

"What are you so happy about?" Marjorie, the head nurse, asked him when he got to the NICU. "Are you on drugs?" She smiled at him. He was nice to work with, and the nurses liked him, and he was a good-looking guy.

"I have a date," he confided, looking like a kid. It was hard to believe that was a big deal to him.

"Lucky girl," the nurse said to him. She was married and ten years older than he was, so she wasn't interested, but they all thought he was a catch. One of them said he was a "hunk," unbeknownst to him. He was unaware of the things they said about him, which was just as well.

"Lucky me," he corrected her. He could hardly wait for Saturday night. And as Sasha walked into the labor room to check on her patient, she was smiling too.

Claire and Morgan met at Max's restaurant for dinner that night. Claire had stopped at the apartment to change her clothes, and Morgan came straight from work. Max was happy to see her and kissed her when she walked in.

"Who are you having dinner with?" He had seen her name on the reservation list and was curious.

"Claire. She wanted to talk to me privately. I think about work." He nodded and walked her to the table. The restaurant was busy that night, and Claire walked in a few minutes later with a distracted look. She kissed Max on her way in, and saw Morgan waiting for her with a glass of wine.

"Thanks for having dinner with me," Claire said as she sat down. Meeting away from the apartment made it seem more official, but she hadn't wanted to be distracted by Abby crying over Ivan, or Sasha coming home from work. She wanted Morgan's attention and her always-sound work advice. Claire had no one else to talk to, and never liked worrying her mother, who wanted to believe she had a stable job. Claire wasn't so sure, or if she should stay. She was beginning to feel she was killing her future in shoe design with what Walter expected of her.

"So tell me, what's up?" Morgan asked with a warm smile as Claire expressed her concerns.

"I hate the designs I have to do for him. We hardly change the shoes from season to season. They want to stick with what they do. He hates change," she said grimly. "What if people think that's all I can do? And it's so frustrating, I don't get to do anything creative. I never get to design the shoes I want. And he's terrified of everything I suggest."

"Would your customers buy more creative shoes, if he let you do them?"

Claire thought about it. "Probably not. But he won't even let me do one. He hates everything I do. If I make the slightest modification to last year's shoes, he's on my back. I don't even have to design a new season. I could just give him the same drawings three times a year. And he's getting nasty about it. I don't think he trusts me, and I know he doesn't like my style. So what do I do? If I quit, I may not find another job. The market is tough these days, and I can't afford to be out of work. If I stay, I feel as though part of me is dying, the creative part."

"Do you have enough money put aside to coast for a while?" Morgan asked her directly.

"For a month or two. No longer than that," Claire said honestly. She loved pretty clothes, and splurged occasionally, but working in fashion, she liked being fashionably dressed, and clothes were expensive, especially the brands she preferred. She had great taste. "I couldn't make it for six months, if it took me that long to find a job. But he might fire me anyway. I don't think he likes me—he never has. But now we argue all the time. I feel as though we're married."

"That sucks," Morgan said with a smile. "Sometimes you have to take the leap. Only you know if you've reached the breaking point or not. Maybe you should start looking around, and inquiring discreetly about other jobs."

"If he finds out, I'll get canned," Claire said, worried. It was a real dilemma, and Morgan felt sorry for her. Claire obviously felt stymied, and suffocated in her job. "And I have that little twit of an intern he stuck me with, the daughter of some friend of his in Paris. She tells him everything. She's his personal spy." It sounded like a miserable situation to Morgan, and Claire was obviously stressed. She needed to vent, which was why she had suggested dinner with her. "I wish I could have my own brand, but that's never going to happen. It costs a fortune to start a line of shoes."

"Maybe you could find a backer," Morgan said hopefully, to encourage her. Claire seemed desperate.

"I don't have enough experience yet, or a name. And designing shoes for Arthur Adams, I'm never going to make a name for myself that anyone will care about."

"Maybe that's your answer," Morgan said thoughtfully. "If he's not paying you a fortune, and you're not building a reputation, you might be wasting your time there."

"I would take a pay cut to work for a better company, where I get to show my stuff."

"Maybe that's what you should do—dig around at the companies you'd like to work for, and let them know you want to make a change. There's a risk there, if he finds out. But it sounds like you're stuck, if you don't."

"I am. I feel like I'm drowning there, and killing my chances at a better job."

"So stick your neck out a little, and see what turns up." Claire nodded as she thought about it. Morgan was giving her the courage she needed to look around. She knew she could count on her for sound advice. They were still talking about it when Morgan glanced up with surprise. A very handsome man was standing at their table, smiling down at her. He had jet-black hair and gray at his temples, and electric blue eyes. He was wearing an exquisitely cut suit, and an expensive gold watch. He looked like the cover of **Fortune** or **GQ.** He smiled first at Morgan, and then stared at Claire. He was riveted by her. It was obvious that Morgan knew him, but Claire had no idea who he was. She had never seen him at the apartment, or anywhere else, although he had a vaguely familiar face, as though she had seen him in the press. Morgan introduced them. It was George Lewis, her boss. He was incredibly distinguished standing there, smiling at them.

"I decided to see what the fuss is all about, with your friend's restaurant," he said to Morgan. "I just had dinner here with a friend. The buzz is well deserved. The food is great." Morgan smiled. Max would be thrilled when he heard. And George set the bar high. She knew he went to all the best restaurants in town. He turned his attention to Claire again then, with a warm smile that was surprisingly intimate. He was mesmerized by her, and she was in jeans and a simple white sweater, with just enough cleavage showing. The sweater was Céline, and she had spent a fortune on it, and it showed. Her nails were perfectly manicured, and her long blond hair hung loose down her back. She appeared even younger than she was, at twenty-eight, and was beautiful. Morgan could see that he was taken with her, which didn't surprise her. He had a weakness for pretty women, particularly young ones. He was one of the most sought-after bachelors in town. And at a glance, she could see that there was a good-looking older man waiting for him at the door. But he seemed to be in no rush to join him.

"It was wonderful to meet you," he said to Claire, lingering for an instant, before he left them reluctantly.

"He's not at all what I expected," Claire commented after he was gone. She had seen easily how taken he was with her, or pretended to be, and it had unnerved her slightly. "I thought he was older. He looks like a playboy."

"He's turning forty in December. And he's actually very serious about his work. But he likes beautiful women, kind of as an accessory, I suspect. I've never known him to get serious about anyone. He doesn't talk about his private life at work, but he's on Page Six a lot, and he dates some very well-known women, mostly actresses and models. I think Valentina went out with him once a while ago."

"I vaguely remember that she hated him. I don't know why."

"He's not bad enough or old enough for her."

Morgan laughed. Valentina went through men like Kleenex. She used them once and threw them away. "I don't think he's flashy enough for her. He's around town with famous women, but he's pretty discreet. He never talks. And he looked fascinated by you." Morgan thought that Claire was attractive, but not as showy as he usually liked. She was a real person, and it showed. He was probably just playing with her, and being flirtatious, although he had never done that with Morgan at work, which she respected about him. He never fooled around in the office.

They went on talking about Claire's job problems then, and Morgan's final advice was for Claire to start hunting around discreetly, put out feelers, and let some of the higher-end shoe companies know that she was open to a change. The plan wasn't without risk, but there would be no improvement without it, and Claire said she felt ready to take the chance. She couldn't go on the way things were. She felt like she was killing her career just for a paycheck, and not a huge one at that. She had wanted Morgan's support and encouragement, and she had gotten that. Morgan never disappointed her, and she had great respect for her advice. And when the check came, Claire treated her, to thank her for her help. They had both forgotten about George by then—it seemed like an unimportant encounter, although Morgan was touched that he had tried Max's restaurant and liked it. And Max kissed both women when they left. And he said he'd stop by later to spend the night with Morgan.

They walked slowly back to the apartment, and Claire felt better than she had in months. She had a plan, and knew it was the right one. She made a list that night of the companies she wanted to approach. The future was looking brighter.

And Max showed up to spend the night as he had said. He and Morgan made love in the morning, because they'd both been too tired the night before, and Morgan was a few minutes late for work, but she had no meetings that morning. All she had was research and desk work until the afternoon. She was poring over several files on her computer, when George walked into her office, and she smiled up at him.

"Thanks for trying Max's restaurant last night. I'm glad you enjoyed it."

"I love it. I'll be back. It's great for a casual meal." He had a legendarily beautiful penthouse in the Trump Tower uptown, but she knew he ate downtown often, and had friends in Tribeca and Soho, and he loved trying new restaurants. He loved to impress the women he went out with, with new finds. And his reputation as a generous date and man-about-town was well deserved. "I liked your friend," he said simply. And for a moment, she thought he meant Max, but the look in his eye said something different. "She's a very pretty girl." That instantly corrected Morgan's first impression. "Do you know her well?" He was curious about her. She looked like a model.

"Claire?" Morgan asked, still startled by the question. "We've been roommates for five years."

"What does she do for a living?" He had never asked Morgan about any woman before, and she was surprised.

"She's a shoe designer. We were talking about it last night. She's very talented, but stuck in a boring job."

"That doesn't sound like much fun. Is she single?" Morgan knew that the question encompassed if she had a boyfriend.

"Yes. She works very hard, though, and doesn't go out much. She's very intense about her career."

"So am I," he said with a broad grin. "I still make time for dinner. Who does she work for?" He was being very direct.

"Arthur Adams," Morgan said in a small voice. She didn't know if Claire was up to dating a man like George, or if she'd even want to. She felt uncomfortable answering his questions, but Claire could take care of herself, and a moment later he left her office.

Three dozen white roses arrived on Claire's desk that afternoon, in a tall vase, with a card that said, "It was wonderful to meet you. George." She was floored. No man had ever sent her flowers like that before. They were exquisite, and very lavish, from the best florist in town.

"Who died?" Walter said tersely when he walked into Claire's office later that afternoon to discuss some price points. She had suggested an increase in their prices, and he didn't agree, as usual.

"They're from a friend," she answered vaguely, looking embarrassed by the enormous bouquet.

"He must be crazy about you," Walter said through pursed lips. "You should get things like that at home." She nodded, and didn't know what to say, but once he left her office, she stared at them, wondering why George had sent them. She knew the names of the women he went out with. She was nowhere in their league, and it felt strange to be the object of his attentions. She almost called Morgan to tell her about it, but decided not to. It didn't mean anything. He was just a rich, successful guy playing a game, and she had no intention of playing it with him. But the flowers were beautiful. She sent him a short, polite e-mail to thank him, and went home at the end of the day. She had convinced herself by then that she would never hear from him again. And she didn't really want to. George Lewis's world was light-years away from hers. And she intended to keep it that way. She never said a word about the roses to Morgan.

The day after he sent the roses, George sent Claire a beautiful coffee table book about the history of shoes. It was a thoughtful gift, and she was touched, but uneasy too. He was obviously trying to woo her, although he hadn't called and asked her out, but she was afraid he would. She had no idea how to deal with someone like him. He was so totally out of her league. She was hoping he'd lose interest in her before he called her or sent any more gifts. And she still hadn't said anything to Morgan about him, nor had she mentioned him to the others. He was rapidly becoming a dark secret.

Claire had sent out several e-mails that week, with her résumé, to her favorite shoe companies. Two of them had written back to tell her they had no positions open, and three more hadn't responded. She hoped they would, but at least she was trying. Walter was annoying her more than ever, and being constantly critical, and in her face.

George was the bright spot in her life at the moment, although his attention made her nervous. He was just a player flirting with her, she was sure, and she reminded herself to keep her eye on the ball, which was her job. But the roses and the book kept distracting her. He was a hard man to ignore.

Chapter 6

As it turned out, Sasha was on call at the hospital all Saturday afternoon. They called her in at one o'clock, and she did three deliveries back to back, dashing from one to the other, but all of them were simple and went smoothly. And she finished just before seven. She and Alex were supposed to have dinner at seven-thirty, and she had no time to go home and change.

She called Alex from the hospital, and was going to offer to postpone the date if he wanted to, since even if she went out to dinner, she might get called back again, although he had known she would be on call that night and said he didn't mind and would take his chances.

"You get your wish," she said to him when he answered. "I'm in scrubs and Crocs. I've been in L and D all day, and I just finished three deliveries. And it's kind of late to go home and dress. What do you want to do? Do it another time?"

"Have you eaten?" he asked her simply.

"Not since breakfast, and two PowerBars between deliveries."

"Perfect. I'm starving. I'll pick you up at the ER in ten minutes. Are you done for now?"

"Yes, until they call me back in the middle of dinner." She was smiling, he was so reasonable and easy to talk to. Men always made a big deal of it when she had to cancel or change plans. But he lived the same life she did, and the women he dated hadn't liked it either.

"Fine. I'll wear my scrubs if it makes you feel better. We can play doctor." And then they both started laughing. "Sorry, that didn't come out the way I meant it. Or maybe it did," he teased her. "Do you like sushi?"

"I love it."

"There's a great place down the street. The food is good, the service is fast. If you get called in, you'll at least have eaten. See you in five minutes."

He was waiting for her outside the emergency room, in jeans and a clean, neatly pressed starched blue shirt and loafers, which looked like formal wear to her. She was wearing her hospital garb, and he told her she looked lovely, and meant it. And they walked down the street in the warm September evening. It was nice to get out of the hospital and felt like a vacation day to her, just being with him, talking about things other than work. And he was right, the food at the restaurant he'd chosen was delicious, and they served it quickly. They sat relaxing afterward, talking about skiing and sailing and their favorite books. They liked some of the same authors, and confessed with some embarrassment that both of them had been good students.

"So what's your idea of the perfect date?" he asked her, still wanting to know more about her.

"We just had it. Good talk, good food, no pressure, someone nice to talk to, who isn't having a fit that I was late, and might have to go back to work in five minutes, and doesn't care what I wore to dinner. I like getting dressed up sometimes, but most of the time I'm too late to dress, and I'm too tired to care when I come home from work. And I fall asleep at the dinner table because I never got to bed the night before." He had met all her criteria for the perfect date.

"I'm a little disappointed," he said, looking slightly woebegone. "You never mentioned sex. That's not part of your dating plan?" he asked hopefully, and she burst out laughing.

"I forgot," she said honestly. "Do people still do that? Who has time for sex with jobs like ours?"

"I hear some people still do it," he assured her mock seriously. "It's an antiquated notion, I'll admit, but I'm kind of an old-fashioned guy, and I like the old traditions, though not on the first date. Maybe second or third? Or nineteenth?" He looked at her hopefully, and she was smiling. She really liked him, and she could tell that he liked her, exactly the way she was, not in clothes she borrowed from her sister, and Claire's ridiculous high heels. She had never been so comfortable on a first date.

"Yeah, sex on date nineteen sounds about right," she teased him. "By then you might be married and could give it up completely." Her parents hadn't slept together in years before their divorce and had separate bedrooms.

"I don't know if I agree with that," Alex said seriously in response to her comment. "My parents still seem like they're in love with each other, though God knows how, with my brother and me driving them crazy when we were growing up. But they seem to have survived it, and get along pretty well. I'd like to have a relationship like theirs one day. I suspect you have to work at it." She nodded, and was fairly sure her parents hadn't, and had slowly grown apart, until their marriage imploded. Her father had admitted to her that he'd been miserable and wanted more than he'd had with his ex-wife. He'd been starving for affection, which made sense, knowing her mother. "So do we have a plan here? Sex on date nineteen? Does lunch in the cafeteria count if the intention to date is there? If so, that makes this date two, which means we only have seventeen to go. Are you free for the next two and a half weeks? I could clear my calendar if you want me to." She was laughing at what he said.

"Maybe we could stretch it out to three weeks," she countered only half in jest. It was just talk, and easy banter between them. She liked his sense of humor, and his stories about his brother and parents. They sounded like the kind of family she wished she'd had, instead of her constantly angry mother and absentee father.

"Actually, the last date I had, I fell asleep on the couch watching a movie. When I woke up, my date had gone to bed without me, locked her bedroom door, and left me a note telling me to let myself out. It was the third time I had done that to her. She said 'Call me after you get some sleep.' I never did, I figured three strikes you're out, and she was really boring. Maybe if we'd ever talked to each other, I could have stayed awake. The notion of sex as a sport you can play with a stranger, or a form of gymnastics, has never appealed to me. I'm a hopeless romantic and have this ridiculous idea that you're supposed to care about each other. Maybe that sounds stupid to most people, and the last person I said that to, an ER nurse in the trauma unit, asked me if I was gay after I said it. She was sleeping with guys she met online, on the first date, and she thought I was a weirdo when we didn't wind up in bed the day I met her. That's fun at eighteen. After that, it's nice if you care about, or at least know, the other person. Sleeping with strangers is too much work." She liked what he was saying and agreed with him. His values were similar to hers, unlike Valentina, who openly admitted to sleeping with men on the first date. And she had been just as sexually adventuresome in high school. Love wasn't necessary for her in order to have sex. Sasha was more old-fashioned, and so was Alex.

"I agree with you," Sasha said quietly. "I think we're kind of a throwback to another time. A lot of people don't think like we do. The guys I've gone out with think sex is what you give them in exchange for a hamburger or a steak." Alex smiled and was familiar with the theory too. He hadn't felt that way since college.

"By the way, it's okay if sex isn't on the schedule until date thirty-six, or never. I like you, and I like the idea of getting to be friends first. Maybe we could get together and fall asleep in front of the TV sometime, or at a movie. Put me in the dark, after three nights on call, and you can count on me snoring in five minutes. I wake up for the credits, though. I like to know who made the movie I missed." She laughed and admitted to doing the same thing.

"That happened to me at the symphony last year. Someone gave me tickets, and with the lights off and the music, I slept through the whole thing. I figure I'll wait till I finish my residency before I try it again. It's kind of wasted on me."

"That's why sports are so great. You can't fall asleep playing touch football. Although I did fall asleep at the U.S. Open with my brother last year. He nearly killed me and said he wouldn't waste a seat on me again. I'm actually pretty impressed we both stayed awake through dinner tonight, aren't you?" He was beaming at her, he loved talking to her, and she was so beautiful it took his breath away, and he would have loved to sleep with her, but he didn't want her to feel pressured, and preferred to move slowly. It made her feel comfortable and safe with him, and he could sense that. She was not a woman who was going to leap into anything.

The hospital hadn't called her all through dinner, and she decided to go home when they left the restaurant, but she invited him to dinner at the loft the next day. She was off duty and so was he. Max was cooking, everyone was coming, and it would be a nice opportunity for Alex to meet them in a low-key way. She hadn't had time to mention him to them, but for the moment they were just friends, and he said he'd like to meet her roommates. He put her in a cab after dinner, and promised to be at the loft the next day.

"Thank you for dinner. It was terrific," she said, smiling at him. And the conversation had been even better than the food.

"See you tomorrow," he said, and waved as the cab drove away. She had given him the address in Hell's Kitchen, and he was looking forward to the evening and seeing her again. And her roommates and extended family sounded like a fun group to him.

* * *

On Sunday, Morgan went to the park with Max, before he came over to cook dinner. Claire went uptown to go shopping, and she wanted to check out the shoe department at Bergdorf's to see if there were any brands she'd missed to send her résumé to. Abby was supposed to spend the day with Ivan, but he had called that morning to say he had the flu, so she hung around the apartment, working on a new play for him. And Sasha slept until early afternoon and caught up on sleep. It was a sunny September day and the weather was starting to turn cool.

Sasha set the table for dinner before the others came home, and by six o'clock, everyone was back, Max had arrived with the groceries, and Oliver and Greg turned up shortly after. And they were all milling around the loft laughing and talking, as Max and Morgan poured the wine, when Alex appeared. Sasha had told them he was coming, and said that he was a friend from work. No one thought much of it, and anyone was welcome at their Sunday-night gatherings.

"Where's Ivan?" Oliver asked Abby.

"He's sick." And then everyone's attention turned to Alex as Sasha introduced him, and he looked a little overwhelmed at first. Sasha explained who her roommates were, and that Oliver was Morgan's brother, Greg was his partner, and Max was Morgan's boyfriend, and she said he owned a terrific restaurant nearby.

"The only one missing is my sister. She's still in St. Bart's, and she'll be home tomorrow." But other than her and Ivan, everyone was there. Alex talked to all of them, and after the first few minutes, he was totally relaxed discussing hockey with Oliver and Greg, and said he'd been to several Rangers games the previous season and saw Greg make the winning save in the play-offs and said it had been sheer genius.

And in a quiet moment, when he wasn't paying attention, Claire glanced at Sasha and raised an eyebrow in the direction of Alex and whispered to her.

"What about him? He's cute."

Sasha seemed embarrassed and tried to appear nonchalant about it. "We worked on a delivery together this week."

"Never mind that—he's great-looking, and he seems nice." Sasha nodded and didn't tell her about dinner the night before, or lunch in the cafeteria earlier in the week. She didn't know where it was going, if anywhere, and she liked his idea of becoming friends first. But she was happy he'd come to dinner so everyone could meet him and he could see where she lived, and with whom.

As usual, dinner was delicious. Max had made a French-style leg of lamb, with lots of garlic, mashed potatoes, and string beans. And he had brought tiramisu from the restaurant for dessert. Whenever Max cooked, it was their best meal of the week, and the red wine he had brought was exceptionally good. He loved cooking for their family-style dinners, and thought Alex was a great new addition. They talked about French wines, and Alex said he liked to cook too. And after dinner, Morgan, Max, Oliver, and Alex played a few hands of poker, while the others cleaned up.

After Max and Morgan went to her room at midnight, Alex and Sasha were finally alone. The others had all gone home or to bed by then.

"What a terrific evening," Alex said warmly. "I love your roommates, and Max is a great guy. I'd like to try his restaurant sometime. He's a wonderful cook." He felt like he'd spent the evening with a family, not just a group of friends, which is how they always felt about it too. And they always had a good time. Alex said he liked the apartment too, and Sasha told him that Claire's mother had helped to make it look and feel like home.

They talked for a long time, and then regretfully he got up, hating to leave, and she walked him to the door. He felt lucky to have met her, and that she had invited him to dinner with her friends.

"Thank you for including me, Sasha. I haven't had that much fun in years. What's your schedule like this week?"

"I'm on duty and on call for the next five days, but I have a day off next weekend."

"Let's figure out something to do."

"I'd like that," she said quietly, and then he gently

pulled her into his arms and kissed her. It was the perfect end to a lovely evening, and she looked up at him with wide eyes after they kissed.

"I'm not sure if that's the right protocol for date three," he whispered, and she giggled. "But it seemed pretty great to me. What do you think?"

She nodded and he kissed her again, and they lingered at the door for a few minutes, kissing, and then hating to leave her, he disappeared down the stairs. Date number three had gone extremely well, and Alex could hardly wait for the rest.

Chapter 7

Valentina came back from St. Bart's the next day, and called Sasha to tell her about all the fun she'd had. She was crazy about Jean-Pierre and said he had treated her like a queen. They had flown back on his private plane, which was nothing unusual for her, but she said that Jean-Pierre was different from any man she had ever known, and he seemed to know everyone in the world.

Sasha had heard all of it before, but she was pleased that her sister was happy, as long as he was a decent guy. Sasha was never sure with her.

"When am I going to see you?" Sasha asked her.

"I'm leaving for a shoot in Tokyo tomorrow, with Japanese **Vogue.** That's why we came back." The Japanese loved her, and were crazy about her blond green-eyed looks. She no longer did the ingenue shoots, where they used fourteen-year-old models, but there was still plenty of work for her, and her agency booked her for great shoots all the time, even for American **Vogue.** She told Sasha that they were pissed at her for staying in St. Bart's for so long, but she'd had a ball.

"Do you want to come over after work tonight?" Sasha offered.

"I can't. I'm going to a gallery opening with Jean-Pierre, and a dinner with the owner after." She mentioned one of the most prestigious galleries in town.

"I'm working today." Her twin had reached her at the hospital. "Do you want to meet me in the cafeteria for lunch? At least I'll get to see you before you leave."

Valentina didn't sound enthused about it, but she agreed. She wanted to see Sasha too.

"See you at noon," Sasha suggested, and Valentina said she'd be there.

Valentina was twenty minutes late, as Sasha sat eating a yogurt and a banana at a table, when her sister appeared. She was wearing a one-piece black stretch jumpsuit, a vintage Dior real leopard coat from the fifties that she'd found in a secondhand shop in Paris, and dizzying high heels. She created a sensation the minute she walked in, and headed for Sasha's table, carrying the coat. She looked rail thin in the jumpsuit, and like the star she was.

"Someone is going to kill you for wearing that coat," Sasha said in a low voice.

"Fuck them. It's Dior couture. I paid a fortune for it."

"Can't you get arrested for that?" Sasha looked nervous, and Valentina laughed. Their faces were identical, and their bodies, and they both had long straight blond hair, but everything else was as different as it always was. And Sasha was wearing scrubs and clogs.

"They should arrest you for wearing those shoes. Can't you wear decent shoes to work?" she asked, disgusted by her sister's choice of footwear.

"Not when I'm on my feet eighteen hours a day." But in spite of what she said, Sasha was happy to see her and gave her a warm hug. She had been gone for almost two weeks. "I missed you. How long will you be in Japan?"

"Three or four days. I'm going to meet Jean-Pierre in Dubai on the way back, for the weekend. He has business there."

"What exactly does he do?" Sasha asked, sounding concerned, as Valentina helped herself to the banana and said it was all she wanted for lunch, with a sip of Sasha's Diet Coke. She had to work in a few days, and she always ate very little before she did. "He's not a drug dealer, is he?" There had been one or two in the past ten years, high-end ones, and one of them had gone to jail. Valentina had never been in trouble with the law, but the men in her life sometimes were.

"Of course not. He's completely respectable. He's a businessman. He doesn't like to talk about his work."

"That's never a good sign," Sasha reminded her, but Valentina brushed her off. She told her all about

St. Bart's, the movie stars and important people she'd met. It wasn't new to Valentina, in her line of work, but she was always impressed. And she said Jean-Pierre had the biggest plane she'd ever seen. Sasha laughed, and said innocently, "I thought you were going to say the biggest something else."

"That too," Valentina said, looking far less innocent. She was a fiercely sexual being, and she liked her men a little kinky and on the edge, which had never appealed to Sasha.

Sasha got a text then from labor and delivery and said she had to go back to work. They had only had half an hour together, but it was better than nothing.

"When are you coming back?" Sasha asked her as they walked out of the cafeteria with Valentina in the leopard coat. All heads turned, not so much because of the protected species, since most people would think it was a fake, but because Valentina was a very striking woman and looked ten feet tall in the high heels.

"In about a week, depending on how long we stay in Dubai. I'll introduce you to Jean-Pierre when we come home." Sasha wasn't sure she'd enjoy the meeting and doubted that she would, but she wanted to see who her sister was going out with, and what she thought of him. She had a more discerning and critical eye than her twin, who was willing to overlook almost anything once she was interested in a man. And she sounded besotted with Jean-Pierre.

They were hugging each other goodbye, when Alex came down the hall on his way to the cafeteria for lunch, and he smiled the minute he saw Sasha. But he was startled by the outfit and her scarlet lips, and she seemed to have grown about a foot.

"Sasha?"

"Hi, Alex," the Sasha he knew responded, while his eyes were riveted to her twin, and they stood side by side, as he suddenly realized there were two of them.

"Holy shit!" was all he could say at first, staring from one to the other. It was the same face, the same green eyes and blond hair, but one of them looked like she was dressed for Halloween, or the cover of **Vogue** in 1956.

Sasha introduced them, and he scolded her for not telling him that her sister was an identical twin. Both girls laughed at what he said and at the stunned expression on his face. Valentina was vastly amused. He looked shocked. And admittedly, her outfit was a jolt, like an electric charge. For Valentina, it was tame.

"I forgot you didn't know." Sasha smiled at him. He had just gotten a full-on dose of her twin. One picture was worth a thousand words.

"How was I supposed to know?" he said to her and then turned to her twin. "Well, I'm very happy to meet you," he said sincerely. "Maybe the three of us can have dinner sometime."

"That would be nice," Valentina said politely. She

had no idea who he was or if he meant anything to her sister. Sasha hadn't told her about him. "I'll be in Tokyo and Dubai this week. Maybe when I get back."

"Of course," he said, impressed. Sasha had to go then, and the two women left Alex to eat his lunch and ponder the creature he had met. With their two very different styles, despite their identical faces and bodies, at least he couldn't get them confused.

Sasha walked her through the lobby and kissed her again at the revolving door. "Take care of yourself," she said to her, sounding like the older sister that she technically was, even if only by three minutes. But she had always been the sensible one. "And don't get too deep into it with Jean-Pierre until you know more about him."

"Don't be such an old lady," Valentina scoffed at her. "I know all I need to know. He's a terrific guy. And a billionaire," she added for good measure.

"Not everything is what it seems. You don't know him yet."

"Don't be such a wiener," she said to her sister, and Sasha laughed. Valentina was a little crazy and had always been wild, but they loved each other unconditionally. "See you in a week," she called out to Sasha as she stepped into the revolving door, and then strode across the sidewalk to hail a cab and disappeared as it sped away. Sasha went back upstairs, and a few minutes later Alex came to find her, when she was outside a labor room checking a chart.

"How could you not tell me you have an identical twin?"

"Maybe I just assumed you knew. She's a character, isn't she? She used to drive me nuts when we were kids, and embarrass the hell out of me. She always used to get me into trouble with our parents. She blamed everything on me. She and my mom are still pretty close. My father is on to her, and they don't get along. And she hates his wife and kids."

"She's a handful," Alex said, still looking shocked. She had made a big impression on him with the leopard coat, the bright red lipstick, and the towering high heels. "At least I'll be able to tell you apart, unless she puts on clogs and scrubs."

"She does that too. She loves confusing people. She used to love driving my roommates nuts, pretending to be me. Claire is the only one who can tell us apart. No one else can, not even our parents, they never could. It was kind of fun being a twin, except when I was taking the rap for her. I'm glad you met her before she left town."

"Me too," he said, but was still a little rattled by it when they both went back to work. Valentina was definitely something else. There was no question in his mind which twin he was falling in love with, and it wasn't the supermodel in the leopard coat.

* * *

After sending Claire another amazing bouquet of flowers, George started calling her. He was very smooth. He called her several times, just to say hello and see how she was, before he asked her out. And then finally after a week of calls and flowers, he invited her to dinner and she gently explained to him that she had to work. His pursuit of her was so determined that she was scared. He was a force to be reckoned with when he wanted something. It was written all over him, and he wasn't willing to take no for an answer. He just tried again.

"What are you afraid of, Claire?" he finally asked her one night on the phone. "I'm not going to hurt you. I just want to have dinner with you and get to know you." But they both knew that what he said wasn't true. He might hurt her, if she fell in love with him, or disappoint her. She didn't want to take the chance. And she didn't want anything to interfere with her work. If she fell for him, it might dilute her energy or alter her focus and jeopardize her work, which was what had happened to her mother. She had let a man rob her of a promising career. Claire was never going to let that happen to her. She had decided that as a young girl. And George was much too seductive. It was easy to imagine falling for him, with all his generous attention and lavish gifts.

"I'm too busy to go out," she said quietly. "I'm working on our spring line."

"You have to eat," he reminded her, slightly tongue in cheek, "to keep up your strength. I promise we won't stay out late. I just want to enjoy an evening with you. Something tells me this could be important for both of us." He was incredibly convincing, and infinitely charming, and the following day, when he made her laugh through an entire conversation, using a lighter touch, she succumbed, and agreed to have dinner with him the following night. She was furious with herself and terrified when she hung up. He was much better at the game than she. He was a master at it. And he always got his way.

She wore a simple black dress for their date, and a gorgeous pair of high heels. Her blond hair was in a sleek bun, with a tiny pair of diamond studs on her ears that she had bought herself. She looked simple and elegant and very striking when he picked her up.

"Wow" was all he could say at first, which was hard to believe, since he had been dating well-known actresses and supermodels for twenty years. He was a pro at this, but Claire was so impeccably put together, and her natural beauty shone like a beacon at the restaurant. He picked her up in the black Ferrari he drove to work every day, and took her to his favorite uptown restaurant, La Grenouille, for a fabulous meal. He asked her a million questions at dinner. He wanted to know everything about her, and he was impressed by how dedicated she was to her career. She didn't tell him about her mother, and why she considered any serious relationship a threat to her goals. After her second glass of champagne, she asked him why he hadn't married yet, and he was pensive for a minute.

"To be honest, I think I've been looking for the perfect woman. My father left my mother when I was an infant, and she died when I was five. I think my memory of her was as the ideal woman, and I've been searching for that all my life, and I've never found it."

"How awful for you," Claire said, about his losing his mother as a five-year-old. "Who did you grow up with?"

"My grandmother, who was fabulous. She was widowed at an early age, and she died the summer I graduated from high school. I was on my own after that. It made me very independent, and maybe a little bit afraid to get too involved, unless it was with the right person. I've never met that right person." And then he added so softly she could barely hear him, ". . . Maybe until now." He looked deep into her eyes then, with a serious expression. "Something happened to me the night I met you with Morgan. I don't know what it was, but I felt as though the world had turned upside down. I've never met anyone like you. You light up from inside. I don't know if we'll be the right people for each other, or what will happen between us, but I know that I've never come as close to perfect as you. My heart stopped the moment we met." He held her hand quietly under the table then.

Her heart nearly skipped a beat as she listened to him. She was terrified. What if he meant it? What if he was the "right one" for her, and they fell in love? What would she have to give up? She almost cried as they held hands. But you couldn't ignore the power of what he said. He was a man who had lost everyone he'd ever loved, and his entire family by the time he was eighteen, and he was willing to admit that he had never fully given his heart ever since, and now he was tentatively offering it to her. She had no idea what to do, and her first instinct was to run, but he was so loving and so gentle and so kind to her that all she wanted to do was melt into his arms.

He told her funny stories after that, and made her laugh, as though he had never made the serious confession he had a while before. And he put her totally at ease. They had a wonderful evening, and an exquisite dinner, and then he drove her back to Hell's Kitchen in the Ferrari, and she felt special just being with him. Everything about him drew her to him, and the pull of it was intense. He said nothing more about his feelings for her, but kissed her tenderly on the lips, and then walked her to her door. He hadn't touched her, he didn't want to rush her, and he kissed her again at her front door, but kissing him was like making love. And then he hurried back down the stairs as she walked into the apartment in a daze.

It was after midnight, and everyone had gone to bed. She sat at her drawing board for a while, trying to focus on the sketches she had left there, and all she could see was his face. She wanted to tell him to go away, not to tempt her, not to pull her into his life, but she wanted to be with him. She turned off the lights and went to bed, thinking of him and the way he kissed her.

She lay on her bed in a half sleep, and all she could think of was George. He was both her fondest hope and her worst nightmare all rolled into one.

She was still thinking about him the next day on her way to work. She picked up the **Post** in the train station, and there it was, on Page Six. "Who was the stunning blond beauty at La Grenouille with George Lewis last night? George looked like he was over the moon, and something tells us we'll be seeing a lot more of her very soon. Stay tuned." Her heart sank as she read it, and she felt terrible about not telling Morgan. She had never done that before, and they were best friends.

She called Morgan at her office as soon as she got to work, and made a clean breast of it immediately.

"I had dinner with George last night," she blurted out.

"George Lewis?" Morgan sounded stunned. She remembered they had met the night she and Claire had dinner at Max's restaurant, but she hadn't heard anything about it from either of them since, although George had questioned her about Claire the day after they met. Morgan had forgotten about it.

"He's been calling me, since I met him with you. I refused to have dinner with him, and he finally wore me down. We went to La Grenouille." As she listened to her, Morgan knew that Claire turning him down would only make him more determined to make her say yes. There was a long silence at the end of the phone.

"Be careful, Claire. He's good at this. Maybe it will be different with you, but he's broken a lot of hearts over the years. The minute they're hooked, he runs. I think it has to do with losing his mother as a kid. One of his girlfriends told me that once. I met her at a party after they stopped dating." Claire remembered what he'd said the night before, but she had to admit that she felt something for him. She didn't know if it was as strong as what he felt for her, but something had happened to her too when they met. Maybe he was right. But she didn't want to share that with her friend. She felt suddenly protective of him and wanted to be discreet.

"Don't worry. I'm more terrified than he is. I don't want any guy interfering with my career. That's more important to me." Morgan understood what she was saying. She felt that way too, although she was in love with Max. But if he had jeopardized her career in any way, or insisted on marrying her, she would have ended the relationship immediately. "He's not going to break my heart."

"Good. And I don't want you breaking his either. He's a good guy."

"It'll be fine," Claire reassured her, with a confidence she didn't feel, but at least she had wanted to tell Morgan that they were dating, or had gone out. What happened after that was up to them. Nothing had yet, but she still remembered the searing kiss and how it made her feel. George had magic powers, and he was a sexy, experienced man.

He called Claire a little while later, and told her how much he had enjoyed the evening. He said he wanted to take her on an outing on Saturday, just to get some air. He made it sound like a drive in Connecticut. "I can have you back by dinnertime if you like, if you have work to do this weekend." She was pleased that he had listened to what she had said about her work, and he was so sweet about it that she couldn't turn him down. He said he'd pick her up at nine o'clock on Saturday morning, and told her to wear casual warm clothes.

The week flew by as she thought of him, and he called her several times, first thing in the morning, when she woke up, or late at night. He sent her funny text messages throughout the day to make her laugh. And he told her that all he could think about was her. He never said a word about it to Morgan in the office, nor did she. This was clearly his private life, and he never shared that with her. He never talked about who he was dating, and was always discreet.

He picked Claire up on Saturday morning at nine o'clock sharp. She was wearing a sheepskin coat in a natural color, and good-looking boots, with jeans and a heavy sweater, with her blond hair down her back like a young girl. She was surprised to find he was driving her to New Jersey, not to Connecticut as she had guessed, but she knew there were beautiful small villages there too, and probably some good restaurants for lunch. But half an hour later she found herself at Teterboro Airport, as he drove the Ferrari up to his plane. It was huge, and she stared at it and then at him, and for a moment she looked scared again. Where was he taking her?

"I thought we'd go to Vermont for the day," he said as he leaned over and kissed her. "There are some beautiful walks, and pretty inns where we can have lunch. We'll come back this afternoon." She looked stunned as she walked up the stairway to his plane, where a stewardess and purser waited to greet them. The captain and copilot had clearance for takeoff, and said they'd be leaving in a few minutes, as they sat down in the big comfortable seats. A few minutes later they took off, and the stewardess served them breakfast.

"Are you okay?" George asked her gently, as he

leaned over to kiss her. The breakfast was delicious. She had scrambled eggs, blueberry muffins, and a cappuccino, and he had waffles and bacon and black coffee. They chatted on the brief flight over New England, and an hour and a half after they left Teterboro, they landed in Vermont, at an airstrip near a tiny village. He said he skied near there in winter, and had discovered the village the previous year. The leaves were red and orange and yellow, and the pilot had rented a car for them that was waiting when they landed, so they could drive around alone. George stopped the car after they left the airport and kissed her passionately, and she responded, as she felt his hand on her inner thigh. And all she wanted when he touched her was more. And she could feel his passion rising.

"You do crazy things to me," he said hoarsely, and she smiled.

"You do the same to me," she whispered, and he began driving again before they could get carried away in the car. He teased her about it, and they both laughed.

"You make me feel like a kid again, a very badly behaved kid at that. I'm sorry, Claire." But she wasn't—she loved being with him.

He parked the car at the edge of a forest, and there was a small lake with swans on it. They got out and walked for a while. It was chilly—autumn had already come to New England, although it wasn't as cold yet in New York.

They went to a small country inn he knew for lunch. They were both sleepy after that, and George glanced at his watch. "I guess we should head back, if you want to get back to New York tonight." He looked at her mischievously then, like a naughty boy. "Or . . . we could stay here. We don't have to, I didn't plan anything, but now that we're here, I hate to leave. It's up to you, Claire, you're the boss. I'll do whatever you say." It was only their second date, and she wanted to be reasonable. She wasn't a slut, and didn't want him to think she was. But the inn where they'd had lunch was magical, and all she wanted now was to be with him, and never go back. She hesitated for a long moment as she gazed at him, and then whispered as he held her hand.

"Let's stay." He closed his eyes for a minute as though the words were too sweet to hear and then opened them and looked at her.

"I love you, Claire. I know that sounds crazy to say so soon, but I think we're meant to be together." And she was starting to feel the same way. She didn't feel panicked, or terrified now—she wanted to be with him. He went to the front desk, and reserved a room, and then he called the crew and told them where to stay that night. And then, laughing like two kids, they went to the local drugstore to buy toothbrushes, and whatever else they needed for the night. Neither of them had planned to stay in Vermont. It wasn't a seduction scene he had sprung on her, it was a decision he had let her make, so she felt comfortable and not forced. And then they rushed back to the inn, and checked in to their room. It was an adorable little room with a fireplace and flowered chintz. There was a big antique four-poster bed, with a down comforter.

George and Claire couldn't get their clothes off fast enough, as their bodies intertwined, their hands searched desperately for each other, and they kissed frantically as they got into the big comfortable bed and began to make love. It was the most passionate sex Claire had ever experienced, born of desire and need and a desperate hunger and thirst for each other.

"I've been looking for you all my life," he said to her as he kissed her, and only moments later was aroused again. They made love again and again that night, and she held him in her arms against her breasts as he fell asleep. It was the deep peaceful sleep of a sated, happy man. She had sent a text to Morgan earlier saying only that she wouldn't be home that night, she was in Vermont for the weekend and everything was fine.

They hated to check out the next day, after making love again. They stood next to the four-poster bed, feeling as though it had become their home. It was where their love had been born, and their life together had begun, and they both knew they would never forget it.

They flew back to New York late that afternoon,

and before they landed at Teterboro, George smiled at her and kissed her.

"Thank you for coming into my life," he said to her.

"I love you," she responded. They had proved it amply the night before.

"This is just the beginning," he said to her as they flew over the lights of the city. Everything looked so beautiful. She felt as though she were seeing it through new eyes. The plane landed gently a few minutes later as they held hands. And whether she had wanted it to or not, Claire knew that a whole new life had begun.

Chapter 8

Alex and Sasha were trying to spend time together whenever their schedules would allow, which wasn't as often as they liked. They had lunch in the cafeteria, met for midnight snacks when they were both there at night, and had dinner on their days off. It was working pretty well so far, and they even went to a movie, which they both enjoyed, and congratulated each other for staying awake. And if dinner out constituted a date, they agreed that they were up to date five or six, and it was going well.

Neither of them wanted to rush anything, they were in no hurry, and they wanted to learn everything about each other so they knew fully who they were involved with.

When Valentina came back from Dubai, she asked about him, and Sasha said primly that they were dating.

"That means you're fucking, right?" Valentina asked bluntly, and Sasha groaned.

"Isn't there some other word you can use? I don't

mind it when I stub my toe, or something goes wrong at work, like they cancel my day off, but I hate that word as a substitute for making love."

"Don't be such a prude," Valentina said to her. It was always the word she preferred, and in her case Sasha knew it was probably the right one.

"And to answer your question, no, I'm not. We don't want to rush it."

"Is he gay?" Valentina looked shocked, and disappointed.

"Of course not. We just want to get to know each other."

"How long have you been dating?"

"I don't know, a couple of weeks. It depends how you figure it."

"You're crazy."

"Neither of us wants to make a mistake." Sasha looked sure of what she was saying, even if it sounded like Chinese to her sister, who always rushed in where angels feared to tread, especially with men.

"So what if you do? Then you end it and move on. It doesn't have to be The One every time."

"Maybe it does for me, and for him," Sasha said to her. She respected Alex for how he viewed it, which was how she felt too.

"Oh, for God's sake," Valentina said, rolling her eyes. "How long has it been since you got laid?"

"None of your business," Sasha answered. And her sister was right, it was longer than she wanted to admit. Now there was Alex, so there was hope on the horizon, all in good time. "So when am I going to meet Jean-Pierre?" She changed the subject. They were in Valentina's apartment in Tribeca, on Sasha's day off.

"In about ten minutes," Valentina answered with a grin. "He said he'd be here, and he wants to meet you too. He's going to Paris tonight. I'm meeting him there next week while I do a shoot for French **Vogue.**" And she'd said that the shoot in Tokyo had gone well.

The doorbell rang a few minutes later, Valentina went to answer it, and a moment later, Jean-Pierre walked into the living room, looking as though he owned it. He was a tall, powerful-looking, heavy-set man with gray hair and piercing dark eyes. If Sasha had met him on the street, she would have said he had a mean face, but he was wreathed in smiles when he gave her a hug and kissed her on both cheeks and looked like a teddy bear. A teddy bear who would eat his young. The smile was wide, but the eyes were fierce.

"I've been wanting to meet you," he said effu-sively to Sasha and sounded as though he meant it. "The beautiful young doctor who delivers babies. Your parents must be very proud."

"Not really," Sasha said, smiling at him. "Our mother wanted me to be a lawyer—she thinks what I do is a pretty messy job. And my father is very proud of Valentina. His wife was a model too." He brushed off what she said as though she were joking, although there was truth to it, and he put an arm around Valentina and kissed her. She was wearing a black leather skirt that barely covered her crotch, and thigh-high black suede boots with high heels. Sasha thought her outfit looked a little S&M, but Jean-Pierre seemed to love it as he slipped a hand up her skirt. Sasha was used to men who behaved that way around her sister, they all did, and Valentina liked it. If Alex had done that to her in public, she would have slugged him. And she smiled when she realized he hadn't done it in private yet either, which suited her just fine.

"I am very much in love with your sister," he told Sasha with a soulful look. "She's a wonderful woman and she makes me very happy." Sasha tried not to think of what that meant. "I have not been this happy since I was a young man." To Sasha, that meant he was using Viagra, but she didn't want to think of that either. He looked a little more respectable than Valentina's usual consorts. He was wearing a serious business suit and a dark tie from Hermès, and he was a tad younger than her last boyfriend, but there was still a toughness to him that scared her, and she knew instinctively that it would be dangerous to cross him. And Valentina had no idea what he did for work.

"Do you do business in the States?" Sasha asked him, fishing, but he was too smart for that.

"I do business all over the world. The world is very small now. Your sister and I were in Dubai last week, and we'll be in Marrakech in two weeks, for a little vacation."

"How fun," Sasha said, trying to look as though she meant it, but something about his eyes truly scared her. He looked like he had X-ray vision. And she wouldn't have trusted him farther than she could throw him. He hadn't said or done anything wrong, but something about him just didn't feel right.

They chatted for a while, sitting on the couch in Valentina's apartment, and finally Sasha got up and said she had to go. She was meeting Alex at the apartment. The others would be out and she had promised to cook him dinner, which she had warned him he might regret, but he said he was game. She told him he was a very brave man.

Jean-Pierre hugged her and kissed her on both cheeks again when she left, and Valentina was beaming at her, convincing herself that Sasha loved him, which was not the case. Sasha just didn't know what was wrong about him and what to object to, but she was sure that something was wrong. But hopefully Valentina would never find out, and he'd be gone long before he caused a problem. Whatever he did for a living, she was sure that he was good at it, and if it was illegal, maybe he wouldn't get caught.

She took the subway north to Hell's Kitchen, and Alex arrived at the loft a few minutes after she did, carrying the groceries they'd agreed on for dinner.

He looked at her closely after he kissed her and asked if everything was okay. She seemed distracted.

"Yeah. I just met Valentina's boyfriend, and I can't tell you what's wrong with him, but something didn't feel right. That always happens with her, and later we find out they were dealing heroin to small children. This one's a little better, or a little smoother maybe, but he's got the meanest eyes I've ever seen. The good news is that they never last long. She's crazy about him, but that doesn't mean anything with her."

"I don't know how twins can be so different," he said as he unpacked the food. "It doesn't get any more different than you and your sister." And he thought that was a good thing.

"I know, it's weird," she agreed. "She's crazy, and she has the worst taste in men in the world, but I love her anyway." Alex understood that, and he had been respectful of her and was careful of what he said.

The two of them started to make dinner, enjoying the night because they knew the others would be out, so they had the place to themselves.

Claire still hadn't told anyone but Morgan, but the romance with George was going well. They were going to Palm Beach on his plane the following weekend. There were suddenly a million plans that all sounded like fun to her. He wanted to take her to the Super Bowl where he went every year, the World Series, skiing in Courchevel and Megève, Aspen, Sun Valley, the Caribbean, and the South of France in the summer. There were a thousand things he promised to do with her, and in between he told her he wanted to spend his life in bed with her. Claire was trying not to be, but she was distracted by him. Every time she sat down at her drawing board, at home or in the office, her mind drifted off, and she could see him naked in front of her. She had even done a sketch of him, which she had hidden in a drawer at work. And all he kept saying to her was that he knew that this was it. And even though she didn't want to believe it yet, she knew it was true. This was it. She just hadn't expected him to come into her life so soon. She wondered sometimes if this was what had happened to her mother, when she had fallen head over heels in love with Claire's father, and followed him to San Francisco. But Claire also knew that this was different. George was a legendary success on Wall Street and a brilliant businessman. People said he had the Midas touch. And he would never ask her to give up her career.

She was beginning to think of things she had never thought of before, like getting married and having children. He was opening new horizons and previously locked places in her heart. It was too soon to think about any of it, or making changes in her life, but she was falling madly in love with him.

The following weekend, when he took her to Florida, they spent a night in Miami, and the second night in Palm Beach, and had even more fun than they had had in Vermont. They already knew each other better, and were learning more every day. He didn't like talking about his childhood, but Claire had finally told him about her depressing father, and her mother giving up her career for him. It explained how desperate she was to remain independent and do her work. She never wanted to be dependent on a man, even him. And George understood.

They went water-skiing in Miami off a yacht he had chartered for the day, and ate at all the best restaurants. She felt like a fairy princess living in a dream with him.

"What's happening with Claire?" Sasha asked Morgan on Saturday morning, when they were making coffee in the kitchen. Abby was still asleep. She had been at her computer working constantly on the new play and staying up late, so Sasha and Morgan were alone at the kitchen table. "She's out all the time, and away for the weekend," Sasha commented. Morgan was quiet for a moment and didn't know what to say. She didn't know the details, but she was aware that Claire was with George for the weekend.

"She's seeing someone," Morgan said simply.

"Wow, she didn't say anything to me. Do you know who it is?" Sasha asked her.

Morgan nodded, trying not to look worried about it. "It's George." It took a minute to register, and then Sasha's eyes opened wide.

"Your boss?" Morgan nodded. "How did that happen?"

"We had dinner at Max's restaurant, George was there, and stopped at our table. I introduced him to Claire. And the rest, as they say, is history. They've been crazy about each other ever since." It hadn't been long, but it was intense. And Claire looked like she was walking on air whenever Morgan saw her. She just hoped it would last, but she wasn't sure. George was hard to read, and even harder to predict.

"Do you think it's for real with him?" Sasha asked with concern.

"I don't know. It could be. One of these days, some woman will land him, and it might as well be Claire. He has a history of short relationships, but just from the little I know, and can sense from her, I don't think he's ever been this serious before."

"Wow," Sasha said again. "Where is she this weekend?"

"Florida, I think. They went on his plane."

"What a cool thing for her, if this works." Morgan smiled at what she said, and hoped so too.

"What about you?" Morgan asked her as they sat

at the table with their coffee. "How's it going with the young doctor?"

"Nicely. Slow but sure. Neither of us wants to make any fast moves and screw it up."

"That sounds good."

"It works for us." Sasha stayed in the kitchen after Morgan went to get dressed. She was going to help Max with his books at the restaurant. They all had relationships now, in various stages, three of them with good, interesting, worthwhile men. The only rotten apple in the barrel was Ivan, and all Sasha could hope, for Abby's sake, was that she'd get rid of him soon.

Chapter 9

In October, when Morgan was going over research for a presentation, she asked for some files from accounting, and realized within a few minutes that they'd given her the wrong ones. She called them to have them send her the right ones, and something caught her eye on the balance sheets while she waited for them to pick them up. There had been a transfer of a hundred thousand dollars, and a withdrawal of twenty thousand that didn't look right to her. The money didn't belong in that account. She could see that a week later there had been an unexplained deposit of the twenty, and the hundred thousand had been moved back again, into the right account. It didn't make sense to her. She wondered if it had been an error in accounting that they had corrected. All the numbers looked right at the end, but there had been some moving and shifting that she couldn't explain. She thought about telling George about it, but since the money had all ended up in the right place, it didn't really matter. But it seemed odd to her. A lot of money came in and out of their office for clients, and she knew George had a remarkable head for numbers and a keen radar, and he kept a close eye on their books. It was important to do that in a firm like theirs, so maybe he knew about it, and had demanded the correction. It wasn't really worrisome since no funds were missing, but she couldn't explain it to herself. Just to be sure, if the subject came up later, she xeroxed the file before they came to pick it up, and she put the xeroxed pages in a locked drawer in her desk. And then she got to work on the research she had to do for the next day.

The error in accounting slipped her mind entirely after that. They had a number of new clients, and she had a lot of work to do.

She had noticed what good spirits George was in since he'd started seeing Claire, and he didn't say anything to Morgan, but he looked like a man in love. She had never seen him as happy or as relaxed, and Claire was like a field of flowers in spring. She had even stopped complaining about her boss.

And Sasha was happy too. She was busy, content, and at peace, and she and Alex were having fun. They laughed a lot whenever he came to the apartment, and they had dinner at Max's restaurant at least once a week. And Alex and Max were cooking dinner together now on Sunday nights at the loft. Max was still the master chef, and Alex was the sous chef, anxious to learn new tricks from him.

Alex fit in perfectly to their self-made family, and the others hoped that he'd stick. It was too soon to tell.

The only one who clearly wasn't happy, and seemed downright miserable, was Abby. Ivan was torturing her, and there were even more excuses than before about why he wasn't around, or was out of range. He was sick, he had a migraine, he had put his back out moving scenery, he had to meet with backers or his accountant, he was reading new plays, he was exhausted from reading new plays, his cell battery had died, and he lost the phone itself once or twice a week, or there was no cell service wherever he'd been. He was like chasing quicksilver across the floor. Abby was constantly looking for him, and listening to his excuses when he turned up. And Daphne was around increasingly, while he claimed he was trying to teach her the business. And her father was supposedly eluding Ivan, and constantly traveling for business, so they hadn't met yet. And their bank account was nearly empty. Their financial situation was desperate.

And at the theater, while Abby continued to paint scenery and clean up, Daphne was constantly underfoot, but Ivan didn't want her to help. He told Abby she had asthma, and it would be bad for her health, and her father would be pissed. So Abby remained the slave, doing everything for him, and Daphne was the new fairy princess. Abby was trying to be patient about it, but her nerves were frayed. And he was either too sick, too tired, or too busy to come to the apartment to be with her, or he hadn't slept in days, and didn't want her spending the night at his place. It had become ridiculous, and even Abby knew it. But Ivan wouldn't 'fess up about what was going on. Abby was tired of his excuses. He was beginning to seem like the liar he was.

And when Abby asked Daphne about her father one afternoon, to be polite, and where he was traveling these days, Daphne looked at her blankly, and with a wistful expression said he had died two years before. The jig was up. Abby said nothing to her, but she was waiting for Ivan at the theater when he got there that night. He had a meeting in his office with Daphne that lasted for nearly an hour, and when she slipped out of his office looking flushed and sweaty, Abby quietly went in. She was not going to be put off anymore. It had gone on for too long, and he had played her for a fool.

He was adjusting his belt when she walked in, and it didn't take a genius to figure out what they'd been doing. She tried not to think of it when she confronted him. She could feel tears choking her throat.

"Where were you this afternoon?" And then she baited him. "Were you with Daphne's father, discussing the angel money with him?"

"Yes, I was." Ivan looked serious and dignified as he faced her and stared her straight in the eye. "He wants to give it some more thought."

"That must have been a difficult meeting for you," she said sympathetically. Her hands were shaking, but he couldn't see them.

"And why is that? He's a very nice man, and grateful for what we're doing for his daughter." She nodded and went on after Ivan spoke.

"Were you at a séance?" she asked in a solemn voice.

"Of course not. Why would you ask that?"

"Because he's been dead for two years. You should have checked with Daphne before you lied about her father. You seem a little foolish after that. And actually, more than foolish, you look like a shit, because you are one. You're having an affair with her, and I know it." He interrupted her, and he was pale.

"Did she tell you that too?" He was panicked.

"No, you just did. I figured it out the first time she walked into the theater, and you told her the same lies you told me three years ago about producing my play. And you're never going to produce hers either. Why bother to keep me around once you had her? Just to clean the floors and paint the scenery? Why lie to me about where you are, who you're with, your migraines, your back, your lost cell phone, and all of it? You know what? I don't care. I don't care who you're screwing or who you're lying to. I've closed my eyes and my ears and my mind for three years because I loved you and I believed you. I don't love you or believe you anymore, and one day she won't either, and you can find another young blonde to give you blow jobs in your office and screw you. You're pathetic. You really are what everyone says about you, you're a pathetic, arrogant dick. And I am through with you. Take Daphne, take her play, and all your lies and bullshit, and you know where you can put them. I hope she won't be as stupid as I was. And good luck getting the money out of her dead father because he's so grateful to you. Fuck you, Ivan Jones," she said clearly, yanked open the door to his office, walked out, and slammed it behind her. She hadn't felt this good in months. And as she walked across the stage to leave the theater, she saw Daphne standing in the wings.

" 'Bye, Daphne," Abby said as she strode past her.

"Are you leaving?" Daphne looked surprised.

"Yes, I am."

"Who's going to clean the theater before the performance tonight?" She seemed worried as Abby smiled at her.

"You are. This place isn't just fun and blow jobs, you know. You have to work too. Have a good time."

Ivan had walked out of his office by then, and was staring at her, unable to believe what she had said. He actually thought he could keep both of them on the hook. Abby realized now that she must have been out of her mind to love him and believe what he said.

"You can't leave," he said to her weakly, acting as though he'd been mortally wounded.

"Yes, I can."

"You'll turn into a sellout like your parents, and write crap for the rest of your life," he said ominously.

"Maybe I will," she said with rage in her eyes, "but I won't be a starving bullshitter when I'm forty-six, having other people do all the work. Grow up, Ivan, get a job. You're out of money, and you just ran out of slaves." Daphne was looking nervous at what she had just heard, and she was staring at Ivan with apprehension.

"I'm not going to clean the theater," she told him, as Abby picked up her bag and left. "You told me you'd produce my play." Daphne was nearly in tears, and Abby slammed the door to the theater as she left.

"You have to," Ivan said to Daphne, sounding stern.

"Fuck you," Daphne said, and followed the trail Abby had just blazed, and as Daphne left right behind her, she had just saved herself years of pain.

Abby was walking back to the apartment by then, at a rapid pace, with adrenaline pumping in her veins. There were tears running down her face, but she didn't know it and wouldn't have cared. When Daphne came on the scene, it made her realize she'd never had him, he had just used her, and he wasn't worth having anyway. She had been a total fool.

She flew up the stairs on Thirty-ninth Street to the loft, and the others were all at home when she walked in. She looked like a madwoman with her hair flying and tear-stained face.

"What happened?" Sasha asked her immediately, worried about her.

"I just told Ivan to go fuck himself." There was a look of astonishment on her face as she told them. "I finally realized he was cheating on me with Daphne, and I finally couldn't stand the lies and excuses anymore. He lied about everything. I'm done." A cheer went up in the room as she said it, and they all hugged her. She knew she'd be sad that night, when she thought about it, and remembered the good times, whatever they were, but she was twenty-nine years old and couldn't let guys like him use her anymore. She had to start over, she had to do it right next time, and she had to work with people who kept their word.

Abby had also been writing a lot lately, and had gone back to work on her novel. She had begun to realize that the experimental style she had adopted for him was stifling her own voice. She was not going to let Ivan kill her career by turning her into a puppet for his own use. All she wanted was to get back to work, follow her own path, and try to forget his. In every possible way, personally and professionally, she had wasted three years.

"How could I have been so stupid?" she said to her three best friends as she sat down on the couch and looked at them. "You tried to tell me, and I didn't believe you. I wanted what he said to be true."

"He's a clever guy," Morgan said sensibly. And the name Rasputin hadn't been so far off the mark.

"He plays on the naïve and gullible, and women who fall in love with him. It's all smoke and mirrors, like the Wizard of Oz."

"And I was the idiot in red shoes. What am I going to tell my parents? I threw three years of my life away." It was all coming clear to her, and it was horrifying, but at least she finally saw the truth.

"They probably knew, and they were waiting for you to wake up. They'll be happy you did," Claire said gently, and put her arms around Abby and gave her a hug.

"I think Daphne walked out too. I saw her leave the theater after I did. But there will always be another Abby or Daphne, willing to believe him and become his slave."

"Sooner or later he'll run out of slaves. He already has. He's a lot less convincing and appealing at forty-six than he was even at forty-three, when you found him," Morgan added.

The four of them had dinner together that night, and talked about it. It was like having three sisters who were there for her when it counted. She was going to call her parents and tell them too, but not yet. They all drank a lot of wine that night and went to bed early. Abby didn't know what she was going to do now. She was going home for Thanksgiving in a month, as she always did, and she was planning to do a lot of writing on her novel before that. She needed to get her own voice back, and get him out of her head.

She cried as she lay in bed that night, but she was tired and drunk and ashamed. Things could only get better after that.

Abby waited a few days before she called her mother and told her what had happened. Joan Williams wasn't angry at her—she was relieved.

"We knew he wasn't right, but you had to see it for yourself," she said gently.

"I wish I hadn't taken so long. Three years. What a waste of time," Abby lamented.

"I'm sure you got something out of it, and it will come out in your writing," her mother said confidently. She had faith in her daughter, her talent and fine mind. Ivan couldn't take that from her. And much to her amazement, she found that her mother was right. With the pure rage that was spewing out of her for Ivan, her writing was stronger, clearer, and more honest than it had ever been. Her anger fueled her, and she was doing the best work she'd done in years, as she holed up in the apartment, writing day after day while the others went to work. But she wasn't shirking. She was writing. This was what she had been meant to do all along, and she put her fury on paper. It was her way of driving Ivan out of her head and life forever. At long last. And healing would come when she had.

Chapter 10

Claire felt as though she were living a fairy tale, and her mother could hear it when she called her. She could tell that something had happened, and she asked if she'd gotten a promotion at her job. It never even occurred to her mother that a man had come into her life and Claire was in love. Her dating life had been so nonexistent for so long that her mother could only assume that the lilt in her daughter's voice was related to work. Claire never lied to her, although she said very little about George, even to her roommates. She didn't want to jinx it, and just wanted to enjoy what they were sharing privately for a while. But sounding hesitant, she told her mother about George.

"When did that happen?" Sarah was stunned, but happy for her. She could hear how elated Claire was.

"A few weeks ago, about a month."

"How did you meet him?" She was equally cautious, not wanting to intrude on her daughter.

"He's Morgan's boss."

"The one who's a whiz on Wall Street?" She seemed shocked.

"Yes."

"He has a lot of money," her mother said, dazed for a minute, and Claire laughed.

"Yes, he does. We've been flying all over the place on weekends in his plane. Florida, Vermont." He was taking her to a party in Boston the following week. And there were all the other places they had talked about in Europe. They had a lot of dreams and plans.

"That must be a little overwhelming, isn't it, dear?" She was worried about her, but pleased too. She didn't want her to wind up with a broken heart, and Sarah vaguely remembered that he was something of a playboy, which wasn't surprising for a relatively young man who had made a fortune. He had the world at his feet, and now her daughter in his arms. She hoped he was sincere about her, and not just playing.

"Is this serious?" her mother asked, adjusting to it rapidly, and hopeful.

"It's very new, but it seems like it, for both of us. He says he's been waiting for me all his life." Sarah smiled at her end of the phone. She was thrilled for her daughter. It was what every woman wanted to hear.

"That would certainly be life-changing for you," Sarah said thoughtfully.

"Yes, it would," Claire responded.

And then she thought of something. "Are you still coming home for Thanksgiving?"

"Of course." She always went home for both Thanksgiving and Christmas. She didn't want to disappoint her parents, especially her mother. The holiday would have been awful for her without her only daughter, alone with a morbidly depressed husband who barely spoke to her.

"Do you want to bring George home with you?"

"I don't know. We haven't talked about it." But she didn't want him to see how dreary her parents were. Their holidays had been grim for the last several years, with her father making constantly gloomy comments, about the state of the economy and the world. She didn't want to drag George into it, although she might have to someday, but not just yet. She was planning to warn him that she had to go home for a few days. She hated to leave him, but she had no other choice.

As it turned out, when she mentioned it to him, he was relieved too.

"Don't give it another thought," he reassured her. "I hate holidays with a passion. They always upset me. I hated them even as a kid." **No wonder,** Claire thought, **with his parents dead and living alone with his grandmother,** but she didn't say that to him. "I usually go skiing in Aspen for Thanksgiving, and the Caribbean for Christmas and New Year. You spend it with your family and don't give it a second thought." And he seemed delighted she hadn't invited him to join her. He wouldn't have gone anyway, but he didn't want to be asked and have to turn her down. It was working out perfectly for both of them. Thanksgiving was still a month away, but he was pleased to have the conversation behind them. Now they could go their separate ways for the holiday, and he promised they'd fly out to San Francisco for an ordinary weekend, so he could meet her parents.

But for all other things except the holidays, he wanted to be with her constantly, and they were seeing each other almost every night. She had spent several nights with him in his penthouse at Trump Tower, and he planned fun weekends for them. He loved going to parties with her, but he put his foot down on spending a night with her and her roommates at the loft.

"I'm too old to spend a night with all your roommates." He liked his privacy and his comfort, and all the luxuries he was used to. And he liked sleeping in his own bed, preferably with her. He told her that she was welcome to stay at his apartment anytime, and assigned a drawer to her for her things, and the use of a guest closet. But she hadn't left anything there yet, it seemed too soon. She took a small bag with her when she spent the night and took it all home with her afterward. She didn't want to be presumptuous and look like she was moving in. She respected his space. He had been a bachelor for a long time, and he was set in his ways. He had a houseman and a maid at his apartment, and they took good care of him. She still felt a little awkward when they served her breakfast in the morning, but they were very nice to her. It was an easy way of life to get used to. And he talked as though he expected her to be there for a long time, hopefully forever. He had never mentioned marriage to her, and she didn't expect him to, or want him to, but it was constantly implied that she was the woman of his dreams, the one he had waited for all his life. He even asked her one day, when they were walking on the weekend, how many children she wanted to have, and she was honest with him.

"None." He looked surprised. "I've never really wanted to have children. They seem like such a burden." All she could remember was her father complaining about it when she was growing up, and feeling unwelcome in his life. "I'd rather have a career."

"You can do both," George said gently.

"I'm not sure I could, and be fair to my kids."

"It's a lot easier to have children when you have money," he reminded her. "We could hire a nanny. To be honest, I've never wanted children either, but I've been rethinking it since I met you. If I were ever going to do it, I can't think of a more perfect mother for my children than you." She felt dizzy when he said it. It was the ultimate compliment. Everything was moving so fast, at his instigation.

He acted as though they'd been dating for a year or two, instead of a month. And no one had ever said "I love you" to her as fast. It panicked her sometimes, and she would try to take a little distance from him, just so she could keep some perspective, but as soon as she did, he sensed it, and did everything he could to pull her closer again.

He knew she was worried about her career if she got too involved with him, but he assured her he wouldn't interfere. And in spite of her fears, and occasional panic, she loved what he said. Who wouldn't? And he texted and called her three or four times a day. It annoyed Walter whenever he became aware of it, and told her in a loud voice to tell her boyfriend to cool his jets. He was unspeakably rude, and increasingly so as he saw the mentions of their romance on Page Six. It was as though he resented what was happening to her, and he made slurs about her boyfriend and said she probably didn't care about her job anymore, which she assured him wasn't true. She was still supporting herself, with no help from anyone, and needed the money. But the atmosphere at work just seemed to get worse. George compensated for it lavishly on the weekends, and for two days she could forget Walter Adams and his ugly, boring shoes.

She had sent out several more e-mails with her CV, but no one had offered her a job yet. So she was still dependent on him. And George was the sweet spot in her life. They were in the honeymoon phase, where everything looked perfect and rosy to both of them. And so far, they had never had even the hint of a disagreement or a fight. She hoped they never would.

Sasha and Alex were doing well too. They spent as much time together as they could, and talked a lot about their work. They had both tried to negotiate their schedules, so they could work and be on call on the same days, and have the same days off, and some of the time it worked, and they did fun things. They went to concerts at Lincoln Center, and she met his friends, most of whom she liked when they had dinner with them. He rented a small sailboat one weekend, and they sailed on Long Island Sound. They went to Union Square's farmers' market to buy food, and to the flea market in Hell's Kitchen. They bought pumpkins for the hospital and carved them for Halloween. She put two at the nurses' station in labor and delivery, and they took the rest to the pediatric ward, where the kids loved them. And by then he reminded her that they were on about date twenty. They had lost count, but the right opportunity to spend a night together hadn't turned up. Like George, he felt awkward spending the night at the loft with her roommates, or at least for the first time. And he said that his studio was a mess, and too small even for him, let alone for both of them. Valentina had asked her if they'd had sex, and told her she was ridiculous when Sasha said no. She told Sasha that she and Jean-Pierre had sex constantly, in every possible location, even on his plane. And she said there was something wrong with them, and insisted Alex was probably gay or couldn't get it up, which Sasha told her was rude. But Alex and Sasha were in perfect harmony with each other, and they weren't upset about the delay. And just before Halloween weekend, he had an idea.

"Why don't we go to some cute inn in Connecticut or Massachusetts for the weekend? We're both off. It would be nice to get away, and out of the city for two days." She loved the suggestion, and he made a reservation at a bed and breakfast one of the other residents had told him about in Old Saybrook, Connecticut. He and his wife had spent their wedding night there.

They left the hospital together on Friday night at midnight, and at nine A.M. on Saturday, they were on the highway to Connecticut in his car. When they checked in to the tiny inn, which was on the water, they could smell the salt air and hear the seagulls from their room. And there were several quaint restaurants nearby. Sasha had brought a small suitcase with her, and Alex set it down in their room. An old couple ran the place, and their niece cleaned the rooms after school. It was just what they'd wanted, and they talked about going for a walk on the beach, but Alex stopped her before they left the room and kissed her hard on the mouth. They had been kissing for over a month, but now they were away together for a weekend. Their intentions were clear. He had wondered if she would be shy with him, but she smiled as she unbuttoned his shirt, and unzipped his pants, and he did the same for her. It had been a long, respectful wait, and now they were like old friends. There were no secrets or mysteries or hidden agendas, they knew everything about each other except their bodies, and Sasha wanted to discover the rest now. Suddenly she couldn't wait another minute, and neither could he. They climbed into bed rapidly and laughed when it creaked, and they instantly forgot about it in a rush of desire that surprised them both. After a month of waiting while they got to know each other, now this was all they wanted, and they were both breathless afterward as they lay in bed and he admired her body. She was exquisite, and she thought he was beautiful too. They lay smiling at each other, and then they kissed again.

"I love you," he said softly. He had waited until now to say it, but they had said it in countless ways and thoughtful gestures in the last month.

"I love you too," she said happily. She felt as though she belonged to him now. The final bridge had been crossed. "My sister thinks we were crazy to have waited, but I'm glad we did." They lay in bed for a long time, and then showered together, put their clothes on, and went outside to explore the small town. They took a long walk on the beach hand in hand, and then they went back to the inn and made love again before going to dinner in one of the nearby restaurants, which was romantic and sweet and entirely candlelit. It was a perfect honeymoon. They spent two days of total bliss.

They were quiet on the ride back, listening to music, and thinking about what had happened that weekend. She leaned over and kissed him, and he smiled at her. He had never felt more elated or at peace in his life.

They took their time driving back to the city, after a last walk on the beach at the end of the day. "Do you want to sleep at the apartment?" she asked him as they drove toward New York. He hesitated, but he didn't want to spend the night without her now after what they'd shared that weekend.

"Yes, I do." And he had another idea, but he wanted to ask his parents first.

They found a parking space right outside her building, and they walked upstairs. All three girls were home, and Max had cooked dinner for them, and Oliver and Greg were there too. It was nice finding all of them there. It was like coming home to a loving family after their honeymoon. They hadn't had dinner, and Max had enough left for them, and poured them both a glass of wine. Morgan and Claire were still sitting at the table, and Abby was deep in conversation with Greg on the couch about her book. George had come for dinner but had already gone home. He had an early meeting the next morning, and Claire had decided to stay at the apartment, so they could get some sleep. They'd had a busy weekend. They had gone to Bermuda on his plane, and stayed on a yacht he had chartered.

"Where were you two all weekend?" Max asked as they ate the pot roast he had prepared, which everyone loved. It was his grandmother's recipe from the old country, and he'd made it with mashed potatoes and creamed spinach, and chocolate soufflé for dessert, with crème anglaise.

"We went to Connecticut," Alex said cryptically as he smiled at Sasha, and everyone understood and looked pleased for them. There were no secrets in the group.

As they always did, they sat talking for a long time. The candles burned low on the table, and everyone was full and relaxed when the others went home. And after Sasha helped with the dishes, she and Alex went to her room and got into bed, as though they'd been doing it for years. They cuddled under her comforter, and they made love again, and just before they fell asleep, he told her he loved her, and she snuggled up to him and kissed his cheek.

"I love you too, Alex," she said softly, and a moment later she was purring in his arms like a kitten. The next thing he knew, it was six o'clock, the alarm had gone off, and it was time to go to work. They were on the same schedule that day.

She showered first, and then made him breakfast while he showered and dressed. She had it on the table for him when he walked out of her bedroom. The others were all still asleep. She and Alex had to be at work by seven, and they were on duty until ten that night.

"Thank you," he said, smiling at her. Staying with her had worked out better than he had expected. No one made an issue of it, and he felt as though he fit right in. Max had spent the night too, and the loft was big enough for all of them, especially with different schedules. Sasha shared a bathroom with Abby, who wouldn't be up before noon. "I feel like I'm in college again," he said grinning, except that he was there with the woman he loved, not a bunch of guys he barely knew.

"Sometimes I feel like that too. But I think I'd be lonely having my own place." She had been there with all of them for five years, and she couldn't imagine living anywhere else.

They left the apartment quietly at a quarter to seven, and he drove to the hospital and put the car in the garage. And then they walked into the hospital together, kissed, and wished each other a good day. Sasha was smiling when she got to the nurses' station, and looked at the chalkboard on the wall to see who was in active labor, who had delivered, when, and how many patients they had.

"Full house," she commented to the nurses.

"You can say that again. We delivered six babies

on Halloween. Two C's and four vag. The place was hopping all night. Lucky for you you were off." She smiled and nodded. It had been more than lucky. It had been their honeymoon. She grabbed one of the charts and went in to check on one of the women who had delivered the night before.

She checked on four of them, and then Alex showed up with a cappuccino for her, and hurried back to work.

"What did you do to deserve that?" one of the nurses teased her. She had seen them together before, and Alex looked smitten with her.

"You don't want to know," Sasha said with a guilty grin, and they all laughed.

Chapter 11

Alex called his parents about their Thanksgiving plans. His parents always hosted dinner, he and his brother were there, and a few friends of his parents who had nowhere else to go.

"I'd like to bring a friend with me, if that's okay with you," he told his mother on the phone, and she immediately made it clear that any friend of his or Ben's was welcome. He had brought friends home from college several times, but no one since and never a woman. This was a first for him. Ben had had a girlfriend for two years, and she had joined them, but she and Ben had broken up that summer. So now it was his turn, and he had suspected his parents would be welcoming about it, but he still wanted to give them the courtesy of asking before he said anything to Sasha.

"Who is it? Is it someone we know?" his mother asked him.

"No, it's someone I'm going out with. Her name is Sasha Hartman, she's a resident at NYU too, and she's from Atlanta." It was as much information as he would give her.

"She sounds interesting," his mother said pleasantly. Helen Scott loved her boys, and always welcomed their friends warmly.

"Can she stay with us, Mom?" He felt like a kid again as he asked.

"Of course. You don't think I'd make her stay at a hotel, do you? And everyone's grown up now. She can stay in your room, if you want her to, the way Angela stayed with Ben. I'm going to miss her." It was an all-male household, except for her, and she had always missed having a daughter. And neither of her sons was married, so she had no daughters-in-law either. She had thought that Ben would marry his girlfriend, but she had had serious issues with his demanding schedule as an orthopedic surgeon, and had ended the relationship because of it. And even his mother realized that Ben was a little obsessive about his work, and he took too many patients, but he loved what he did, and Helen had told him that the right woman would understand it, and apparently Angela wasn't it for him. But he had been very upset about the breakup, and had only just started dating again recently, but there was no one important in his life yet.

Alex talked to her for a few minutes, and was excited to speak to Sasha that afternoon when they left work together. He had been staying at the apartment with her.

"I called my mother today," he told her as he drove home with her. "I wanted to clear it with her, before I asked you, and she's delighted. I'd like you to come home with me for Thanksgiving," he said, smiling at her. And then he added gently, "You're the first woman I've ever taken home." She leaned over and kissed him, and she was thrilled.

"I'm very touched and flattered." He told her he was proud of her, and couldn't wait for her to meet them. And she was excited about it. She knew it was a big deal to him, and it was to her too.

"Should I bring Valentina?" she teased him, and he groaned at the image.

"I'm not sure they're quite ready for her yet," he said as Sasha laughed at him.

"Neither is our family, and we're related to her," Sasha said simply. She hadn't been planning to go home anyway, so she didn't need to explain it to her mother. Going home for holidays now was just too unpleasant, being pulled between her parents while they competed with each other. She didn't enjoy her stepmother, although she was a sweet woman, and her mother was just too difficult and hadn't done Thanksgiving dinner in years. She went to a friend's house every year, and was happy not to be bothered, so this was going to be the first family Thanksgiving Sasha had had in a long time. She was going to Chicago with Alex, and it sounded wonderful to her.

"I may have to buy a dress," Sasha said, thinking about it as they walked into the apartment. "I don't think I have the right thing to wear." Or she could borrow something from one of her roommates, which she did often. Abby was too small, and shorter than all of them, but Morgan and Claire were about the same size, and Valentina, which would have been exotic, but definitely not the right look.

"My father and brother are doctors. You can wear your scrubs and Crocs if you want to." He grinned at her. He was ecstatic that she was coming home with him. And he wanted to show her all his favorite haunts in Chicago. It was going to be a fantastic weekend. Sasha called Oliver that night to tell him about her change of plans and that she wouldn't be at their Thanksgiving dinner, and he was happy for her.

George and Claire had their first fight two weeks before Thanksgiving, over a trade show she had to go to with Walter in Orlando. George wanted her to go to a black-tie dinner at the mayor's mansion, and she said she couldn't go.

"That's ridiculous," George said to her over dinner at Le Bernadin, the finest fish restaurant in New York, and another of his favorite haunts. "Tell him you can't. I can't tell the mayor you won't come to dinner because you're selling shoes in Florida." He made it sound like a Moroccan bazaar.

"And I can't tell Walter to sell his own ugly shoes because I'm having dinner with the mayor."

"You don't even like the shoes he sells."

"No, I don't, but it's my job." It was the first time George had put pressure on her, but the dinner was important to him. The mayor and his wife were clients, and he didn't want to offend them. But she didn't want to offend her boss. Walter was difficult enough as it was, and he would read about the evening in the papers. He was scanning them daily now for mention of her, so he could complain that she was out partying too much to do her job. She wasn't going to add fuel to the fire by refusing to go to an important trade show with him, even if it sounded insignificant to George.

"You don't even like your job," he reminded her. "You want to quit."

"That's true. But I don't want to get fired. It may sound tacky to you, but I need the money, and this is what I do."

"I didn't say it was tacky, I said it was ridiculous to cater to that ogre you work for. Let him sell his own damn shoes in Orlando."

"This is what he pays me for." There was no way to resolve the argument unless she agreed to go with George, and she couldn't do that, whether George understood it or not. This was exactly what she'd been afraid of since the beginning, that he would try to force her to quit her job at some point, and then she'd be dependent on him. That was precisely what she didn't want, and surely not this early in the relationship, or even later on. She had to have the ability to work and earn her salary, whether he liked it or not. She was sorry to miss the party with him, but if she didn't want to get fired, she had no choice. And she didn't want to give up her job with Arthur Adams until she had another one, hopefully a better one, which she wouldn't get if she got fired from the one she had. She knew that George understood the concept, he just didn't like her saying no. The word was unfamiliar to him.

They finished dinner in silence, and he took her home to Hell's Kitchen in the Ferrari in a huff, and went back to his apartment after he dropped her off. He never stayed at the loft with her anyway, but he didn't invite her to stay with him uptown that night. He was mad. And she held her ground. But she was depressed the next day about the argument, and she looked glum at her desk, when a messenger walked in carrying an enormous bouquet of roses with a card that said, "I'm sorry I was such a jerk last night. Go to Orlando. I love you. G." She smiled the minute she saw it and called him immediately, and thanked him for being understanding.

"I'm sorry, Claire. I was just disappointed. I wanted to go with you and show you off."

"I'd much rather be with you than in Orlando," she said honestly, and then noticed that Walter was standing there, listening to her, and she told George she had to get off. This was a headache she did not need.

"So are you coming to Orlando or not?" her boss asked her angrily.

"Of course I'm coming."

"Then what are the flowers about?"

"He loves me, that's all," she said nervously.

"You're going to wind up marrying him and quitting," he said, looking sour.

"I'm not going anywhere," she said firmly, "except to Orlando with you."

"Fine," he said gruffly, and stalked out of her office. She always felt like she was on thin ice with him now, but better with him than with George. And she was relieved that they had resolved their first big argument nicely, and he had backed down.

And that night, George told her he was taking her away for the weekend, and it was a surprise. He told her to pack summer clothes, and she couldn't wait to find out where they were going. He was a good secret keeper, and she didn't find out till Saturday morning when they got on the plane. He was taking her to the Turks and Caicos. He had told her to "think beach," so she had brought the right clothes. He had rented a private villa with their own pool, at the best resort on the island. He still felt guilty about their fight and wanted to make it up to her, which he did. They hardly put their clothes on all weekend, and spent most of it in bed, and the rest lying naked by their private pool, making love in it, or having dinners served on their private patio at night. It was a fabulous weekend.

And two days after she got back, she went to Orlando with Walter, in coach on a commercial flight, to stay at a Holiday Inn, and George went to the mayor's black-tie dinner. She called him as soon as she checked in to the hotel.

"You've ruined me," she teased him. "Do you know what it's like to fly coach again and stay at the Holiday Inn after our incredible weekend? I feel like Cinderella after the ball, with no glass slipper. This sucks." He laughed at her and told her it served her right for not coming to the dinner with him. But he also said he missed her, and couldn't wait for her to come back in two days.

The trade show was as boring and tedious as ever, and exhausting, and George took her to dinner the night she got back. They had dinner at Max's, and he told her all about the dinner she had missed. He had sat next to the mayor's wife and Lady Gaga, and said he'd had a boring time without her, which was hard to imagine and flattering, given who was there. He wasn't angry at her anymore, just happy to have her back in New York. And the following week he was going to Aspen, and she was going to San Francisco for Thanksgiving with her parents. She hated to leave him for that too, but she knew he'd have fun on the slopes, and he had friends there. He went several times a year, and was an expert skier. He was going to have a lot more fun than she was, without a doubt.

On Tuesday night before the Thanksgiving weekend, George had their own Thanksgiving dinner catered by "21" for them at his apartment, and the meal was delicious, better than most Thanksgivings. The turkey wasn't dry, the stuffing was perfect, there was cranberry jelly, mashed potatoes, an assortment of vegetables, and pumpkin, pecan, and apple pie for dessert, with whipped cream.

"I thought we should have our own Thanksgiving dinner, since we won't be together," he said lovingly to Claire. "I'm sorry I'm such a no-show about holidays. They just upset me, and Christmas is even worse. It's the worst day of the year for me. It brings up all my old stuff. I'd rather just ignore it, and ski my ass off in Aspen, but I'm going to miss you," he said, and kissed her. And after dinner they went to bed. They had agreed that she wouldn't spend the night, since he was leaving too early the next morning. He was planning to get up at five and leave the apartment by six. But he wanted to make love to her before they both left.

"I want to give you something to remember when you're in San Francisco," he teased her. And he made it a memorable evening for her. They made love as passionately as they had the first time. He was an incredible lover, and she was learning a lot from him. He was patient and gentle and had learned her body well, and everything that pleasured her, and

at other times he was so passionate he was almost
rough, but everything he did to her made her body
keen for him again and again. He made love to her
twice, and the second time, he lay in bed looking
at her afterward, and said something that touched
her deeply.

"I want to have babies with you one day, Claire.
Please tell me you'll be the mother of my children."
He looked so serious when he said it that she didn't
have the heart to refuse him, and for the first time
in her life she nodded and said yes, and meant it.
And he clung to her after that like a drowning child.
"I love you so much," he said to her, and then regretfully they got up, and he drove her home, and
kissed her for a long time before she got out. "I'm
going to miss you. Take good care of yourself. See
you Sunday." She walked into the building and felt
like she was on a cloud, remembering what he'd
said. It was already two o'clock, and he had to get
up in three hours. It was going to be a short night
for him. But he could sleep on the plane on the way
to Colorado. Her flight was leaving at ten o'clock so
she had to get up early too.

It had been a beautiful evening, he had seen to
that, and she kept thinking about what he had said
to her after they made love the second time, about
wanting to have children with her. It was not something she had ever longed for, but she could see herself having children with him now, and now it was
her hope too. He hadn't proposed to her that night,

but he had said he wanted her to be the mother of his children, which was almost the same thing. Her future was linked with his now. And she knew it was going to be a beautiful life with him. Of that she was sure. He was someone you could count on. He was the kind of man one should marry, not like her father. George was her dream come true.

Chapter 12

Claire and Abby shared a cab to Kennedy Airport, since their planes were leaving at almost the same time, Claire's to San Francisco, and Abby's to L.A. Claire thought that by the time her flight left, George might have landed in Aspen, but she hadn't heard from him yet. She was going to have a quiet Thanksgiving holiday with her parents, as she always did. She no longer saw her old friends when she went home for a few days. She had been gone for ten years since she left for college, their lives were too different now, they had nothing in common, and she was closer to her roommates in New York. Sometimes she ran into her high school friends when she went out with her mother, and she was always surprised by how little their lives had changed. They had married the people they had dated, or were living with them. A few had children now. Some worked for their parents, or at unexciting jobs. It was a small city, and other than the high-tech world of Silicon Valley, there were very few interesting opportunities. Her more enterprising friends had moved to New York and L.A. And there was no fashion milieu to speak of, so there would have been no jobs for her. She was glad she had gone to design school in New York, and stayed. And even though she missed her, her mother was pleased that she had opted for a life in New York. Her father never understood why she didn't move back to San Francisco and find something to do there. She no longer tried to explain.

Abby and Claire chatted on the way to the airport. They had hardly talked since her breakup with Ivan. She had been plunged in her writing night and day. It was as though freeing herself had fueled her, and she had a lot to talk about with her parents. They had always given her good advice in the past, and she needed to decide where to go from here. All she wanted was to finish her novel. It was going well.

Ivan had called a few times to make weak excuses for his behavior, and told her he was all alone. She stopped taking his calls, and he gave up calling quickly when he realized she wasn't sympathetic to his cause and hadn't changed her mind. He wanted her to feel sorry for him, but she didn't. She was just angry at herself for the time she had wasted, and for being such a fool. It had taken her years to realize what a loser he was, while he pulled her into the swamp with him, and used her in every way he could, and she had let him.

"See you on Sunday," Claire said as they hugged each other outside the terminal. Claire was going to check her bag at the curb, and Abby only had carry-on. Claire always took too much with her. And Abby disappeared into the terminal a minute later. Claire glanced at her phone while she checked her bags. George hadn't called her yet, so they probably hadn't landed. She hoped the weather was decent. George had told her that the airport was dicey in Aspen, coming in over the mountain for a sharp landing, but she wasn't worried about it. His pilot had been there with him many times before.

Alex and Sasha's flight to Chicago left two hours later, and she had packed even more than Claire for their four days in Chicago. She wasn't sure what to wear, so she had brought a multitude of options, mostly borrowed from Morgan and Claire, in varying degrees of dressy to casual, and conservative, which Morgan had for work. Sasha wanted to make a good impression on his parents, and every time she asked him, Alex said they wouldn't care what she wore. He described their dress code as preppy, which was what he wore too when they went out. His father and brother would wear suits for Thanksgiving and he would do the same, otherwise a blazer and slacks, and his father always wore a tie and looked like a banker. He said his patients expected it of him. And as a surgeon, his brother wore scrubs most of the time. Sasha informed Alex proudly that she hadn't brought hers, nor clogs or

Crocs. She packed sneakers in case they went sailing on his brother's boat, since they were die-hard sailors, but he said it was probably too cold for her. She could stay home with his mother, or explore the city on her own. His parents' home was on the lakefront, and his brother lived in the Wicker Park district, comparable to lower downtown New York. He said his brother was doing very well. He said it without envy, only pride, and she knew they were very close.

They landed at O'Hare Airport at one o'clock local time, which was an hour earlier than New York. His parents would still be at work, and his brother was coming for dinner that night. Alex knew they would all be curious to meet her, but he didn't make an issue of it to Sasha—she was nervous enough as it was.

The airport was jammed, and it took them an hour to get their luggage, and another hour to get home. A housekeeper let them in, and threw her arms around Alex the minute she saw him, and glanced at Sasha with curiosity and a polite smile. The house on Lake Shore Drive always looked the same to him, and was his boyhood home. It was elegant and traditional, with serious antiques and warm-colored fabrics. There were flowers in the living room, and a comfortable country-style kitchen, where the family often gathered. And then he showed her his boyhood room, filled with sports trophies and mementos of his school years. His diplomas from Yale and Harvard were on the wall as she looked around and smiled at him. And his brother's room looked much the same right next door. The two boys shared a bathroom. Their rooms were done in navy and plaids with a view of the garden, down the hall from their parents' big sunny bedroom. And he led her to a guest room across from them, where he and Sasha would be staying. His old room had a narrow single bed, and he would have felt strange staying in that room with her anyway, even with a bigger bed. The guest room was neutral ground, and he had never stayed there with anyone. He set her suitcase down. The room was done in blue and yellow floral chintzes. And she could tell they had used a decorator, unless his mother had decorating talent, and it was very pretty. The style was somewhat English, and the walls were a pale yellow, which made the room look sunny even in Chicago winter weather. They were predicting snow for the weekend.

They stopped in the kitchen and made a sandwich, and Alex suggested they go downtown and look around. He wanted to show her the city. He still had an old Toyota in the garage, which he kept there, and hadn't let his parents sell. He used it when he came home, and the housekeeper drove it for errands and to buy groceries. It started easily, and they headed from Lake Shore Drive to Michigan Avenue, on the scenic tour he had been planning for days. He was excited to have her with him, in his native city, and she had never been to Chicago before.

"There's the Wrigley Building and the John Hancock Center. My mom's office is in that tower, and my dad's is at the University of Chicago Medical Center in the Hyde Park area. Ben's in the same building, on another floor." It was the medical building where most of the high-end doctors were. Ben had joined a practice there as soon as he finished his residency.

They drove around the city, which seemed smaller than New York but had the same electric buzz. It was very different from Atlanta, where she grew up. And the shops on Michigan Avenue all looked sophisticated and were the same big-brand names and luxury stores as in New York, which was true of most cities today. But there was still a distinct flavor to the city, the buildings were even taller than in New York, and he explained that they were designed to accommodate the weather, so one had to brave the elements as little as possible. An office building would occupy the first twenty floors, topped by four floors of a department store, with possibly a restaurant above it, and then thirty or forty floors of apartments, so one never had to go out in the freezing cold or snow.

"It's one-stop living," he said, smiling. "It's very convenient, especially in the winter." Sasha found herself thinking that she wouldn't like living on the sixtieth floor in any city, but it did make sense.

They parked the car and got out and walked for a while. They wandered into a bookstore, and an art gallery, and it struck her immediately how friendly people were. Salespeople were pleasant, anxious to help them, and chatted with them.

They headed back to the house around five-thirty. Sasha started to fidget in the car, and Alex smiled at her and leaned over and kissed her. He understood why she was nervous, although he was certain that her fears were unfounded—he knew his parents and how kind and welcoming they were, and his mother had been pleased he was bringing someone home.

"They're going to love you," he repeated to Sasha for the thousandth time, and she looked worried and unconvinced.

"What if they hate me?" she said miserably. She had never been as anxious about meeting any-one. She loved him, and didn't want to screw it up somehow.

"If they hate you, I'll stop seeing you immedi-ately, and you'll have to go to a hotel," he said with a straight face, and she looked panicked, and he laughed. "Will you stop it? First of all, they're going to love you. Second of all, I'm thirty-two years old, not sixteen. I make my own decisions, and you're the best thing that ever happened to me. And my parents are smart enough to know it. You're the prize here, not me."

"You're their son. They want to protect you from

bad people and conniving women," she said, smiling at him.

"Are you conniving? How did I miss that? Listen, as long as you don't dress and act like your sister, everything will be fine. And knowing them, if I said I loved her and she showed up in a bikini and high heels, they'd be fine too. They're very open people, even if they look conservative. Don't put so much pressure on yourself. You'll see what I mean when you meet them. My mother is the nicest woman alive. She loves everyone. If you introduced her to a serial killer, she would explain to you about his terrible childhood, and say that he was probably having a bad day."

"I wish I could say the same about mine," Sasha said wistfully. "My mother hates everyone, and sees the dark side in every situation. She's the toughest divorce lawyer in Atlanta, and assumes the worst about everyone, including her clients. There's a good person in there somewhere, but she's gotten very hard with time. And she has nothing but bad things to say about my father and his wife. Charlotte's not a very interesting person, but she's a sweet girl and she makes him happy, and they have cute kids. My mother nearly went over the edge when he had them, and never stops telling Valentina and me how little he cared about us when he was setting up his business." He owned the most profitable department stores in Atlanta, and malls throughout the South. "I don't know how my mother got so angry and bitter, but she is, and she's getting worse with age. She gets along better with Valentina, because my sister doesn't take any guff from her. Every time I see my mother, I feel like I've been run over by a train."

"My mom's not like that," he said gently. "She'll probably want to adopt you. She was really sad when Ben and Angela broke up. She always wants us to have the kind of relationship she has with my dad. They're good together." He said it warmly, and as he did, Sasha realized that she had never seen a marriage like that. Her father was nice to her step-mother and protective of her, but they were by no means intellectual equals, and sometimes he acted like she was stupid and couldn't think for herself. She treated Sasha's dad like her father, and relied on him for everything, and all decisions. She had no mind of her own, and participated in none of their important plans. And her mother had been too hard on their father, and verbally brutal with him at times. She had always considered him be-neath her because he wasn't as educated as she was, but he had been very successful in spite of it. He had a good head for business and was a bright guy. Her mother dismissed his business acumen as luck, and being in the right place at the right time, which Sasha knew wasn't true, and was a mean thing to say about him, along with all the rest of what she still accused him of, including being a lousy father, which Valentina agreed with, and Sasha didn't.

Valentina thought their mother was a legal genius, while Sasha thought she was smart, but a bitch, which she certainly was to her. And their mother had more respect for Valentina's modeling career and international stardom than for Sasha's medical career, where she warned her she'd never make a dime thanks to the rigors of modern medicine and HMOs. Money mattered a lot to her, except Sasha's father's, which she dismissed, because it was his. And Valentina had the same profound worship of money as their mother.

"My parents were so mean to each other, and so unhappy," she said honestly, "that I never wanted to get married, and I still don't, if that's how it ends up. It was kind of a relief when they got divorced. Until he remarried and my mother went nuts about it, and she still is. They refuse to be in the same room, and only one of them could be at my graduation." She had never admitted that to anyone before.

"Which one came to your graduation?" Alex asked with interest.

"My father. My mother was trying a landmark case. She won, which justified not being there, to her. I think if I ever told her I was getting married, she'd kill me. Recidivists, as she calls them, are the mainstay of her business. She's handled two or three divorces for some of her clients. They always come back to her because she does such a good job, and gets them a ton of money from the other side. She usually represents women. She doesn't believe in marriage, and always told me and Valentina not to even think about it, just to have fun. Valentina took her seriously." She smiled at him. "And she likes rich guys, no matter how they make their money." As she said it, she thought of Jean-Pierre, who would have terrified her. There was something deeply unsavory about him, but Valentina didn't care or even notice. "It's hard to imagine people like your parents, who've done it all right. No one in my world ever has. All I ever heard about were the disasters, and all my friends' parents were divorced, growing up."

"A lot of my friends' parents were too," Alex said quietly. "My parents married very young. Maybe that helps. They just kind of grew up together, had us when they were young, and expected it to work." His father had just turned sixty, and his mother was fifty-nine, she knew. Her parents were almost the same age, but had a very different life experience. It was hard for Sasha to imagine. Her mother was always telling her about marriages that fell apart in a year. And the high divorce rate nationally supported what she said, that marriage just didn't work, and was an antiquated idea. According to her, women no longer needed to get married if they had careers, and to some extent Sasha believed her. And in her own way, Valentina did too. She had never gone to college and had started making big money at eighteen as a model, and she still made a fortune at what she did, more than Sasha ever would using her skill and brain. But her job had longevity, and Valentina's didn't. One day she'd be too old to model. But she'd made a few good investments, with their father's advice, so maybe she'd be okay, and Sasha knew he would always help them.

They pulled into the Scotts' driveway at six o'clock. All the lights were on, and his mother's Mercedes station wagon was in the garage. And feeling acutely nervous again, Sasha followed him into the house. She was standing just behind him in the front hall, when his mother came down the stairs with a broad smile and ran to hug him. She was a very pretty woman, wearing a simple dark gray suit and high heels, straight dark hair she wore pulled back, and a string of pearls on her sweater. She was everything he had described, except younger, prettier, and warmer. She didn't look old enough to have a son his age, let alone Ben's, and she still had a trim figure. She played golf and tennis on the weekends with friends. And Alex said she'd played touch football with them when they were young. She was athletic and in good shape, and her eyes widened with pleasure the minute she saw Sasha over Alex's shoulder while she hugged him. And a moment later, she was hugging Sasha as though she had known her all her life.

"We're so happy you came home with Alex!" she said, and sounded as though she meant it. "Has he been dragging you around downtown all afternoon? You must be freezing. We just lit a fire in the

den. Would you like a cup of tea?" Sasha nodded,
a little dazzled by the experience of this friendly,
open woman who seemed genuinely kind and
nice, and was so warm to her, even as a stranger.

"I'd love one," Sasha said, and followed them into
the study, lined with beautiful leather-bound books,
some of them first editions. They bought them at
auction whenever they found them. And there was
some very handsome art on the walls, much of it
English, of horses and landscapes, and several of
boats. The whole family loved sailing.

Sasha sat down on a comfortable couch, and a
moment later the housekeeper brought them all tea
on a silver tray. Their lifestyle was more elegant than
Sasha had expected, and Helen Scott took obvious
pride and pleasure in her home. She seemed to be
the perfect wife and mother, and had a major career
as an attorney too. It was impressive. Her mother
had the law career, but had never cared about their
home. She hated to cook, and had sold their family home and bought a small apartment without a
guest room six months after the divorce. She was a
great lawyer, but not a homemaker by any means.
Helen seemed to manage to do both well, and had
recently heard rumors about a possible appointment to the Superior Court bench, which had always been her dream. She would readily give up her
antitrust practice for that, if it happened. She wasn't
counting on it, but the prospect was exciting.

"So what did you see this afternoon?" Helen asked

Sasha warmly. "We have some wonderful galleries and cultural events here. It's a shame you don't have more time. And the lake activities are a lot of fun in summer, before it gets too hot. And whatever you do, don't let the boys take you out in the boat now. You'll freeze!" she warned her, and they laughed. "I'm sorry I wasn't home when you got here," she said to Alex. "I was trying to clear some things off my desk." The things on her desk were always fairly major, he knew, but she never made an issue of it, and made more fuss about his father's practice. She was fascinated by medicine, and always said she was a frustrated doctor, but hadn't had the patience for all the years of medical school and residency. "I know you're doing your residency too, but I don't think Alex told me in what." She turned her attention to Sasha with interest.

"OB/GYN. I want to do high-risk and infertility eventually. Right now I'm doing pretty much everything in OB, but there's a lot of high-risk now, and multiple births with older mothers, so it's pretty interesting." Helen seemed very interested in Sasha's work, and put her at ease with intelligent questions about it.

"Sasha has an identical twin," Alex added, and Helen looked fascinated by that.

"I always wanted twins," Helen said, "but there are none in either of our families," she told her, looking mildly disappointed.

"My father was a twin, but his brother died when

they were very young," Sasha said. Alex hadn't known that, and was interested to hear it. "My sister and I are totally identical," she said to Helen, "except in personality." She laughed. "Our parents could never tell us apart, which was a lot of fun. We used to play on it every chance we got. I used to write papers and take exams for her, and she flirted with boys for me, and got me dates. And then I'd blow it by being boring on a date. But I got her pretty good grades on exams." They all laughed at what she said.

"Is she in medicine too?" Helen inquired as they drank their tea, and there was a plate of homemade cookies that smelled wonderful—they were gingerbread and chocolate chip.

"No, she's a model," Sasha said simply. "She has a much more glamorous life than I do!"

Alex nodded ruefully. "Sasha forgot to mention to me that she had an identical twin when we first met," he explained to his mother. "I saw them at the cafeteria together at the hospital, and thought I was seeing double. She had just said she has a sister. They look the same, but they are day and night."

"She's pretty out there," Sasha admitted comfortably. She already felt at home with them, and she accepted her sister as she was. "She showed up at the hospital that day in a stretch jumpsuit that looked like a leotard, high heels, and a leopard coat, which is pretty tame for her. She fools my roommates all the time, pretending to be me, except one of them can tell us apart. Our parents used to dress us identically but in different colors, and my sister would make us switch clothes. It drove them crazy, and I have to admit, we loved it. No one could ever figure out who was who. But they can now. She wouldn't be caught dead in scrubs and clogs, which are all I own. No one in my family can figure out why I wanted to be a doctor. And some days, neither can I," she said as she smiled at Alex, and he laughed.

"Yeah, me too. They're trying to kill us with the schedule we're on. We go on dates and see who'll fall asleep at the table first." His father and brother had been through it too, so Helen knew what he was talking about.

"I could never go to the movies with your father when he was a resident. He fell asleep during the trailers for future films, and I had to wake him up after the credits. Actually," she said, with a twinkle in her eye, "he still does that now. Nothing's changed."

"What do I do?" a handsome man with gray hair asked as he strode into the room and kissed his wife. "Are you giving family secrets away?" He glanced at Sasha and included her in his smile, and hugged his son.

"It's no secret you sleep at the movies," his wife said, teasing him.

"Did you tell them that I snore?" He pretended to be worried, and turned his attention to Sasha. She was startled by how good-looking he was. He looked like Alex, but taller and older. He was a very handsome man, fit and youthful, as was his wife. Alex's parents made a beautiful couple. Neither of them looked their age, and could easily have claimed they were ten years younger. "Don't believe anything they say about me," he said to Sasha. "Welcome to Chicago. We're pleased you could come," he said, as his wife handed him a cup of tea, and he helped himself to a cookie. "We can't get Alex here often enough. They keep him too busy to come home." They all knew it was true.

"We had to agree to work on Christmas and New Year's to get Thanksgiving," Alex told them, and his parents weren't surprised. They'd been through it too thirty years before, and with young children. Tom Scott had been in medical school, and she'd been in law school when she had them. Looking back, they could never figure out how they managed. Helen thought it made life easier for this generation that they didn't marry as young, although she thought Ben should be thinking about it now. He had been about to get engaged to his girlfriend when they broke up a few months ago. Helen was philosophical about it, and said she obviously hadn't been the right one. She had decided that she didn't want to be married to a doctor who worked as hard as he did. And there was no denying, their older son was married to his work. Alex was a little more moderate, and their father loved his practice, but had always made time for his family too. He had set the boys a good example about priorities, and they'd had a warm home life as a result, and still did, and strong family ties.

"So what's on the agenda for tomorrow?" Tom asked his son. "A little sailing in the morning?" He looked hopeful, and Helen shuddered.

"You're all crazy. You'll freeze. If you go, don't take Sasha. We'll find something to do here. We'll set the table and keep the home fires burning, and maybe crochet a little." She was kidding, and they laughed. "Can't you find something else to do except freeze to death on the boat?"

"It's too cold for tennis," Tom said practically. He played several times a week, and it showed. "And I'm terrible at Scrabble." He grinned. Alex had told Sasha that they had their Thanksgiving meal midafternoon, and his family liked to do an activity in the morning, usually something active. On the weekend, he was planning to take Sasha to a museum and a nice restaurant for lunch, of which there were many, and she wanted to do some shopping, since she wouldn't have time before Christmas, once they went back to work. They had made lots of plans.

They chatted until dinnertime, and right before dinner, Ben joined them. And he was even more handsome than his younger brother. They were the best-looking family she'd ever seen, and Sasha silently wished that her sister would go out with someone like Ben, but she wouldn't have given him the time of day. He was too normal, healthy, and clean.

Ben was obviously curious about Sasha, and talked to her all through dinner. He asked a lot about the orthopedic service at NYU, they talked about the residency programs she and Alex were in, and the conversation was mostly medical all through dinner, and Helen held her own. Her husband talked a lot about his cardiology practice, and she was very knowledgeable and well informed about new developments in experimental surgeries. His father was very interested in Sasha's passion for infertility and innovations they were implementing in Europe, which they discussed at length. It was easy and fun for Sasha to talk to people who shared the same interests she did, and a little while after dinner, Ben left to go back to his apartment, and the elder Scotts and she and Alex retired to their respective rooms.

She flopped onto the comfortable bed and smiled at Alex, and he beamed at her.

"How are you doing? I'm sorry about all the doctor talk at dinner. It's like hanging out in the doctors' lounge. Being with my family is like living at a medical convention."

"I love them," Sasha said with a broad smile. "They're all so nice. My family is like a soap opera—everyone hates someone, they're always fighting or badmouthing each other. You're so lucky. This is great!"

"I like them a lot too," he admitted, and was thrilled that she did, and she had been totally at ease all evening, and he could tell his parents and brother approved, not that it mattered. He loved her anyway, but it was such a good feeling to know that they were pleased for him, and it was a perfect fit.

They were too tired to make love that night, and slept like little kids in the big comfortable bed. His parents were at breakfast, reading the paper, when Alex and Sasha walked in, and his father looked up with a smile. It was a crystal-clear icy-cold morning, a perfect Chicago winter day, with no sign of snow, contrary to the prediction.

"Are you up for a sail?" he asked his son, while Helen rolled her eyes and Alex laughed. And his mother looked pointedly at Sasha.

"Don't listen to them. They're insane. It's a family disease, and it's hereditary. Incipient insanity around boats, particularly sailboats." But by the end of breakfast, Alex had agreed to join his father, they had called Ben, and he was going to meet them at the yacht club.

"If you lunatics freeze to death on the lake, Sasha and I are eating the turkey without you." But when Sasha followed Alex to the guest room and watched him dress, she wanted to go too, and asked him if she could.

"Are you serious? You don't have to, Sash. They already like you. You don't have to prove anything to me or them." He didn't want her to feel uncomfortable or obliged to join them.

"It sounds like fun. Maybe I'm a little crazy too. Do you have a jacket I could wear?" She followed him to his old bedroom, and he pulled several out of the closet that were too big for her but would keep her warm. She picked one, and he gave her a set of long johns that he'd had when he was younger and smaller. She put on the clothes, two heavy sweaters, and the sneakers she had brought just in case, with a pair of wool socks over the long johns, and ten minutes later they were standing in the front hall, ready to go, and she was wearing a wool cap Alex had given her and her own gloves.

"Oh my God, another crazy person in our midst," Helen said, looking at Sasha, who was bundled up like a four-year-old to go play in the snow. "Don't let them kill you out there. I'd hate to eat the turkey all by myself." She kissed them all goodbye, including Sasha, and they drove off in Tom's Range Rover, with Sasha in the back seat excited to be with them.

Ben was waiting at the lake, standing near the boat, which was a beautiful old wooden classic sailboat that was their father's pride and joy. Ben had taken the tarps off while he was waiting, and they all climbed aboard. Alex showed her the cabins belowdecks if she got too cold, and told her not to be a hero if she was freezing, but she loved being on deck, as they pulled away from the dock in the crisp cold air. There was just enough wind to fill their sails, and they spent the next two hours sailing around the lake. Alex looked at her as though he'd found the prize of a lifetime, and Sasha was ecstatic, and he was sorry when they returned to the yacht club after a great sail.

"Your mother will kill me if we don't go back now," Tom said regretfully. Their faces were all red, and they looked healthy and glowing from the cold. Ben went back to his apartment to change, and Tom drove Alex and Sasha home, where Helen was waiting for them with hot toddies.

They were exhilarated after the sail, and Helen assured her younger son that he and Sasha deserved each other if she had enjoyed it, which she sincerely insisted she had.

Ben was back an hour later, and they sat in front of the fire in the den once they were dressed, and then moved into the living room when the guests started to arrive. They had invited four friends. Two of them were widowed women, and the men were alone for the holiday because one was divorced, and the wife of the other one was with their daughter in Seattle, where she was having her first baby any minute. Both men were doctors.

The dining room looked beautiful after Helen had set the table and decorated it with flowers and their Thanksgiving decorations. Their friends were interesting and good company, the meal was splendid, the conversation was lively, and they sat around and talked for hours until the guests left and Ben finally went home. They all said they were too full to ever eat again, but Alex knew that they would be eating the leftovers enthusiastically the next day and all through the weekend. He and Sasha were having dinner at a restaurant with Ben the following night, and then taking her on a tour of their favorite bars and hangouts. With their sail together that morning, she had become part of the clan.

She and Alex talked that night until they fell asleep, after they made love, as quietly as possible so his parents wouldn't hear them. She had called her own parents to wish them a happy Thanksgiving, and she'd tried to reach Valentina, but couldn't and had sent her a text, wishing her a happy Thanksgiving. She had reached Morgan at the apartment before she went to her brother's. Sasha told Alex before she drifted off that it had been the best Thanksgiving of her life, and seeing the look of love in her eyes, he believed her. It had been his as well.

Chapter 13

When Abby got to L.A. on Wednesday afternoon, her parents were still at work, and she let herself into their home in Hancock Park with the key they had put under the mat for her. Maria, their longtime maid, had already left for the day. She only came in mornings now, and the house was quiet, but familiar and comfortable. Her mother had had it redone the year before with strikingly modern furniture and contemporary art. It wasn't cozy, but it was beautiful. Abby wandered around the house, after she put her small tote bag in her room, and went to sit in the garden, thinking about what she would do now, and what she wanted to say to them. She knew they hoped she'd move home, now more than ever, but she wasn't ready to do that. There were writing opportunities in New York too, and she was doing her best work, writing normal fiction, since the breakup with Ivan. She'd done a few short stories and was working on her novel. She hadn't realized it for the past three years, but he had been holding her back, as she tried to meet his esoteric new-wave standards, which no longer felt right for her, and never really had. She was developing her own voice again, and she felt that her writing was getting stronger than ever before. Her parents had been very patient with her for a long time, and she hoped that they would be for a while longer. She still wanted their financial and emotional support to give her the time she needed for her writing.

There was a spare car in the garage that she used when she was home, an old Volvo from her high school days. It was ancient but it still worked. She drove around L.A. that afternoon, looking at familiar places, thinking about her life now without Ivan. It felt good to be home. And when she got back to the house, her parents were both there and excited to see her. She hadn't been home in almost a year, since Christmas, and she was startled to see that her parents had aged a little. She always thought of them as young and vital forever. Her father was complaining about a bad knee he had injured playing tennis, and her mother was healthy, but seemed subtly older. They had been older parents when she was born, as a surprise, and now they were in their late sixties, but still going strong with no thought of slowing down, and Abby was glad to be spending the holiday with them.

They talked about her writing that night at dinner, and were relieved to hear that she had given

up writing experimental plays to please Ivan, and
was writing more traditional material again. They
had ordered in fancy takeout food since her mother
never cooked. They had an offsite chef who dropped
off meals for them several times a week, based on
healthy nonfat meal plans.

"So what do you think, Abby?" her father asked
her gently. "Are you ready to come back and try
your hand out here? Your mother could get you
a job writing scripts on just about any show you
want." They thought in terms of commercial material, which was what Ivan had hated about them.

"I want to try to find work on my own," she said
softly, grateful for their help. And eventually, she
wanted to be self-supporting too, it was her goal.
And she didn't want a job because she was someone's daughter. She wanted to sell her writing or get
work because of her talent, not her parents. "I don't
think TV is right for me," she said honestly. "I'd
like to finish my novel and sell some short stories.
I could try screenplays later, but not yet." She gave
her mother three recent chapters of her novel that
night, and the next morning she told Abby how
much stronger her writing had gotten and said she
was impressed by how much her style had tightened
and matured. And she thought the work was very
cinematic and would make a great film. Abby was
pleased and respected her mother's opinion. Coming from her, it was high praise. Abby knew there
was still a dark edge to her writing, even without

Ivan, but now she felt sure it was her own voice and not his.

"Would you mind giving me a little more time in New York to work on it?" she asked humbly. She was at her parents' mercy financially, but they had always been supportive, and were still prepared to be. They both made that clear to her in their conversations and she was grateful to them. They had always been reasonable and kind, even during her three years of insanity with Ivan, and even more so now that he was gone. And she was clearly making progress with her writing without him.

They were having their usual Thanksgiving dinner the next day, with the strays her parents collected. She had learned her love of eclectic, interesting people from them—the difference was that theirs were often famous ones, not charlatans like Ivan, and Abby didn't always know the difference. Her parents were nontraditional, and their Thanksgiving dinner normally consisted of twenty or so people who had nowhere else to be, and no family, and Joan and Harvey Williams had their dinner catered by Mr. Chow, with fabulous Chinese food, a lot of great French wine, and a combination of actors, writers, directors, and producers, who gathered at their table for an unconventional Thanksgiving. Abby had always loved it, and the people she met there. It was very Hollywood, in the best way. Some of the guests came every year and had for twenty years. Others were new. Some

disappeared for a few years and then showed up
again after they came back to town, finished a
film, or wound up between relationships with no
one to spend the holiday with. There was nothing
mournful about it—in their own way they were
all winners, even if some appeared to be misfits or
very strange. Abby had grown up among people
like them, which had given her an open mind and
broad view of the world. And her parents may have
been too busy to spend a lot of time with her, but
she knew they loved her, in spite of the awful things
Ivan had said about them. She felt guilty for listening to him now, and knew that none of what he
said was true.

Her mother wandered into Abby's bedroom before the guests arrived and hugged her daughter.
"You know we love you, baby, don't you? Sometimes
I feel like we get disconnected with you living so far
away." And they never got to New York, they were
busy in L.A. with their work, and got stuck there.
"And I don't care what kind of work you do. I just
want you to be happy and feel good about yourself.
Don't let anyone pull you off your path or tell you
what to do, not even us. You don't even have to be a
writer if you don't want to be. Life is about following your own dream, not someone else's, whatever
that dream is. You know what's right for you, better
than anyone else. And we're here to support you,
whatever choice you make." It was what they had
done for the past three years, while Abby drank the

Kool-Aid with Ivan, and she was so grateful they hadn't given up on her, and were there for her now, stronger than ever.

"Thanks, Mom," she said, touched by what her mother said. "I'm really trying."

"I know you are. You'll get there. I didn't even start writing for TV until I was thirty-five. I was writing literary novels before that, and novellas, and believe me, they were awful. Your father was the only one who liked them, and that was because he loved me. So just hang in, and you'll find the right writing form for you, and the right vehicle, if you really want that." And they both knew it would be a lot easier without Ivan. They had been incredibly kind and supportive about the breakup without a single "I told you so."

"I feel so stupid for wasting all that time with him," she said with tears in her eyes, and her mother hugged her again.

"Don't forget I was married for two years, before your dad. The guy started out normal when we got married, and became a religious fanatic, and founded a cult in Argentina, which was when I left him. We all do stupid things sometimes and get involved with the wrong people. It's good to keep an open mind, but also to know when to cut your losses and close the gate. You did with Ivan. And it takes the time it takes." Abby didn't know what she had done to deserve such understanding parents, but she thanked God that she had them. She had forgotten about her mother's first marriage. She never talked about it. There was no reason to. Her parents had been happily married for more than thirty years, and they still liked surrounding themselves with unusual people. It had never occurred to them that it would rub off on their daughter, to her detriment. Her father had said as much to his wife when they first met Ivan in the beginning, but they let her make her own decisions, for better or worse, and it had worked out in the end, after a three-year detour, but she seemed to be back on track again and even more dedicated to her writing, which had improved after what she'd been through.

People started to arrive at six o'clock, and by seven, there were twenty-six guests, in assorted casual outfits, drinking wine, and in earnest conversations in the living room and around the pool. The food was delivered at eight, and people sat wherever they found space, indoors, outdoors, on the floor, in chairs, and on couches, with their plates perched on their knees, enjoying talking to the other guests about various aspects of show business. It was a perfect Hollywood Thanksgiving, and typical of her parents, and seemed normal to Abby.

She was sitting on the floor, in jeans and sandals, wearing a Guatemalan peasant blouse that her mother had brought her back from a trip when she was fifteen, when a man with a beard and jeans and a camouflage jacket sat down next to her on the floor, and introduced himself as Josh Katz. He said he had produced a TV show with her mother, and was now making a feature film on location in South Africa, about the early days of apartheid. She knew it was the kind of project her parents respected. He had warm dark brown eyes and a slight accent, and later said he was Israeli, and he had a strong interest in work about oppressed people, particularly women. For a minute, she wondered if he was a better version of Ivan, with a more convincing line, but she also knew that if he was sitting in her parents' living room, he had the right credentials and was for real. Her parents were allergic to phonies, which was why they had hated Ivan.

"How come you're here?" Abby asked him, and then realized how that sounded and apologized. "I mean alone on Thanksgiving. Do you live in L.A.?"

"Some of the time. Tel Aviv, L.A., New York, and wherever I'm shooting. Johannesburg right now, but I'll be back in a few weeks for postproduction. I have two sons here. I'm spending the weekend with them, but I was free tonight, so your parents were nice enough to ask me when they heard I was in town. And I'm starting a film here in six months, so I have to find an apartment, to finish this film and the next one. I'll be here for a year and a half."

"How old are your sons?" She liked him. He seemed interesting, nice, and offbeat, like her parents.

"Six and eleven," he said proudly and showed her a photograph of them on his phone. They were cute boys. And he looked to be about forty. "My wife lives here. We got divorced two years ago, but I try to see my kids whenever I can. It will be nice living here for a while. I hear you're a writer." She nodded, looking vague for a minute. "What do you write?"

"I've been writing plays for experimental theater for the last three years. Now I'm working on a novel and some short stories. I've gone back to a more traditional style." She smiled. "I'm trying to figure it out. I'm in transition," Abby said and laughed.

"Sometimes that's a good thing. It leaves you open to change. Sometimes you have to tear everything down to build a stronger structure. I find that to be true in life and movies too."

"Then I'm right on track." She laughed ruefully, and he smiled. He liked her, and he liked her parents too. They were good, honest people with talent and integrity, which were rare in Hollywood.

"Can I read anything you've written?" He was always looking for new material and found it in surprising places.

"My stuff isn't representative of my current style and what I'm doing now. And my novel isn't finished."

"Have you ever written a screenplay?" She shook her head in answer. "It's a pretty short jump from plays to screenplays—you'd probably find it easy. Can I see something you're working on now? A few chapters of your novel?" He handed her his card before she could answer. "Send me something. You never know. I may know someone who's doing something you'd be perfect for. That's how it works. Networking. That's how I met your mother, and I did some shows for her, which got me started. She gave me a chance." Joan had always been brave about that, and had discovered some real talent, people who were famous now, and a few duds. She was willing to make mistakes, which made her more forgiving of others.

"Okay," Abby said thoughtfully. He was very convincing, in a nice way, and very positive. She got pulled away by her mother then, to talk to someone else, an old friend of theirs she hadn't seen since high school, who looked a hundred years old now, and was nearly unrecognizable after a face-lift. She was grateful her mother hadn't had any work done and still looked like herself, even if slightly older.

Abby found Josh's card in her pocket when she got undressed, and wondered if she should send him some short stories or a couple of chapters of her novel. She mentioned it to her mother the next morning when they had breakfast by the pool, sitting in the sun. Her father had gone to play golf, which he could still do with his bad knee.

"Why not?" her mother said easily. "He's a very talented guy, and very open to new ideas. I knew we'd never keep him around for long. He's too unconventional, and too creative, and he doesn't like playing by network rules." Her mother was good at doing that without compromising her talent or

ideas, but not everyone could pull it off. She had
a rare knack for walking a fine line between commercial and sheer genius, and the ratings showed it,
despite what Ivan said about her. "Send him something," Joan encouraged her. "Maybe he'll have
some good suggestions for you, and introduce you
to someone making an indie movie, if that's what
you want."

"Maybe it is," Abby said, looking thoughtful. "I
don't know where I'll wind up, maybe novels or
film." She knew she hadn't reached her final goal
yet. Her current writing was a work in progress.

Abby opened her computer that afternoon, and
sent Josh an e-mail of the first two chapters of her
book and one short story and said she'd enjoyed
meeting him, and then forgot about it, and went
shopping with her mother at Maxfield, and some
of the vintage stores they both liked. Their ward-
robes were very eclectic, and they loved borrowing
strange pieces from each other.

The weekend flew by, and she was sad to go back
to New York on Sunday. Her parents had told her
that they were going to Mexico for Christmas and
had invited her to join them, but she thought she
should stay in New York and write, and she didn't
like Mexico as much as they did, she always got
sick. In some ways, her parents acted like people
who didn't have children. They treated her more
like a friend, and always had. But the flip side of
that was that they accepted her independence and

had always given her her freedom. They had always treated her like an adult, even as a child. And they were delighted to include her in anything they did now, but they had never adjusted their life to her. She was welcome to follow along, but they made their own plans, regardless of hers, like Mexico over Christmas.

She promised to come back soon, and her father drove her to the airport and hugged her tight when they got there.

"We love you, Abby," he said, holding her for a moment. "Good luck with the writing."

"Thank you, Dad," she said with damp eyes. Even after the last three years of insanity with Ivan, which had been like joining a cult, they still believed in her. It was amazing, but that was the kind of people they were—always engaged in the artistic process, and profound believers in the power of the creative, even if they weren't perfect parents. She loved them anyway. She waved as she walked into security, and a moment later she disappeared, and went to board her plane to New York. It had been a great four days.

When Claire got to San Francisco, nothing had changed. And the occupants of the house never changed either. Her parents' house was a small, slightly shabby Victorian in Pacific Heights. It needed a coat of paint, but Sarah kept it looking fresh inside, even when she had to paint a room herself, which she sometimes did. And she used her least expensive upholsterers to re-cover the furniture so her husband wouldn't complain about the expense. Her father looked depressed, and was grousing about the real estate market. He hadn't sold a house in eighteen months, which Claire thought was due to his personality, not the economy. Who wanted to buy a house from someone who told you everything that was wrong with it and the world? And he hated the broker he worked for.

Her mother was making chirping noises, and had the house looking bright and pretty, with flowers in Claire's bedroom. She had bought a turkey, which was slightly too big for them, as though they were expecting guests, but they no longer entertained, and rarely saw their old friends. Her father had eliminated them over the years, and her mother no longer tried to convince him to have a social life, so she met her women friends for lunch. She did a lot of reading at night. And no one ever mentioned the fact that her father drank too much, which contributed to his depression. He was never falling-down drunk, but three or four scotches at night were too many, and Claire and her mother knew it, and never said it out loud. They just let him do what he wanted, and after the second scotch, he sat alone in front of the TV, which he did every night until he went to bed.

Claire's mother wanted to know all about George

when Claire got there, and she could see how excited she was about him. He hadn't called her yet from Aspen.

When Claire didn't hear from him when she arrived, she assumed that George was already skiing, or afraid to intrude on her with her parents, and she was sure she would hear from him later that night. When she didn't, she called him from her room on her cell, and the call went straight to voicemail. With the time difference between San Francisco and Aspen, she figured he was already asleep, so she left him a loving message.

He didn't call the next day on Thanksgiving, probably for the same reason. He was skiing for sure that day, and he knew she would be having Thanksgiving dinner with her parents, and he didn't know what time. Claire sent him a text, and he didn't respond.

It didn't start to worry her until the next day. They hadn't spoken since he dropped her off late Tuesday night, which was very unusual for him. He liked to keep track of her all day, with calls and texts, and to know what she was doing. After three days of silence, she wondered if he hated holidays so much that he had retreated into his cave in a mild depression. She didn't want to push him, or intrude or insist. So she sent him another loving text and said she missed him, without trying to make him feel guilty for not calling. He obviously needed space, and they would be home in two days, on Sunday night, and were planning to spend the night together.

Her mother's questions about him continued through the weekend, and Claire tried to answer as honestly as she could, that she had no idea what the future would bring, but that it appeared to be serious for both of them, and he was wonderful to her. She didn't tell her that he had asked her to be the mother of his children the night before she left, or that she hadn't heard from him in three days. She was sure that that was a momentary aberration— they had never been closer than the night before she left for San Francisco.

On Saturday, she felt a mild flutter of panic, and began to worry about him, and that something might have happened. What if he was sick, or had been seriously injured skiing? He might have broken both his arms and couldn't use his cell phone, or had a head injury, since he said he didn't wear a helmet but was an avid skier. But she thought he would have had someone call her if he was hurt, or texted her himself if he was sick. She had to believe that holidays were even harder for him than she had thought. He had cut off all communication with her, and was obviously depressed. She was concerned that she might have offended him without realizing it, but nothing on their last night together indicated it. He had hardly been able to tear himself away from her when she got out of the car on Tuesday night, and an hour before that said he wanted to have babies with her. How angry could he have been, and over what? Clearly, his silence was not her fault, but it was alarming anyway.

She was careful not to let her mother see how upset she was, as she continued to field her questions, and gently deflect them. And by Saturday night, Claire tried calling him several times, and left him messages saying how worried she was about him and how much she loved him. He did not respond.

She still hadn't heard from him when she boarded the plane to New York on Sunday morning. She was due to arrive at JFK at four o'clock, and to meet up with him after that. She called him from the car, and neither his cell phone nor the landline at his apartment answered. She knew the staff was off, and she didn't want him to feel that she was stalking him, but there was a knot in her stomach the size of a fist now. What had happened, and why wasn't he calling her?

She never heard from him that night, waiting at her apartment. Abby came back from L.A. and said she'd had a great weekend with her parents, and Sasha and Alex were back from Chicago, and Sasha said it had been a perfect Thanksgiving. Claire's weekend at home had been predictably depressing, and even more so faced with George's inexplicable silence, but she didn't say a word to her friends. And Morgan said they'd had a lovely Thanksgiving dinner at Greg and Oliver's. Everyone's holiday had gone well except her own. She was sure there was a simple explanation, and George would apologize for his lack of communication when he called. But in the meantime, not knowing the reason for it was agony, and she lay awake until four A.M., hoping to hear from him. Even a booty call after midnight would have been welcome—some sign of life from the man she loved who had wanted her to be the mother of his children only five days ago, and hadn't spoken to her since. It made no sense.

She woke up two hours after she fell asleep, long before her alarm, and waited until eight A.M. to call him. His staff didn't come in until nine on Monday mornings, so no one answered when she called his apartment, and he still wasn't answering his cell, and he had to be home by then, unless something serious had happened.

She dressed for work hastily, without coffee or breakfast, and felt disorganized and a mess and distracted when she got to her office. She waited until just after nine and called his office, knowing that he always got there by eight-thirty to prepare for the day. His secretary answered on the private line and said that he was in a meeting. Claire said to just tell him she had called. And now she was sure he would call her.

She could hardly think straight until lunchtime, and she snapped at Monique when she set foot in Claire's office. She was in no mood for her today. And providentially, Walter never came into her office.

Claire called George again at lunchtime and was told that he was out to lunch, and would be in meetings off-site all afternoon, and would not be back in the office. His assistant's voice gave nothing away. She was pleasant and cool, and when Claire hung up, there were tears running down her cheeks. Something was clearly very wrong. But what? And why? He was stonewalling her, and she had done nothing to deserve it. She was so panicked and in so much pain from worrying about it, she was breathless.

She left work half an hour early and told Walter she was coming down with the flu and had a fever. It was easily believable, she looked awful.

She went to bed as soon as she got home, and just lay there, until she heard Morgan come home hours later, and went to find her in her bedroom.

"He won't talk to me," she said in a hoarse whisper, as Morgan stared at her in amazement. She looked like she had been beaten, or had a serious illness.

"Who won't talk to you?" She couldn't imagine.

"George. I haven't heard from him since I saw him on Tuesday night. Everything was fine, and I haven't heard from him since then. He won't take my calls or answer my texts. Nothing. Silence. Do you think he dumped me?" She could hardly bear to say the words, but Morgan might know more than she did. Maybe he had told her.

"Of course not." She brushed the thought aside.

"He's crazy about you." She looked puzzled for a moment. "I know he gets weird about holidays, and sometimes he just disconnects for a few days. If things get too stressful at work, sometimes he takes off and goes somewhere for a day or two, and when he comes back, he's fine. Did you two fight about something?"

"Not at all."

"I saw him in the office today, and he looked normal. He was laughing with one of our clients. I think he had a busy day, but I'll admit, that doesn't explain it. Maybe leave him alone, and see what he does. Don't chase him. He's not injured, he's not dead, he's alive. He'll call you."

But two days later he still hadn't. She hadn't heard from him in eight days, and there was no explanation for it.

Claire had taken two days off from work, still claiming to have the flu. Everyone in the apartment knew by then, and they were tiptoeing around as though someone had died. Claire emerged from her room as seldom as possible, not wanting to see anyone, and Morgan asked Max what he thought about it that night.

"I don't know," he said honestly. "Men do strange things sometimes. Sometimes they move too fast and scare themselves to death, and then they run. But he's a serious guy, with a responsible business. You'd think if he was backing out, or changed his mind, he'd have the balls to tell her."

"Maybe not," Morgan said quietly. They were having a late dinner at the restaurant, and the crowd was thinning out. She just hoped George didn't walk in with some other woman, but she couldn't imagine he'd have the bad taste to do that. And she couldn't ask him at the office. He was her boss, and had never discussed the relationship with Claire with her. Whatever she knew, she had heard from her roommate. George was not one to discuss his private life with his employees, no matter what they read on Page Six. "He's dumped a lot of women over time. I think he's somewhat relationship-phobic. But there's no reason to just cut her off. He should say something. The poor thing is going nuts, and she looks like she died." Morgan was upset about it, and even knowing him as she did, she couldn't figure out what was going on.

"I can imagine," Max said, looking sympathetic, and then Morgan thought of something she'd been meaning to ask him, but kept forgetting and hadn't found the opportune moment.

"I know this sounds crazy, but a few weeks ago, I found something unusual in a file the accounting department gave me by mistake. It jumped out at me off the spreadsheets. Money that was put in the wrong account, another smaller amount that was withdrawn and then returned a week later. Nothing was missing, but it was shuffled around and in the wrong accounts. What do you make of something like that? Do you think some kind of funny business is going on there?" George was always so meticulous about their accounts that it had surprised her. "And he invested funds in a company where one of the directors was indicted by a grand jury a few years ago, and then it was dropped. Do you think something weird is happening?"

"No, I don't. He's too smart to do something dumb like that, and he's a standup guy. He's got a golden reputation. He's not going to screw that up and risk getting in trouble. I think more likely someone just messed up in accounting, and then fixed it."

"I thought that too," she said honestly, "but you never know. Sometimes strange things happen in my business. Look at Bernie Madoff." He had been the ultimate financial criminal of all time, and had been sentenced to 150 years in prison, for bilking banks and clients out of billions. But not in her wildest dreams could she imagine George doing something like that. Nor could Max, which reassured her. She trusted his judgment, and he had keen instincts about people.

"George is no Bernie Madoff." Max smiled at her, and then looked serious again. "I'm not worried about his cooking the books, but I am worried about Claire. After eight days, it's not looking good, and there aren't a lot of possible explanations, except a bad one for her. I feel terrible for her," he said gently. He was very fond of Morgan's roommates. They were all nice women, and he liked them better than some of his own sisters.

"I feel awful about it," Morgan said too. "It's a hell of a blow. I think she trusted him completely and is really in love with him. I don't know how she'll get over it if he never shows up again."

"She may have to," Max said sensibly. "He owes her an explanation, but it doesn't sound like he wants to give it to her. By now he would have contacted her, if he was going to." Morgan nodded, as they both thought about it.

It pained Morgan to see how normal George looked in the office. He acted as if nothing had happened. And while he joked and chatted and went in and out of meetings, Claire was dying a thousand deaths in the apartment, staying in bed, and looked like a zombie.

Two weeks after Thanksgiving, Claire had still never heard from him. She had thought of going to his office to demand an explanation and confront him, but it seemed too melodramatic. She wrote him a letter asking him what she had done to offend him, and told him how much she loved him, and dropped the letter off at his apartment. She had written him several e-mails. It was impossible to understand. He had told her he loved her, that she was The One, and he wanted her to be the mother of his children, and then he had vanished. It made no sense and sounded crazy to all of them. If he had changed his mind, it would be awful, but all he had to do was tell her. It was obvious to everyone by then, and most of all to Claire, he had scared himself to death, panicked, and run. But he had been the one to set the pace and move so quickly. He had been the one to pursue her and convince her while he wooed her, and tell her he loved her almost on their first date. But whatever his reasons, he was gone, in silence. After two weeks, Claire could no longer make excuses for him—it was over. And she had never lived through as much pain. It was like a death, of hope and dreams, and love, and everything he'd promised. She had lost ten pounds and looked like a woman in deep mourning.

She had gone back to work after a week, and to make matters worse, Walter was torturing her. And even he could see that something terrible had happened.

"What's going on?" Alex asked Sasha the first time he saw her after Thanksgiving. "Did one of her parents die?" He couldn't imagine any other explanation for the way she looked, unless she was sick herself, and he hoped not.

"It would appear that she got dumped. George never said anything to her—he just disappeared."

"What do you mean disappeared? As in left town?"

"No, as in he wouldn't talk to her or see her. He just shut her out without a word of explanation."

"What a shithead," Alex said, looking angry. "He

was giving her the full-court press the whole time we've been dating. How can he not say something to her?"

"I don't know. But that's what he did." The others were trying to comfort her just by being around. But Claire was going straight from work to bed every day, and sleeping all the time.

And two days later Walter called her into his office. It was ten days before Christmas, and she thought he was going to hand her her end-of-the-year bonus. She had worked hard, and their numbers had improved slightly. And much to her delight, Monique was going back to Paris. Her internship was over.

"I've been meaning to talk to you for a while," Walter said, playing with two paper clips on his desk, which seemed to have his full attention. "I was going to talk to you two weeks ago, but you were out sick. You still look like hell, by the way. You should get checked out."

"I'm fine," she said bleakly, waiting for him to hand her the check so she could leave his office.

"I know you don't need this job anymore, with your fancy boyfriend waiting in the wings. You're going to be a billionaire any day now." Claire wanted to throw up as he said it, but it was none of his business that George had dumped her, and she didn't intend to tell him. She didn't comment. "But whether you marry the guy or not, I know this isn't the kind of company you want to work for. You want to work for one of the big high-fashion companies, Jimmy Choo, Manolo Blahnik, one of the sexy brands." He glanced up at her then. "And to be honest, you've got the talent. I hear you've been sending your CV around, and I'm sure one of them will snap you up. The truth is, your talent is wasted here, and I can't afford you. I'm letting you go, Claire. I'm sorry. It's not personal, it's business. We do best with our own classic styles. We just don't need a high-powered designer on staff, who wants to make changes. And our numbers are going to be a lot better without you. I can make whatever modifications we need myself." She was staring at him as though she didn't understand him, as though he were speaking another language.

"You're firing me?" Her voice was a squeak, and he nodded. "Because I've been sending my résumé around?"

"No, I've wanted to let you go for six months. Keeping you doesn't make financial sense. You need to go make your sexy shoes for someone else. I'm sorry. Good luck. You'll probably marry the guy anyway, and won't want to work anymore. But whatever you do with him, I can't afford you. I wish you all the best." He stuck out his hand to shake hers, and she shook it, feeling numb, and then turned in the doorway.

"Are you giving me my end-of-the-year bonus?"

He shook his head. "Severance?" She had worked for him for four years, and hated every minute of it. She should have gotten combat pay for that.

"Two weeks," he responded in a flat tone. "It's not personal, it's business," he said again. He was giving her as little as he could get away with. She couldn't believe it. She was in shock. She walked into her office, put her sketches and personal belongings in a cardboard box, and walked out carrying it, and once in the street, she hailed a cab. It was snowing, and she was soaking wet when she got in.

"You look like you've had a rough day," the driver said, glancing at her in the rearview mirror.

"I got fired," she said with tears and melted snow running down her face with her mascara. She looked a mess.

"I'm sorry," he said, and threw the flag on the meter to stop it. He took her home and didn't charge her when she glanced at the meter. It was blank. "Merry Christmas," he said, looking sorry for her, and she wished him a merry Christmas too, with tears pouring down her cheeks as she walked upstairs to the apartment. The other girls were there when she walked in, saw her, and were startled by how bad she looked.

"What happened?" Morgan asked her as she came to help her with the box, and Claire stared at her in amazement.

"I just got fired. 'It's not personal, it's business.' Two weeks' severance, no end-of-the-year bonus."

It was one blow too many after the hellish weeks of mourning George after he dumped her. And she had no idea what to say to her parents when she went home.

And that night, as though he had radar and needed to add insult to injury, she finally heard from George. He sent her a text. She read it in disbelief, but now nothing surprised her. "I'm sorry, I got in over my head. It's my fault not yours. I've thought about it carefully. This is the right decision for me. We don't belong together, Claire. I don't want a long-term relationship, marriage, or kids, or a partner. I'm a lone wolf at heart, and want to be. Best of luck. Merry Christmas. G." She stared at it for a long time and read it over and over, and then she started laughing hysterically. She walked into the kitchen, holding her cell phone, while the others stared at her, terrified that she was finally losing it.

"It's official. I just got a text from George after almost three weeks. He dumped me. By text. He said it was the best decision for him. And merry Christmas." She sat down at the kitchen table with them, feeling mildly hysterical. "Wow, dumped and fired in the same day," she said, sounding as though she was in shock. Abby put an arm around her without a word as Claire burst into sobs. But she was strangely relieved to have heard from him. At least it was nothing she had done. He had set the pace, he had wanted her so desperately and convinced her to go out with him, said he loved her and wanted to have babies with her, and now he had dumped her. The irony and the cruelty of it was almost unbearable, and she knew that she would never trust any man again. Her roommates put her to bed that night, and sat with her. Sasha lay on the bed next to her. Abby sat on the floor and stroked her hair. Morgan sat at the foot of the bed, looking miserable, watching her, and occasionally patting her foot under the covers. They were there with her—there was nothing else they could do. And Claire finally cried herself to sleep.

Chapter 14

Claire was the only one going home for Christmas. The others were all staying in New York. Morgan's office was always closed from Christmas until after New Year's, and she helped Max at the restaurant during the Christmas rush, seating people at the tables, when he needed her to, and helping him with the books. It was the only way to see him during the holidays, since he worked night and day, seven days a week, and was grateful for her help. She had no family to go home to anyway, and Oliver and Greg were skiing in New Hampshire with friends.

Abby's parents were in Mexico, and she stayed in New York to work on her novel. And Alex and Sasha were on duty at the hospital over both Christmas and New Year's. At least they'd be together.

Claire was sorry she wasn't staying with them too. By the time she left for San Francisco on the twenty-third, she felt like she was moving under water and drowning with the shock of everything that had happened. She wasn't even angry—she was in despair.

Morgan was furious at George. Although she had respected him before, she no longer did. It was impossible to respect a man who could be so cruel to her friend. Claire was reeling from having her heart broken into a million pieces. She could barely face the thought of Christmas and wished she wasn't going home. She would rather have stayed with her friends in New York, but didn't want to disappoint her mother. Before she lost her job, Claire had bought her mother an expensive handbag she hoped she'd love, and her father a sweater, neither of which she could afford now, but it was Christmas and she hadn't told them she'd been fired. She dreaded spending the holidays with them. They had no idea that George had dumped her and she'd lost her job. She was going to tell her mother while she was there, after Christmas, and ask her to tell her father after she left. She couldn't face dealing with his concern, and depressing view of life. Failure was familiar to him.

The flight was delayed by three hours due to weather in San Francisco, and there were storms all across the country, which made for a turbulent flight. She didn't care. If the plane crashed on the way out, it would be a relief. She wouldn't have to collect unemployment then, or look for a new job, or spend the rest of her life without George, hating him for what he'd done.

She was planning to send her CV out again when she got back, and tell them she was available immediately now and had left her job. When they checked her references, they would know she got fired. She was sure that Walter would tell them, but there was nothing she could do to stop him.

She took a cab from the airport, and her mother was waiting for her at home. They had finished dinner, and her father was already in front of the TV, watching the Discovery Channel with a drink in his hand, and her mother followed her to her room while she unpacked.

"You've gotten awfully thin," her mother said, looking worried. Claire had lost ten pounds or more in the four weeks since Thanksgiving.

"I had the flu. We all had it at the apartment," Claire lied to her, not ready to tell her the truth. She couldn't put the horror of it all into words.

Her mother had put up a tree in the living room, as she always did, and her father complained that it was a fire hazard. Claire had no idea how she was going to get through the four days she planned to be there.

"How's George?" her mother asked with a gentle smile as she watched Claire unpack. This time she had brought very little, and seemed to be living in jeans and black sweaters. She was in some kind of mourning, for George, and her heart, which had died.

"He's fine," she said vaguely, pretending to look

for something in her suitcase so her mother didn't see her face.

"What did he give you for Christmas?" **A kick in the teeth** was the only answer she could think of, as she continued to dig through her suitcase. Sarah had been wondering if he would give Claire an engagement ring, or maybe he was waiting for New Year's, which Claire had originally said she'd be spending with him.

"A purse" was the insane response that came to mind as she turned to face her mother. "I hate to do this to you, Mom, but it's three hours later for me, and I'm still tired after the flu. Would you mind terribly if I go to bed?" She knew her mother counted on her for company when she was home, but she just couldn't do it tonight. And she still had Christmas Eve and Day to get through.

"Of course not, dear. We can talk tomorrow. Would you like a cup of herbal tea?" Her mother was always so sweet to her that Claire felt terrible shutting her out, but she needed to be alone, just for tonight.

"I'm fine." Claire gave her a fierce hug, and a minute later her mother left to go back to her own room, to read as she did every night. And twenty minutes after that, Claire was sound asleep.

She helped her mother bake cookies the next day, and watched her prepare the turkey and stuffing and put it in the oven. Claire set the table for her, and Sarah had decorated a beautiful Christmas table for the three of them, as she always did. And afterward the two women would go to midnight mass, at Grace Cathedral. Claire's father hadn't gone with them in years.

It was cold when they came down the steps of the cathedral across from Huntington Park, with brightly colored lights hung in the trees, and Claire tucked a hand into her mother's arm as they looked at it for a minute. Sarah didn't ask her anything, but she could sense that something was very wrong, and she had seen Claire wipe away tears during the service. They got into the car to drive home, and Claire was very quiet.

"Thank you for coming out here," Sarah said softly, as they pulled up in front of their garage. "I know it's not fun for you."

"I like being with you, Mom," Claire said honestly. That much was true, and then she couldn't lie to her anymore. She turned to her mother in the car. "George dumped me, and I got fired. I didn't want to tell you on the phone, and I'm sorry to tell you now." Her mother silently put her arms around her and held her as she cried.

"I'm so sorry," she said soothingly. She didn't ask what happened. It didn't make any difference. The end result was all that mattered, and her daughter's broken heart. "I'm so sorry."

"Yeah, me too," she said to her mother, as she pulled away and smiled through her tears. "He said he's a lone wolf. But he's the one who rushed into everything, and acted like we'd been together for years. He scared the shit out of himself, and then he ran away."

"Do you think he'll calm down and come back?"

"Not a chance." She was bracing herself to see his name any day, linked with someone else, on Page Six. She knew it would happen sooner or later. He was finished with her, and she didn't want to give herself or her mother false hope. His text had made it clear. "And Walter is an asshole, and I hate his shoes." She laughed and blew her nose in a tissue her mother handed her, and this time Sarah laughed too.

"Even I wouldn't wear them at my age," she said to Claire, and they both chuckled.

"I'll start sending my résumé out after New Year's. Something will turn up." And she had the credentials to design more than just shoes. Footwear was her strong suit and her passion, but she was willing to design clothes too, and had the training for it from Parsons. "I'm sorry to tell you all this tonight. I was going to wait until after Christmas." But she was relieved that she had told her now. Her mother was always so comforting and positive. She was suddenly happy to be home, with her broken heart. "Don't worry about me, Mom. I'll find a job." She didn't want her mother to think she was going to be a burden on them. At twenty-eight, she wanted to stand on her own two feet. And her parents didn't have the money to help her. She expected nothing from them, except her mother's love. "And could you do me a favor, and don't tell Dad until after I leave? I don't want to hear about it from him." Sarah nodded, she understood.

They went into the house then and had a cup of chamomile tea in the kitchen. Claire's father had gone to bed, and the house was quiet as the two women sat talking. Sarah was looking pensive, thinking of what Claire had shared with her, and a little while later, they went to bed.

In the morning, Claire and her mother exchanged gifts sitting next to the tree. Sarah loved the Chanel bag and was touched by what it must have cost her, especially now. And Claire gave her father his sweater when he got up. He actually liked it and thanked her for it, and everyone was in a good mood.

Claire went into her room then, and sent e-mails to her roommates, wishing them a merry Christmas, and as she turned the computer off, her mother walked into the room, and quietly shut the door behind her, and then sat down on her daughter's bed. She looked as though she had something important to say. She had thought about it all night.

"Is something wrong?" Claire was instantly worried, but her mother shook her head.

"No, there's something I want to share with you that I've never told anyone. You know, I've been doing a lot of small decorating jobs for years. Your father never knew about most of them, but it gave me money for you for school, and some pocket money. Well, I did some bigger jobs too, and I've been putting the money away for many years." Claire could see where her mother was going, and she shook her head.

"I don't want money from you, Mom. I have a little saved up, and I can live on that and my unemployment until I find another job. I'm going to see a headhunter when I get back. I want you to keep your money for you."

"I want you to hear me out," she said with a determined look. "I have more than you think put aside. No one knows about it, except you and me now. I have an idea. I'd like to invest that money in a small shoe company. I know how to run an interior design business, and shoes can't be that different. We could start very small, on a tight budget. And you could design the shoes you want to. If we're successful, you can pay me back one day. But I don't expect that. I'd like to be partners with you." Claire was looking at her in amazement, and then her mother stunned her further. "I could come to New York for a few months, maybe even six months or a year, and help you get it off the ground. I could stay with you, if that's all right with you and the other girls, and we could work on it together." She told her then how much she had put aside, and Claire nearly fell off the bed. It was more than enough to get a small shoe company off the ground. She knew the figures of Walter's business, and her mother had more than that. And with that much to capitalize the venture, they could get a loan if they needed more.

"What about Dad?" She couldn't imagine her leaving him for as long as she said.

Sarah hesitated before she answered. "I think it's time for me to go back to New York and take my life back. I've been thinking about it for a while. This would be a perfect opportunity for both of us." She smiled at Claire, who came over to hug her fiercely.

"You are unbelievable, Mom. And I'd love to have you stay with me, if you don't mind sharing a bed. I'll ask the others, but I'm certain they'll say yes. But are you sure? That's a big step for you to take." She had been in San Francisco for thirty years, and unhappy for a long time, and she wanted to do something before it was too late. And if she could help her daughter in the process, it felt like the right decision to her. She had no doubts.

"It's time for your father to look at his own life, and figure out what he wants to do, before he's too old to enjoy himself. And if he doesn't want to, that's up to him." She looked sad as she said it, but smiled at Claire.

"Holy shit, Mom." Claire was grinning at her. "I can't believe you'd do this for me."

"Who else would I do it for? You're my only child." Sarah was beaming, and so was Claire as they hugged each other again. It was a plan.

"You know, we could use the same factory Walter does in Italy. They do great work, and they're reasonable. We could try Brazil, but I like the finish work better in Italy." Claire's mind was already racing ahead. Her mother had just turned the worst Christmas of her life into a hopeful one. She was going to start her own shoe business, and she was going to do everything she had to to make it a success. And then Claire was serious again. "When are you going to tell Dad?"

"After you leave. You don't need to be part of that. I'm going to tell him that we're starting a business together. He doesn't need to know where the money comes from. And I intend to tell him I was leaving him anyway. I don't want you getting blamed for it. And it's true. I was going to tell you before you left that I'm leaving him. It's long overdue."

"Do you still love him, Mom?" Claire asked quietly. She knew what a big step this was for her mother. She had protected him for thirty years, like a child, and sacrificed herself and everything she wanted in the process.

"I don't know," she said honestly. "He's hard to love the way he is. Not just the drinking, but his whole outlook on life. I love the way he used to be before his business ventures failed. He believed in himself then, but he's become a very sad, bitter man. I don't want that poison in my life anymore. It's too toxic. It's bad enough to get old—I don't want to do it with a miserable old man. I'd rather be alone.

Maybe this will jolt him into making some changes. And I want to try living in New York again. I have wonderful decorating clients here, but I'd love to play in the big leagues again. Or I thought that was what I wanted—now we're going to do shoes!" She almost giggled as she said it, and Claire grinned. "But I want you to ask the girls about my staying in the apartment. I'll understand if they say no. It would save some money if I can stay with you, but I don't have to. I can get a small place of my own for a few months, if that's better for you."

"It would be fun to have you at the loft with me, and they all love you. I'll ask them, and tell you the truth. When do you want to come?"

Sarah thought about it for a minute. "Would the first week in January be too soon? We should get moving." Claire felt giddy as she listened to her. She was starting her own shoe business! She had never even dreamed of something like this.

"That sounds fine," Claire said about her arrival. "What'll we call it?"

Her mother didn't hesitate for an instant. "Claire Kelly Designs, of course. What else would we call it?" The two women hugged again, and Claire thanked her profusely and opened her computer again when she left the room. She wrote a joint e-mail to all three of her roommates, told them she was starting her own shoe company with her mother, and asked how they would feel about her staying with them for a few months until they got it off the ground, and she told them she wouldn't be angry if they said no.

All three responses came back immediately. They were thrilled for Claire about the shoe company, and delighted to welcome her mother. Morgan had added, "I hope she cooks better than you do," but they had Max for that. Claire went to report their answers to her mother. She was in her bedroom sorting through her closet, and Claire knew why. She was getting organized for New York.

"It's a go," she said cryptically to her mother, "unanimously." Sarah beamed at her and gave her a thumbs-up. And Claire had to hand it to her. She was fifty-five years old and she was starting a shoe company. "I love you, Mom," Claire said as she left her mother's bedroom again and went back to her own. She was leaving in two days, and now she could hardly wait to go back and get started. They had a lot of work to do, and they'd have to go to Italy to meet with the factory, make production arrangements, and sign a contract. It was too good to be true, but it was happening. Two weeks before, she had lost everything, and now a whole new life was beginning. A miracle had happened, all thanks to her mother. And Claire hoped it was going to be a miracle for Sarah too. And who knew, maybe her father would wake up.

*   *   *

Alex and Sasha were on duty at the hospital on Christmas Eve, sitting in the doctors' lounge, sharing a sandwich. She had two women in early labor with first babies, who she knew were going to take forever and probably wouldn't be born until morning, but she was stuck there anyway. And everything was quiet in neonatal ICU. Three babies had gone home the day before, and the others were all stable. The nursing staff was keeping an eye on them while he and Sasha talked and ate the turkey sandwich he'd gotten for them downstairs.

"Merry Christmas," she said, grinning at him. "Maybe next year we'll actually have a turkey dinner instead of a sandwich." But neither of them looked unhappy, and they were grateful to be together. She'd been telling him about Valentina and her French boyfriend. They were in Paris and due back in two days. "I can't believe she's still with him," Sasha told him. "They usually don't last this long. It's been three months."

Alex's parents had called them earlier on his cell phone and wished them both a merry Christmas. She had loved spending Thanksgiving with them, and sent his parents flowers to thank them, and a five-pound box of chocolates for Christmas. She and Alex hadn't exchanged gifts yet and wanted to do it when they went off duty on Christmas night. She had bought him a warm hat and gloves, and a pair of Crocs as a joke.

He pulled a box of cookies out of his pocket then, that he'd gotten for her in the cafeteria, and he handed them to her when she finished her half of the sandwich.

"Dessert," he said as she hesitated.

"Maybe I should save them for later. It's going to be a long night." She eyed the box thoughtfully.

"Go on, I'll get you more if you want. The cafeteria's open all night." She weakened and dug into the box and couldn't reach the cookies. They were stuck inside. She peered into it and saw a black velvet box instead, and she looked at Alex with startled eyes.

"What's that?" Her heart was pounding as she pulled it out and looked at him in amazement.

"The cookies must have come with a prize!" he said with a wide smile. She had the box in her hand as he got down on one knee in the doctors' lounge and spoke softly. "Sasha, I love you with all my heart and being. I pledge you everything I have and am. Will you marry me?"

"Oh my God," she said, and started to cry, as he opened the box for her, and slipped a beautiful diamond ring onto her shaking hand. "Oh my God . . . I love you . . . What number date is this?" she asked, laughing through her tears. They had only been dating for three months, but he was absolutely certain she was the love of his life. He had told his parents over Thanksgiving what he intended to do, and they heartily approved. His father had lent him the money for the ring, and Alex was going to pay him back.

Alex kissed her then, and looked at her. "You haven't answered me. 'Oh my God, what number date is this,' is not a conclusive answer."

"Yes! Yes . . . oh my God. What am I going to tell my mother? She doesn't believe in marriage." She was panicked.

"Tell her we do," he said quietly, and put his arms around her, and she held up her hand to admire the beautiful ring he had just given her.

"When are we getting married?" she asked him. She was overwhelmed by the whole idea.

"How about June?" She nodded, and they were talking and hugging and laughing, when one of the labor nurses walked in and saw them. It was Sally, the one they both liked best.

"What are you two doing in here?" She liked them both and always enjoyed working with Sasha when she was on duty.

"We just got engaged," Sasha told her, beaming.

"Congratulations!" she said heartily, and then went back to business. "We're getting some action in Room Two. Heavy labor, we're at ten. She's ready to push. We need you."

"How did that happen so fast?" Sasha stood up quickly. "She was at two the last time I looked."

"Maybe the baby got tired of waiting. What do I know? You're the doctor, so get your ass in there and get to work. If you'll excuse me," she said, turning to Alex with a broad grin, "your fiancée is on duty. She's the doctor here tonight. And give him back the ring," she said to Sasha. "You can't wear it when you're doing a delivery." She was right. Sasha handed it to him, and he put it in the box and slipped it in his pocket.

"Don't lose it!" she said as she kissed him quickly and hurried after the nurse with a wave at her future husband.

The baby in Room Two was already through the birth canal and crowning when Sasha hurried into the labor room. She was just in time to catch the baby, a little girl who came out with two pushes, as her parents laughed and cried at the wonder of her. Sasha cut the cord and put her on her mother's stomach, and then to her breast, as the new mom held her close and looked adoringly at her husband and told him how much she loved him. And all Sasha could think of, as she watched them, was that one day that would be her and Alex.

Chapter 15

When Alex and Sasha came off duty on Christmas night, they met the others at Max's restaurant, after they went back to the loft to shower and change, and make love to celebrate their engagement. They were both glowing when they walked in to meet the others, and Sasha was wearing her engagement ring, but she was not going to tell them until they saw it. She was drinking a glass of wine since she they were off call for the night, and holding the glass with her left hand, when Morgan let out a piercing scream as she stared at it.

"Oh my God! What is that?" Max looked instantly terrified, thinking she had seen a mouse or a cockroach, and then Abby saw the ring and let out a shriek.

"What's wrong with you two?" Max shouted at them, and by then Greg and Oliver had seen it too and were laughing.

"We're engaged!" Sasha shouted at them. "We're getting married."

"Oh, for God's sake, I thought we had rats." Max turned to Morgan. "Don't ever scream like that again, unless someone shoots a customer." But they were all laughing and hugging by then, and Max ordered their best champagne for the table.

"When did he ask you?" Morgan wanted all the details, and Sasha told them. And Alex looked like a proud man as they all congratulated him.

"Have you told your mother?" Morgan asked her, and Sasha shook her head.

"We called Alex's parents and brother last night. I thought I'd call mine, and Valentina, tomorrow. I wanted to give us some time to enjoy it first."

"That should be fun with your mom," Morgan teased her. Morgan knew that Sasha's mother was no advocate for marriage, and would try to talk her out of it. She thought Sasha's father was a nice guy, but her mother was hell on wheels and rarely nice to Sasha, or anyone else.

"I think Valentina is coming home from Paris tomorrow, or the next day. And you're all bridesmaids," she told Morgan and Abby, "and Claire, of course. I have to send Claire an e-mail to tell her. We think we'll get married in June." She gave them all the details, as they drank the champagne. And Valentina would be the maid of honor, of course.

"Who's going to plan it?" Morgan asked her.

"I don't know yet. We haven't thought about it." It hadn't even occurred to Sasha.

"You need a wedding planner. You'll go crazy without one. You're too busy to do it. And I can't see your mom planning a wedding. That would be like hiring Cruella De Vil to be your dogwalker." They all laughed at that. "She'd be handing out pamphlets on divorce law in church." Listening to her, Sasha realized that they had a lot of decisions to make—about church wedding or not, Atlanta or New York, big wedding or small one—not to mention who was going to pay for the wedding. For now, she just wanted to enjoy the moment with Alex before all hell broke loose and they had to figure it all out. And it sounded like Morgan was right, they would need a wedding planner.

They talked about their e-mail from Claire about her mother moving in with them for a few months, so Claire could start a shoe business with her. They were all happy for her, and the three women said they liked her mother and thought it would be fine. She was a quiet woman, and if Claire didn't mind sharing her bedroom with her, it would work.

They all had a good time at dinner that night, and went back to the apartment. And the next day Sasha called her mother. She was already back in her office the day after Christmas.

They made small talk for a few minutes, which was never easy with her, and then Sasha decided to bite the bullet and cut to the chase.

"I have something to tell you, Mom," she said,

feeling ten years old again and as though she'd gotten in trouble at school.

"You're giving up medicine to go to law school? Now that would be good news." Muriel was only half-joking.

"Actually, no. I've been dating someone wonderful, and we're getting married. I'm engaged."

"How long have you been dating him, and why don't I know about him?" **Because you're a sour old bat,** Sasha wanted to say to her, but didn't.

"We haven't been dating for very long, and I wanted to be sure it was serious before I told you."

"How long?" Muriel Hartman asked, sounding as though she were cross-examining a witness.

"Three months."

"That's ridiculous. You don't know each other. Do you know the success rate of people who get married after three months?"

"I'm sure sometimes it works out. We've spent a lot of time together."

"What does he do for a living?" The inquisition was on.

"He's a resident at NYU, like I am, in pediatrics."

"I hope you're prepared to starve. He won't make any money, and you won't either. What do his parents do?" She hated the way her mother viewed things and the things she said. But none of it surprised her. This was why she rarely called her mother.

"His father is a cardiologist, and his mother is an attorney, in Chicago." It was all the information Sasha could give her. "They're very nice people. I met them at Thanksgiving."

"Well, I'm not paying for the wedding. I don't believe in marriage."

"I didn't call you to ask you to subsidize my wedding," Sasha said, annoyed. "I just called to tell you I'm getting married, and I was hoping you'd congratulate me, if that's not too much to ask."

"Congratulations," Muriel said tersely. "I'm sure your father will pay for the wedding," she added, sounding angry. "Have you called him?"

"No. I called you first."

"That was nice of you," she said, surprised. "When are you getting married?"

"Maybe June. We don't have a date yet. It just happened."

"Well, congratulations," she said again, "even though I think you're making a mistake. You should live together for a few years, and by then you probably won't want to get married. And don't have children!" she said sternly, which was a direct slam at Sasha and Valentina. **How about just not having a mother?** Sasha wanted to ask her. Sasha thought her mother was truly the most unpleasant woman she'd ever met. "Don't forget to give me the wedding date so I can put it on my calendar."

"Thanks, Mom," Sasha said, and hung up. She

had waited until Alex had left the apartment to call her, so he wouldn't be shocked by the exchange, and Sasha was glad she had.

She called her father after that, and her father said he was thrilled for her, congratulated her immediately, and said he couldn't wait to meet Alex. He said all the right things, and then put his wife on the phone to congratulate her too, which was a lot better than the conversation with her mother.

"Where are you getting married?" he asked her.

"We don't know yet, Dad. Maybe New York. I've lived here for a long time, all my friends are here now, and destination weddings are hard."

"Well, wherever you decide to do it, remember I want to pay for the wedding. Whatever it costs. And you need to hire a wedding planner. They're expensive but you don't have time to do it yourself." It was exactly what Morgan had said. And she was touched by her father's constant generosity to her. He was still helping her financially at thirty-two, and never complained. He knew how hard she worked, and one day, after her residencies, she'd be self-supporting, though not for a while. "Do you have a date yet?"

"Sometime in June. We have to figure it out." He hesitated for a minute when she said it, and then said it would be fine, whatever worked for her. "Thank you again, Dad." She was touched that he had been so quick to offer to pay for the wedding, unlike her mother, who would be a guest and nothing more.

"You two have to come to Atlanta now, so we can meet the groom."

"We will as soon as we can. Our schedules are pretty tough."

"We'll give you an engagement party when you come down."

She thanked him again and hung up, relieved that it had gone so well with her father, and according to expectations with her mother. At least now they knew and couldn't complain that she hadn't told them. And now they had to choose a location, a date, and find a wedding planner. It felt a little overwhelming as Sasha went to meet Alex for lunch. They were off for the entire day and night. And she smiled as she saw her engagement ring sparkle on her finger. She waved at Abby on the way out. She was sitting at her computer and gave her a thumbs-up.

Abby had been glued to her computer ever since Thanksgiving, working on her novel and short stories. And she was happy with the results. She was dedicated to what she was doing. Her parents had called her from Mexico over the holiday, and were pleased to hear that she was hard at work. As her mother told her, that always paid off in the end.

It had been something of a lonely holiday for her. Her parents were on a trip, Ivan was out of her life, although she hardly ever missed him, Claire was in

San Francisco, Sasha and Alex were always working, Morgan was at the restaurant with Max, and
there were times when she was very sad. Her work
was a good distraction, but it wasn't someone to
talk to. She went out for a walk that afternoon to
get some air, and walked past a pet hospital with
signs on the window, about dogs and cats that were
available for adoption. There were several Chihuahua mixes that looked a little like one of Oliver and
Greg's dogs, a pug mixed with a beagle they referred to as a puggle, and a number of fluffy dogs
with a lot of hair that were also mixes. Her favorite
listed on the poster was a Chihuahua-Dachshund
mix they called a chiweenie, which made her laugh.
And feeling irresistibly drawn to the photographs on
the window, Abby walked inside. There was a sign
indicating that the adoption center was upstairs,
and she followed the arrows to the second floor,
where she found herself looking through windows
at heartbreaking little abandoned dogs. There were
a number of cats too, some of them very old. All
of the pets at the hospital had been rescued, some
found by people and brought in, others brought in
by their owners, to give up. It seemed sad to Abby,
and all of them needed a home. It made Abby's
eyes fill with tears to look at them, they were all so
forlorn. And then she found herself nearly eye to
eye with an enormous black dog who stared at her,
barked, and sounded like he was saying "Take me
home."

"Don't look at me like that," she said to him through the glass, and he barked again. He wasn't taking no for an answer. "I can't," she said, staring him in the eye. "I live in an apartment." His next bark sounded like "I don't care." She walked away from him, and he started barking frantically, as she glanced at a dog whose sign said it was a Lhasa Apso, but she was very old. And suddenly Abby knew she had to leave before she made a terrible mistake and went home with a dog. She had just gone to see them for the fun of it, to cheer herself up, and now they were tugging at her heart. The enormous black dog was still barking, standing up in his cage, and he was as tall as a man.

"What is that?" Abby asked an attendant walking by.

"He's a Great Dane, he's two years old, he was a show dog, and his owner left him here because he moved away. He couldn't find a home for him. His name is Charlie. He's a good guy. Would you like to meet him?" She felt like she was being fixed up on a date. And before she could stop herself, she said "Okay" with a slight feeling of panic. She wasn't afraid of the dog, but of herself.

Charlie emerged from the cubicle she'd seen him in, and he came out politely, sat down in front of her, and held out his paw for her to shake.

"Hello, Charlie," Abby said meekly. "I want to be clear with you. I can't take you home with me. I have three roommates and live in an apartment.

And they'd kill me." His mournful eyes reminded her that it was a loft with a lot of space.

"How much does he weigh?" Abby asked the attendant out of curiosity.

"A hundred and eighty pounds."

"Oh my God," Abby said. Ivan had only weighed one sixty-five. Charlie was as big as a man, bigger in some cases. He sat looking at her expectantly, and she could see that he was very well trained. But what would she do with a hundred-and-eighty-pound dog? "What does he eat? A side of beef?"

"Ten or twelve cups of kibble a day, or a couple of cans of dog food." It didn't sound like a lot to her, given his size. "He sleeps a lot, and he's very well behaved." As the attendant said it, Charlie held out a paw to her again, with pleading eyes.

"Please don't look at me like that," Abby said to the dog directly. "I can't help you out. I told you, I have roommates."

The look in Charlie's eyes said, "So?" She was having an entire conversation with his very expressive face. And he was not letting her off the hook.

"Does he attack people? Has he ever bitten anyone?"

"Never." The attendant looked offended. "He's the gentlest dog here, and he's kind of a scaredy-cat. He hides when other dogs get aggressive. I don't think he knows how big he is. He thinks he's a lapdog."

"I'll think about it," she said to the attendant, said goodbye to Charlie, and headed down the stairs. And as she did, Charlie broke free from the attendant and ran after her, and then lay whining at her feet. Abby was nearly crying as she patted him, and told him he had to go back. And then he put his hands on his head, while he lay there, as though it were the worst news he'd ever heard, and he didn't want to hear it. Abby sat down on the steps next to him, and gently stroked his coat as he gazed up at her imploringly, begging her to take him. She felt a wave of insanity come over her then, stood up, faced the attendant, and said, "I'll take him." The attendant beamed and Charlie barked, and then the attendant asked her a question.

"Do you have a garden? He needs room to walk around."

"I live in a three-thousand-square-foot loft."

"That'll work." He went to get a leash for Charlie, the diet he'd been following, the vitamins he took, a sheet of instructions, and the adoption papers for Abby to fill out. The dog was glued to her side, and she glanced down at him with a stern expression.

"If they get pissed at me and throw me out, it's all your fault. You'd better be nice when we get home." He almost seemed like he was nodding, and the attendant put everything in a shopping bag after Abby signed the papers, and paid the ten-dollar adoption fee for the dog. This wasn't about money, it was about love and finding a good home. "Okay, let's go," she said to him, and he followed her down the stairs, politely. He had won.

Abby took him for a walk on the way back to the apartment, as the dog loped along. He really did look like a small horse, and people gave them a wide berth, not sure if the enormous dog was friendly. But he didn't react to anything on the way home, strollers, kids, bicycles, roller bladers, other dogs. He just trotted next to Abby, and once when a small dog barked at him, he panicked, and she remembered that the attendant had said he was a coward.

He ran up the stairs, and Abby was relieved when she saw that no one was home. Charlie sniffed around the apartment, and then lay down at her feet, as she grinned at him. This was going to be fun, if the others didn't kill her. The way he looked at her, she felt like he was talking to her. And when she sat down at her computer to work, Charlie went to sleep.

Everything was fine until Morgan came home from the restaurant during a break to change her shoes. Her legs were killing her after standing up all through the lunch rush in heels, and she wanted to put on flats. She saw Abby working, and then she saw the enormous beast and let out a horren-dous scream. Abby jumped a foot where she was sitting, and Charlie dove behind a chair, and lay there shaking, terrified by the scream. But at least he didn't attack her, Abby thought gratefully. The dog was cowering behind the chair, shaking like a leaf with eyes that begged Abby to protect him.

"What is **that**?" Morgan asked, advancing on them both with a determined expression.

"That?" Abby said innocently. "Oh, that. It's a dog."

"No, it's not, it's a horse. And how did it get here?"

"It walked up the stairs," Abby said, looking nervous. Abby was a tiny person, which made the dog's size seem even more incongruous, and Morgan was the tallest of the group.

"And why did it walk up the stairs?" Morgan asked her with a fierce stare.

"He was too big for me to carry," Abby answered.

"Why is he here? Please don't tell me he moved in while I was helping Max at lunch."

"Uh . . . well . . . actually . . . his owner moved away, and he had no home, and he looked at me so pathetically, and I couldn't, I had to . . . it's really his fault." Charlie was peeking around the chair by then, since no one had screamed again, and sensing an opportune moment, he walked cautiously over to Morgan and held out his paw. Morgan shook it and almost smiled, which Abby thought was a good sign. And Morgan was relieved to see he wasn't aggressive, even if he was huge.

"His name is Charlie, by the way," Abby told her.

"Abby, please tell me you didn't buy this dog."

"I didn't. I adopted him. It was only ten dollars. And the first week of food was free."

"You can't keep him in an apartment. It's not fair to the dog. He should live on a farm, or an estate, a ranch, or something." And as she said it, he rolled over onto his back with his paws in the air, to indicate how much he loved his new home. "I can't believe you did this."

"Neither can I," Abby said honestly, as Alex and Sasha walked in. Charlie dove behind the chair again.

"Wait till you see what Abby brought home," Morgan said with a look of exasperated amusement, as Alex and Sasha approached. Charlie was invisible behind the chair, cowering again.

"What did she bring home?" Sasha asked with a smile, thinking it was something to eat or a piece of furniture, and as she asked, an enormous head peeked out from behind the chair, and she jumped. "Holy shit! What is that?"

"She claims it's a dog, but it's actually a horse. His name is Charlie." At the sound of his name, he walked out, and came to nuzzle Alex's hand. Maybe he reminded him of the owner who had moved away.

"Great. He likes you. You take him home," Morgan said to Alex.

"Are you kidding? He's bigger than my whole apartment, and I'm never there."

"Neither are we," Morgan pointed out. "We all work."

"I don't," Abby said meekly. "I'm home all the time now. He can stay with me."

"Does he live here?" Sasha asked with a look of panic.

"What are you worried about? You're moving out in June." It was the first time anyone had said it since her engagement, and they all suddenly realized what her wedding meant. She would be moving out. And Charlie had moved in.

"Well, I'm not gone yet. Abby. You can't handle a dog this size," Sasha said practically.

"He's very well behaved," she pleaded his case, while Charlie waited for the verdict, go or stay.

"Why don't you all try him out, and see if it works? If it doesn't and he's a problem, Abby can take him back where she got him," Alex suggested. Morgan looked dubious, but it sounded sensible to Sasha and Abby, who both said okay. And as though he knew what they were talking about, Charlie lay down again with a sigh and stretched his legs and closed his eyes, and a minute later he was sound asleep.

"He's kind of sweet," Abby said, looking down at him, as her two roommates laughed and Alex grinned.

"Never a dull moment around here," Alex commented.

"You couldn't get a Chihuahua or something

small?" Morgan asked her as she went to get her shoes.

"He talked to me," Abby said to Alex and Sasha, as Alex leaned down to stroke him, and Charlie groaned with pleasure. He was one lucky dog. And for the moment at least, Charlie had a home.

Chapter 16

Sasha tried to reach Valentina again that night to tell her about her engagement, but the call went straight to voicemail. Sasha didn't want to just leave her a message about something that important. And the next day, she and Alex were at the hospital, and Sasha had no time to call. All the pregnant women who had held out through Christmas past their due date were delivering that day, two days after the holiday. Alex and Sasha had been engaged for three days.

By ten o'clock that night, Sasha had been on duty for fourteen hours, and she finally got a break. She had just done her last C-section, and put a ten-pound baby boy in his mother's arms.

"There can't be a baby left to deliver in New York. I think I delivered them all today," she said, as Alex rubbed her back in the doctors' lounge. Her cell phone went off as she said it. She looked, and a number she didn't recognize came up.

"Dr. Hartman," she said into her phone, in case it was a patient.

"Lieutenant O'Rourke, NYPD," the voice said, sounding official. "We have your sister here. You're listed as her emergency contact and next of kin." Sasha's heart started to pound as she listened. "She's all right," he said in a gruff tone, "but she's been injured. There was a homicide. The victim was shot in the back, and the bullet went through him and lodged in your sister's leg. It missed the artery, but she's lost a fair amount of blood. She's conscious. She's in the trauma unit at NYU hospital. Can you meet us there?"

"Oh my God, I'm upstairs. I'll be right there," Sasha said, and hung up, and looked frantically at Alex.

"What happened?"

"Valentina. Someone got killed and the bullet went through him and lodged in her leg. She's in trauma."

"Here?" She nodded and ran out of the doctors' lounge to the nurses' desk.

"Get someone to cover for me," she said, trying to sound calmer than she felt. "My sister's been shot. She's downstairs in trauma. If you can't find anyone, I'll come back. We don't have anyone in labor."

"Yet," the nurse added, shocked by what Sasha had told her. "Is your sister okay?"

"I don't know. I think so. She was shot in the leg." She kissed Alex goodbye then—he had to go back to work—and she left the floor at a dead run and went down the stairs to the main floor to the trauma unit. She asked for Valentina, and found her in a cubicle surrounded by policemen, covered with blood from head to foot, and hysterical. "What happened?" Sasha asked her. She was deathly pale, and they were examining her leg, and had given her a shot for the pain.

"They killed Jean-Pierre. We came back today. We were making love, and someone shot him. The bullet went through him and is in my leg. But they killed him." She was sobbing, and was in shock. Sasha watched them sedate her, and left the cubicle when Valentina got drowsy, and went to look for Lieutenant O'Rourke. He was waiting for her outside. After she introduced herself, she watched him do a double take when he saw her. He took her into an examining room to explain. Kevin O'Rourke was a burly Irishman, and he announced himself immediately as "Homicide. NYPD."

"Your sister's boyfriend was an arms dealer," he said simply. "One of the biggest in France. He expanded his operation to the States and the Caribbean several months ago. We've been watching him since he got here. He just did some kind of big deal in France. We don't know what it was yet—we're waiting to hear from Interpol. Someone got to him tonight. They shot him in the back while they were . . . er . . . uh . . . in bed. The bullet went right through his heart, angled downward, through his back, came out his chest, and lodged in her upper thigh, where it is now. That's all we know for the moment. We'll need to talk to your sister to see what she knows, after they get the bullet out. She's in no condition to talk to us now. She's damn lucky—the bullet could have hit the artery, and she'd be dead." He looked serious as he said it.

"Is she in trouble?" Sasha asked bluntly.

"Not that we know of. We've seen her with him for months. She may be able to identify some faces for us. But these big guys don't usually share information with their women. She's not in trouble with us, for the moment, but she will be with them, whoever killed him. She may have seen the shooter. If she did, she's in serious danger. Jean-Pierre was no small dealer—he moved up recently to selling nuclear weapons, to Middle Eastern countries and individuals of assorted nationalities. The French authorities have been watching him too."

"What are you going to do to protect my sister?" Sasha asked in panic, still concerned she could wind up in trouble with the law herself.

Kevin O'Rourke was unhappy when he answered. "Ten minutes ago I thought we had a problem. Now we have two of them. I didn't know she had an identical twin. We may have to help her disappear for a while."

"I can't disappear with her," Sasha said firmly. "I'm a senior resident on the OB ward. I can't take time off while you look for the killer."

"You may have to," he said grimly.

"I can't," Sasha said, without giving him an inch. She was not going to screw up her residency for Valentina. She had worked too hard for it.

"Your life could be at risk too."

"No one has any reason to connect her to me. She hangs out in high-flying circles all over the world. I'm here all the time, delivering babies."

"We'll talk about it," he said, sidestepping the issue, as the surgeon came to talk to Sasha. They were about to take Valentina into the OR to remove the bullet. He said she had lost blood, but her vital signs were stable, and they were giving her a unit of blood. Sasha went back to see Valentina again, she was woozy from the pre-op sedation, but Sasha kissed her and told her she'd be fine, and then they rolled her away. Sasha didn't go into the operating room with her, and a few minutes later Alex joined her. He had found someone to cover for him for a little while. She filled him in on what had happened, and what the lieutenant had told her about Jean-Pierre. It was all seriously unnerving, particularly about any future risk to Valentina from the shooter.

"I had a terrible feeling about him when I met him. I don't know where she finds them. But this one was the jackpot." Sasha was deeply upset.

"Maybe this will teach her a lesson," Alex said, looking unhappy. Sasha nodded, but in the meantime, this was going to change Valentina's life dramatically, if she had to go into hiding, possibly for a long time. And Sasha was not going with her. She didn't tell Alex about the risk to her, and what the lieutenant had told her, and then he went back to work upstairs.

Valentina was in a private room on the surgical floor two hours later, with two policemen outside her door, and a nurse with her in the room to make sure that she didn't bleed again. Sasha spent a few minutes with her, but Valentina was sleepy from the anesthetic and pain medication, and she wasn't making sense. Sasha left her and was about to go back to work when the lieutenant came looking for her again.

"How is she?" he asked her.

"Pretty out of it from the drugs. Otherwise she's okay." The surgeon had told her how lucky Valentina was—the bullet had done no major damage. Anything could have happened—she could have lost her leg or died. It was serious proof to Sasha that her sister's life was out of control, and she had terrible judgment about men.

"Did she ever say anything to you about the guy?" he asked Sasha.

"Only that he was a wonderful person, and treated her like a queen. I met him once and thought he was scary. She's got a weakness for bad guys."

"She won the prize this time," he said, echoing Sasha's own thoughts about her sister. "We're going to talk to her tomorrow about disappearing her for a while, and we want to know if she can ID the shooter. And we need to talk to you too."

"I told you, I'm not going anywhere. I have a serious job here, and he wasn't my boyfriend."

"Maybe not, but you're the mirror image of your sister. If you won't let us protect you, then you're going to have to make some major changes to your appearance. We can help you with that. But you can't go around looking like her, or you may run into the guy by accident and he'll kill you. These people mean business—they don't fool around." She had learned that tonight, and so had Valentina.

"Where would you put her?"

"Someplace safe, out of the city. We have secure locations. She'll have to cooperate with us. And you have to do everything you can to change how you look, so you don't wind up being a decoy. We don't want you to get hurt by these people," he said kindly. She was an innocent, unlike Valentina, who had taken the risk of consorting with criminals, even if she didn't know to what degree. Jean-Pierre clearly wasn't a simple businessman, and she must have known it, even if she knew no details. There was nothing wholesome about him. They had seized his plane that night and found the cargo hold full of concealed weapons. "Are you on duty tonight?" he asked her, and she nodded.

"Until six A.M."

"I'm going to send two of my men upstairs with you, and I'm sending them home with you. I want two cops with you at all times until further notice, and we catch the killer."

"Can they be in plain clothes?" He thought about it for a minute and nodded. It would be better that way. "Good. I want them in hospital scrubs while they're here. I don't want to be the talk of the hospital, trailing policemen behind me."

"You can thank your sister for that," he said tersely, and Sasha nodded.

"I know."

He assigned two policemen to her, and she had them change into blue surgical pajamas before they went upstairs. Their weapons showed under the thin scrubs, and Sasha had them put white doctors' coats over the scrubs. It worked, and the lieutenant laughed when he saw them.

"Just like on TV," he teased his men. "Try not to get sued for malpractice—the department won't pay for it." They followed Sasha back upstairs then. And miraculously, no women in labor had come in. The two policemen in costume followed her around, and sat in the doctors' lounge with her, while she dozed. They were on their feet at full alert, the minute Alex came through the door to check on her. He took her into a corner of the room to talk.

"What's with the two guys in costume?"

"They're here to protect me," she whispered. "I may need them for a while." She realized that she was going to need permission from the head of the residency program. Her sister had put her in a hell of a position. And when she left at six o'clock with Alex, the two cops followed them home, ready to stand at the door of the apartment. She invited them in to have coffee at the kitchen table. The Great Dane looked up with interest, lifted his giant head, and went back to sleep. Alex and Sasha said goodnight, went to her room, and went to bed. He was worried about her and didn't like what was going on.

"What aren't you telling me?" he asked Sasha. She didn't want to lie to him.

"They're afraid the shooter may go after Valentina, if they think she can identify him."

"Shit. And you look just like her."

"But they don't know that. No one in that crowd has ever seen us together. I met Jean-Pierre once. No one is going to come after me. They just don't want the guy to run into me by accident, and mistake me for her."

"So what are they going to do?" Alex asked grimly.

"Disappear her, until they find the killer, maybe with the help of an informant. And I told them I can't go into hiding, so they may change my looks for a while."

"How? With a clown nose?" He was not amused and had never dealt with anything like this before. Nor had she.

"I don't know. They're going to tell me tomorrow."

"What a fucking mess," Alex said, lying on the

bed with an arm around her, worried sick. "I may kill your sister myself."

"I hope it teaches her a lesson. She needs to clean up her act. This better be her last bad guy forever." He nodded, and they lay there together until they fell asleep, with the policemen sitting in the kitchen.

At eight o'clock, Sasha got up quietly, to call her parents in Atlanta to tell them what had happened. Her mother sounded cool about it, although Sasha could tell she was upset, and their father was panicked, and offered to fly to New York. She told him she'd let him know but thought they were going to spirit Valentina away pretty quickly to a safe location.

She talked to Valentina after that, on the hospital line, and she sounded awful, and was crying over Jean-Pierre.

"He was selling nuclear weapons," Sasha said in an angry tone.

"He was wonderful to me," Valentina cried.

"He was killing other people. You have to wake up after this. They could have killed you too."

"I know," she said sadly. "They almost did. The doctor said if they'd hit an artery, I'd be dead."

"Exactly. Did you see the guy who shot him?"

"No. We were making love. I had my eyes closed, and then he was on top of me, bleeding everywhere. I couldn't see anything. What are the police going to do with me now?"

"I think they're going to take you somewhere to keep you safe."

"My agency will be pissed," she said, sounding worried. "I have two shoots next week with **Bazaar.**"

"I'll be more pissed if they kill you," Sasha said, and promised to come and see her later, if the police let her.

The policemen in the kitchen had changed shifts, and Alex got up two hours later and found Sasha talking to the lieutenant who had come to see her, with three police intelligence agents, specialized in undercover work. They were looking her over carefully, her bone structure, her hair, her eyes. It took them an hour to decide what they needed to do. And they made their recommendation to the lieutenant while Sasha listened with a sinking heart. It didn't sound good to her.

Her long blond hair had to be cut short and dyed brown. They had contact lenses to change her eyes from green to blue. They wanted her in flat shoes and loose clothes, nothing tight and sexy like her sister, which she didn't wear anyway, and they didn't want her to appear as tall as Valentina, who always wore heels. They thought the hair color and length and blue eyes instead of green would do it. There wasn't much else they could do. They wanted her to be nondescript instead of striking like her sister, but Sasha was still a pretty woman. And they were debating brown contact lenses instead of blue.

Sasha cried when they cut her hair, and dyed it brown. They cut it short in a boyish cut, which actually suited her, but Alex looked upset. He loved her hair.

"It'll grow back," she told him, and then learned how to put the contacts in. They settled on the blue ones, and they were all shocked at the difference it made. She really did appear like a different person, and nothing like Valentina now, or herself. When Abby and Morgan came in for breakfast, they were amazed, and she told them what had happened the night before. Lieutenant O'Rourke left a little while later with his crew. Two plainclothes officers wearing jeans and T-shirts with baseball jackets to conceal their guns stayed behind. And Sasha felt like her life had been turned upside down. The lieutenant told her she couldn't visit her sister—they didn't want anyone to see them together. And Valentina would be removed from the hospital before noon, to an undisclosed location, until they found the man who had shot Jean-Pierre.

The three women and Alex were sitting at the kitchen table discussing it, and the two policemen had retreated to a discreet corner of the room and were playing with the dog. It had been a hell of a night. And Sasha had to see the head of the residency program to explain it to him before she went back on duty that night.

Morgan went to work at the restaurant then, and Alex went out for a while to get some air and pick some clothes up at his apartment. He was going to stay at the loft with Sasha until the killer had been found. He was back later that afternoon and went for a walk with the dog, while Sasha slept and Abby worked at the computer.

And at five o'clock, Claire came home from San Francisco and was confused. There were two men she didn't know hanging out in the kitchen. Sasha looked like someone she'd never seen before, and there was a dog the size of a horse snoring on the couch.

"What the hell is going on here?" she asked Alex, who looked at her ruefully.

"Good question. Valentina turned our life to shit last night, and nearly got herself killed." Sasha explained it to her, and Claire was stunned. It was the worst story she'd ever heard. And on a lighter note, she couldn't believe the size of the dog Abby had brought home, but she admitted that he seemed sweet. And he held out a paw to her too, and then licked her hand with a tongue the size of a ham. She sat down on the couch after a while and laughed.

"Well, at least it's not boring around here," she said, and Alex laughed.

"No one would ever accuse this place of that." They were allowed no contact with Valentina, and as far as he was concerned, that was a relief. Sasha had told her they were engaged, and Claire congratulated them both. And shortly after, Valentina called from the hospital with a tearful goodbye.

At seven o'clock that night, Sasha went to meet with the head of the residency program, who wasn't happy about the situation, but agreed to let her work since she was heavily disguised, and she would be accompanied at all times by armed undercover policemen. But he warned her that he wanted no disruption for the patients or staff, and Sasha promised him there wouldn't be. All she wanted was to do her job.

And at eight o'clock, she met the others at Max's restaurant, and they had a relaxed dinner, with the two policemen at a nearby table. Claire talked about the shoe business she was starting with her mother, and they were all excited for her. Sasha and Alex had traded their shifts that night, and it was a relief to be together and act like normal people, even though Sasha didn't look like herself, but she got to show off her ring. They all agreed it had been a crazy month, which included an engagement, a murder, and a dog. Not to mention Claire's broken heart, getting fired, and the business she was starting with her mother.

"And what are we all doing for New Year's Eve?" Oliver asked when he and Greg showed up for dessert, and everyone looked blank.

"We're working," Alex and Sasha said in unison. Morgan always helped Max at the restaurant, which left Claire and Abby free, without dates. Greg suggested the four of them go to Times Square to watch the ball drop and then go to Max's restaurant for supper with Max and Morgan when things calmed down.

"Sounds like a plan," Oliver said, smiling at the two women.

"Let's hope it's the start of a great year," Max added, and they all raised a glass to that, and then toasted the newly engaged couple again.

Chapter 17

Two days after Valentina was taken to an unknown location for her protection, Abby was peacefully writing at her desk, with Charlie asleep at her feet. Her cell phone rang. It was Josh Katz, the producer she had met at her parents' on Thanksgiving. She hadn't thought of him in a month, since she'd met him.

"I'm in New York for New Year's." He said he had moved back to L.A. since he'd seen her, but was visiting friends in New York for the weekend. "I read what you sent me. It's strong." She wasn't sure if that was bad or good, but she thanked him for reading it, and told him she'd been working on additional chapters of her novel that were even more cinematic. "That sounds interesting. Do you have time to get together?" he asked her, and she thought about it. She wanted to finish what she was writing that afternoon.

"Sure. When?"

"How about today? Now? I'm staying in Chelsea, and I could come over in half an hour. I'm sorry I didn't give you any notice. I wasn't sure I could get away. I had to meet with some post-production people for the film I'm finishing right now."

"That's okay. I'm just sitting here working. I can take a break." She wasn't sure if the meeting was business or social, but she could make the time.

He was there half an hour later. He was taller than she remembered, and he was wearing a ski parka and a heavy sweater. He noticed Charlie immediately, and stroked him.

"Great dog." He was the kind of dog men loved.

"He adopted me a few days ago. We're still getting acquainted." She smiled at Josh, and offered him a glass of wine, and he accepted a cup of coffee instead. He didn't waste time getting to the point. He wasn't much for small talk, and was all about his work. And now hers.

"I'm here to make you an offer. I liked what you sent me. You write great stuff, a little dark, but I like the genre. I'm working on a movie now, and it's right up your alley. We have a script, but I don't like it. I need someone to take another crack at it. It's based on a book I bought years ago. I've never done anything with it, but I think it's a good time for it. It fits into the mood of the country at the moment. And the minute I read your work, I knew you were perfect for it. I want to hire you to write the script." Her eyes grew wide at what he said.

"Just like that?"

"Just like that." He smiled at her. "I've got great instincts for matchmaking. You're perfect to do the script based on this book." He told her the title, and she laughed.

"That was my Bible five years ago. I used to read it every night."

"Then I was right." He smiled.

"But it's not a little dark. It's very dark," she corrected him.

"So is your work, but there are little touches of levity in it that I like. You know how to laugh at yourself, and it comes through."

"So what would I have to do?"

"You have to come up with a script we can work with. I can show you how. And you told me yourself that you're getting more cinematic. We can work on it together when I finish postproduction on this one. I need you in L.A. for a year, starting in March." Her face fell as he said it, and he saw it. "You can come back here in a year. You don't have to move back to L.A. forever. You can just live there for a year while we do the movie. Then you can do whatever you want, but you'd have an indie film to your credit, and you can call the shots on the next one, if the one we make together is a success. This film could give you a name people will want to hire." He was a good salesman, and for a minute she wondered if her parents had put him up to it, but he was too independent for that. He was kind of a maverick, and she liked that about him. And he seemed like an honest man.

He told her how much he wanted to pay her, and it was more money than she'd ever hoped to make, especially at this stage of her career, with an unpublished novel.

"Why are you giving me this chance?"

"Because I think you're good, and you're fresh. You're not jaded by Hollywood, and you haven't sold out. There's a raw openness to what you write that I really like. Will you think about it?"

"What if I get stuck in Hollywood forever?"

"That would mean that what you're doing is a success. There are worse fates than that, my friend. And you can live wherever you want between films. I do. It's not a bad life. And I don't mind L.A. when I'm working. Everything you need is there." She could hear Ivan's voice in her head screaming "sell-out" as she listened to him. But was that so wrong? To make an indie movie with a guy who wanted to pay her real money for her work? And he seemed to genuinely respect what she wrote and want to keep her style intact.

"I'll think about it," she told him, and he stood up. "How are your boys?" He smiled when she asked him.

"Thank you for remembering. They're great. We just spent the holidays together. They're a good age. I can take them anywhere, and they're fun. I wish I'd had more."

"Maybe you will someday," she said kindly. He certainly wasn't too old.

"Probably not the way I work. It drove my wife insane when we were married. She said I worked all the time, and she wasn't wrong. I'm a little mellower now, but not much. I like spending time with my boys, though. And the rest of the time I'm busy."

"Me too." She smiled at him. And now she was writing what she loved, not to please Ivan, but herself.

"Then come work on my movie. Make it our movie," he said, sounding very convincing, and she laughed.

"I'll think about it and let you know." The money alone was enticing, and she loved the book the movie would be based on. But she wasn't sure. She didn't want to leave New York, but his indie film would be perfect, just what she wanted. If it had been in New York, she would have said yes on the spot. She had shared her reservations with him.

"You can always come back here," he reminded her again before he left. She sat for a long time afterward, thinking about it, and stroking the dog. He looked up at her with a questioning look, as though he knew something was going on.

"Do you want to move to L.A.?" she asked him, and he wagged his tail and laid his head down again, as though he was too tired to figure it out and was leaving it up to her. "Thanks a lot," she said to him. "What do you mean, make up my own mind? If

I move, you do too, so you'd better think about it. L.A. is hot and nasty." But so was New York. But Josh was right, she could always come back, with an indie film under her belt. She was twenty-nine years old, and maybe it was time to take a real job and make some money, and not just talk about it and write for herself. It was a big decision for her, and could be the start of a real career.

The next day was New Year's Eve, and Greg and Oliver picked Claire and Abby up to walk over to Times Square. The crowd was massive when they arrived, and it was a festive atmosphere. When the countdown started, everyone screamed as the brightly lit ball came down, televised around the world. The four of them wished each other a happy New Year, and made their way to Max's restaurant, where he had saved them a table, and he and Morgan joined them at one A.M. It was a perfect way to spend the evening, with good friends.

They drank champagne and were all a little drunk when they left at two o'clock. And Abby found Charlie snoring in her bed when she got home. She gently pushed him aside, and climbed into bed next to him, and thought about the movie Josh had offered her the day before. And just before she fell asleep, she knew she had made up her mind. The champagne had helped. It was a terrific opportunity, and she couldn't pass it up. It was a chance to become financially independent and make a name for herself. What more could she ask?

And it was time to grow up. What she'd done with Ivan had been amateur hour. She couldn't do that anymore. She had to take this project and see if she could make it in the real world. And an indie film based on a book she loved was a gentle way to start a serious career. She couldn't ask for anything better. And when she finished the movie in a year, she'd come back to New York. And she wasn't going "back" to anything. She was moving forward. And she didn't have to leave till March. She had two more months with her best friends, in the apartment. And then she'd go to L.A. for a year. Just a year. And she already sensed that she'd learn a lot from Josh. She promised herself before she fell asleep that if she still felt the same way in the morning, she'd call him.

Charlie nudged her at nine o'clock. He wanted to go out, and he didn't care how hung over she was. She walked him around the block and came back, and then she picked up her cell phone and called. Josh picked it up immediately and sounded as bad as she felt.

"Sorry to call you so early," she said apologetically.

"No worries," he said in a gruff morning voice, deepened by too many shots of tequila the night before. He was staying with a writer who drank a lot. And he sensed that what he was about to hear was important. He had known it the minute the phone rang, just as he had known it when he read the material she sent him. Something huge was about to happen, to both of them.

"I'll do it," she said in a small voice. "I want to. I really want to. And I can always come back."

"Yes, you can. I'm leaving tomorrow. Do you want to have dinner tonight? We can talk about it."

"That would be fine. Do you want to come here? We're all having dinner around seven o'clock, with my roommates, at my apartment."

"I'd like that. And Abby, just so you know it, you're a great writer. We're going to make a fantastic movie together."

"I know. That's why I said yes."

"See you later," he said. He already knew the address since he'd been there to make her the offer. It was just the beginning. Great things were going to happen. And when he hung up, he lay on the bed smiling, knowing he had just made the best deal of his life.

Chapter 18

When they gathered at the apartment on New Year's Day, everyone was hung over. Max brought leftovers from the restaurant. He didn't have the energy to cook dinner. Josh Katz joining them for dinner came as a surprise, but the biggest surprise of the night was when Abby told them at the end of the meal that she had agreed to work on Josh's next movie, and she would be leaving for L.A. in March. There was a moment of shocked silence when she said it, and then a sudden babble of questions. How long would she be gone? When was she coming back? When was she leaving? And Josh felt a pang of guilt as he saw the sadness on her roommates' faces. It suddenly dawned on all of them that Sasha would be moving out in June after the wedding, and now Abby was going to L.A. to make a movie. And there were tears in Abby's eyes when she said she'd be gone a year. But she promised to come back for visits. Suddenly half of the home team would be gone, and they could all figure out that if the movie was successful, she would probably stay in L.A. It cast a pall on the end of the evening. They were happy for her, but it was a shock to realize that in six months, only Claire and Morgan would be living in the apartment in Hell's Kitchen, which had been home to two of them for nine years, and all of them for the last five. It was going to be a big change.

"I think your friends are going to hate me," Josh said quietly to Abby as he was leaving.

"They're happy for me. It's just going to be different." But she was still sure she had made the right decision. And she was taking Charlie with her.

"See you in March," Josh said when he hugged her goodbye. He was glad he had come to dinner and met her friends. He liked them all, they were good people.

The two plainclothes policemen assigned to Sasha had joined them for dinner too. It had been the usual noisy, friendly family dinner, although everyone was quiet after Josh left, at the thought of Abby leaving. With Sasha getting married, and Abby going to L.A. for a year, there was change in the air, which saddened them all. It was a bittersweet way to begin the year.

Morgan slept through her alarm the next morning, and rushed out the door before the others were up. It was their first day back after vacation, and she had a thousand things to do. But when she got to the office, two unfamiliar men opened the door, and when she walked in, there was pandemonium. Half a dozen FBI agents were removing boxes from their file room, and another five men were taking out their computers.

"What the hell is going on here?" she asked one of them, with a rising wave of panic. And then she saw two more agents walk out of George's office with him. He was in handcuffs, and he looked right through her as he walked past her, as though he'd never seen her in his life.

They used the conference room to interrogate the employees, while Morgan waited in her office. They had told them that no one could leave. Their cell phones had been taken from them, and they said they would be returned later, and people were standing around in clusters whispering all over the office. No one knew what was going on. And she didn't know much more after they interviewed her. There were two FBI agents taking notes, and a third one to interrogate her.

They asked her if she knew anything about their bookkeeping system, and the accounting, and precisely what her duties were. They wanted to know which clients she had seen with George, and on her own. She remembered the irregularity she'd seen recently and told them about it, and they wanted to know if she had reported it to anyone, or discussed it with George, and she said she hadn't. She said they had seemed strange to her, but even though the money was in different accounts than she expected it to be, nothing was missing, so she thought maybe it had been a mistake in accounting that had been corrected. And at the end of a two-hour interview, they told her that she was under investigation and could not leave the city. She asked them directly what George was being charged with, since he had been taken out in handcuffs, and they told her he was going to be indicted for running a well-concealed Ponzi scheme, similar to Bernie Madoff's, but on a much smaller scale. He had been cheating his investors, taking in money he didn't actually invest and was never going to return.

"That's impossible," Morgan said in defense of her employer. "He's meticulous in his dealings." And then she remembered the name on the list of directors that she had found disturbing since he had been indicted. But she still couldn't imagine George doing what they were accusing him of. It had to be some kind of mistake.

She was allowed to leave the office at six o'clock, and was told not to return. The entire staff was under investigation, and had been dismissed. The office was closed, and their accounts had been seized. They returned her cell phone when she left the office, and when she exited the building, she felt like she was in a state of shock. She took a cab back to Hell's Kitchen, and stopped to see Max at the restaurant. She desperately needed to see a friendly, familiar face. She burst into tears as soon as she saw him, and told him what had happened. He couldn't believe it either. But it was all over the Internet and TV that night. George Lewis was under investigation, and more than likely would be indicted by the grand jury for stealing millions from his investors. Bail had been posted at ten million dollars in a federal arraignment, and he was expected to get out of jail that day.

Claire was stunned when she heard about it too. She wondered if that had anything to do with why he had dumped her, but she suspected the two events were unrelated and that he was a criminal, or a pathological liar. The lone wolf was a crook. The next morning she and Morgan sat in the kitchen reading the papers, too shocked to know what to say.

"It looks like I'm out of a job too," Morgan said to Claire. She was panicked about her future, and had said as much to Max the night before. "Nobody is ever going to hire me after this." There would always be some question if she had been part of the Ponzi scheme, but she truly had no idea about what he'd done.

Federal agents came to see her at the apartment, and questioned her again. She had already told them all she knew, and said it all again. And they questioned Max at the restaurant too, wanting to know what she had said to him about her job. And he told them about her asking him what he thought of the irregularities she'd found, and he had told her that he thought they were accounting errors, and she had agreed. But neither of them had suspected something like this, the theft of millions from his investors. And he had done it cleverly and well.

She didn't know what to do with herself in the days after the office closed, and to keep her from losing her mind over it, and to keep her occupied, Max asked her if she would help him at the restaurant, and oversee his books. She was grateful for the distraction, and he offered to pay her a salary for doing it, which she wouldn't accept. But she went to work with him every day. It was a terrible time for her, and she clung to him like a rock in a storm.

Claire's mother arrived in the midst of the mess, and was shocked at what she read. He had sounded so perfect from Claire's description of him, and turned out to be a crook, on a major scale.

"Thank God you weren't still dating him when this happened," she said to Claire. "Do you think he knew this was coming?"

"No, I don't. Apparently, they've been monitoring him for months through the bank. Morgan says he had no idea, and neither did she. It's been a terrible blow to her." Morgan hadn't been able to sleep, and was losing her hair, which was apparently a reaction to the trauma she was going through. She still didn't know if they were going to indict her too. They had interviewed her several more times, and nothing was conclusive yet. And she couldn't look for another job until she was cleared, and absolved of any guilt. Claire was sure they would find her innocent of any knowledge of what he'd done, but in the meantime, Morgan's life was in limbo, her future uncertain.

Over coffee the morning after Sarah arrived, Claire asked her mother how her father had taken it when she left.

"He was shocked," Sarah said quietly. "He never thought I'd do it. But I'm glad I did. It's up to him now to figure out his life, without me. I need to take care of myself." Claire had never heard her mother speak that way, and she was proud of her for doing it. She was stronger than Claire had ever dreamed, and it proved to her that you could pick up the pieces and start again at any age. It had been weeks since the breakup with George, and Claire was still reverberating from it, but it had turned out to be a blessing, given everything that was happening to him. And then the two women got to work. They had a lot to do.

With Valentina in hiding from a murderer, her boyfriend assassinated, George being indicted for federal crimes, his startling breakup with Claire, and then Claire being fired by Walter, two plain-clothes policemen protecting Sasha, and Abby's announcing she was leaving in March, and Sasha in June, the mood in the apartment was decidedly somber, despite Claire's elation about starting her business, Sasha's over her marriage, and Abby's film.

Claire showed her mother the sketches she'd been working on since Christmas, and Sarah thought they were very good.

"When are we going to Italy?" her mother asked her, looking excited, and Claire smiled. This was going to be fun.

"Maybe next month, when we have enough designs for our first line. If we go in February, we should have samples by April, in time to take them to a trade show, and take orders for fall." She knew how it all worked, as she explained the various aspects of the business to her mother, and they made a timeline of what they had to do. It was going to be a lot of work. After they met with the factory, they could establish their price point. Claire wanted to try and keep their prices down, while offering a high-fashion look, and it was going to be a challenge. But she finally had a sense of freedom to do the kind of designs she wanted to do, after being stymied by Walter for years.

As the weeks went by, her portfolio took shape, and she made an appointment at the factory for mid-February. And the week before they left, Morgan was informed there was no evidence that she'd been involved in George's crimes, and she was free of any suspicion. It was an enormous relief. But they asked her to remain available for future meetings if

they needed more information for the federal pros-
ecutor's case against George.

"To put it bluntly," Morgan said to Max after the
grand jury had cleared her, "George is in deep shit."
She realized now that she had never really known
him, or what he was capable of. No one had. He
was a classic sociopath, with no conscience about
the people he had hurt, just as he didn't care what
he'd done to Claire, setting her up to trust him and
believe him, while she lowered her defenses and became vulnerable to him, and then he walked away.
Morgan found herself wondering now if he had
planned it that way, just to hurt her, and Claire had
thought of it too. If so, he was even sicker than they
thought.

At the same time, Sasha was staying in touch
with Lieutenant O'Rourke about her sister's situation, but there was no news. He said they were talking to every informant they had, but no one knew
anything. At least her sister was safe. But Sasha was
tired of looking like a freak, and having two plain-
clothes cops follow her everywhere.

She and Alex were working harder than ever, and
by the time Sarah and Claire left for Italy, they still
hadn't gone to Atlanta so Alex could meet her parents. They never got more than one day off at a
time, but they were determined to get there before
the wedding. And they hadn't found a wedding
planner either. Sasha had no idea where to look,
or who to ask. Oliver finally found one for them,

through a client whose daughter had just gotten married, but the wedding had cost a fortune, and she didn't want to take advantage of her father unreasonably, no matter how nice he was about it.

"It's a shame Valentina can't find a decent guy. If you had a double wedding, maybe you could get a group rate," Oliver teased her one night on the phone. She and Alex were going to meet with the wedding planner the next day. It was nice to be dealing with something pleasant for a change. All they talked about at the apartment now was George's indictment, and Morgan being cleared. She had decided to keep helping Max with his books at the restaurant, and Max said she was a genius at it. From looking at the spreadsheets, she had spotted that the bartender was skimming money off the top. Max had confronted him with the evidence, the man had admitted it, and Max replaced him immediately. She was still planning to look for a job, but she wanted to regain her balance and composure before going to a headhunter and searching for something on Wall Street. She didn't feel ready for that yet—what had happened was too shocking, and it was still in the media every day.

Valentina's boyfriend's murder, on the other hand, had disappeared without a trace. He was just another gangster who had been killed by his own kind. It had appeared in the paper the day after the murder, and not again. And the article had said that there had been a woman with him, but Valentina wasn't mentioned by name, by police request, for the benefit of her safety. Sasha still had no idea where she was and hadn't heard from her. There could be no communication between them, by police demand.

And she and Alex weren't sure whether to laugh or cry when they met the wedding planner. She was British, her name was Prunella, and she looked more like an undertaker than a wedding planner, in a severe black suit, with her dyed jet-black hair pulled tightly back in a bun. Oliver had said she'd been a ballerina in her youth, but she looked like a prison guard to Alex, and he whispered to Sasha, when the woman left the room briefly, that she scared him to death.

"Maybe she runs a tight ship," Sasha said hopefully, and she didn't like her either. But they had no one else. The few they had heard about and checked out cost a fortune, and Prunella was only slightly cheaper. She asked them to describe their dream wedding, and they both agreed that small would be better, and said they wanted about a hundred guests.

"Are you sure?" she asked with a disapproving expression, and they nodded. Alex said that his parents had had a hundred people at theirs. And they had offered to hold the wedding in Chicago, with the reception at the house, but Alex and Sasha agreed that they wanted to be married in New York. "Do you have an idea of location?" she asked them.

"You may already be too late for this June, and you may have to wait a year for a prime location."

"We don't want to wait a year," Sasha said firmly, and Prunella raised an eyebrow with an unspoken question. "I'm not pregnant. But we'd like to get married **this** June," Sasha said, looking the wedding planner in the eye.

"I've had quite a lot of pregnant brides recently," Prunella said with a sniff. "Modern times. One of them went to the hospital from the reception. Do you want a garden setting? A restaurant? A hotel? Indoor, outdoor? Afternoon? Evening?" The options were dizzying, and they had come to no decisions when they left her home office on East Sixty-eighth Street.

"I can see why people go to Vegas," Alex said, overwhelmed.

"Maybe we should do it in Chicago," he said vaguely.

"Our friends are here," Sasha reminded him. "I don't want to get married in Atlanta either."

When Oliver called Sasha to see how they'd liked her, she described the meeting and how unnerving it had been. Then she talked to him about what they should do.

"Nighttime weddings are more fun, and dressier," he said. "What about someone's home with a garden? Let me think about it. Do you want a church wedding?"

"Probably." She liked the garden idea, particularly in June, but she couldn't think of any, and then Oliver called her back the next day.

"I don't know if it's a crazy idea or not, but I know a woman with a beautiful roof garden on her penthouse on Fifth Avenue, overlooking Central Park. I've rented it from her before for clients, and she's very particular about who she rents to. I'm not sure how she'd feel about a wedding. She owns the top two floors, so you wouldn't have to worry about the neighbors complaining. She let us go pretty late for our event. It wasn't cheap, but it wasn't ridiculous either. If you want, I'll call her, and it's not like a hotel where it's booked years in advance. Do you have a date?"

"June fourteenth?" Sasha said hesitantly. It seemed like a good date to her, in warm weather, and before the Fourth of July weekend and people's summer plans.

"I'll let you know." He called back ten minutes later, when she was on her way to work. She and Alex were on different schedules that day. "You're in," Oliver told her. "June fourteenth. Evening wedding. She said you can have a hundred and twenty people. You provide all the catering, flowers, band, etc. She provides the hall." He quoted a price that seemed reasonable to both of them.

"It sounds perfect." She was delighted.

"My clients loved it for their events. One was corporate, one was private—it worked for both."

"I wish you were our wedding planner," she said wistfully. He made everything so easy and had such great resources.

"I don't. Weddings are a nightmare. I don't want one. If I ever get married, I'll go to the Elvis Chapel in Las Vegas."

"That's what Alex said yesterday," she said, sounding glum again.

"So should I book it?"

"Yes, I'll tell Prunella." She called her just before she got to the hospital, and told her they had a location.

"Then we need to send out save-the-dates immediately," she said imperiously. "And you have to pick your invitations right away. They have to be printed now. Your wedding is only four months away. That's practically tomorrow. We have work to do," she said sternly.

"Could you send me a list of what we need to do?" Sasha asked, feeling as overwhelmed as Alex had the day before.

"I will as soon as you sign the contract." She had given them a copy of it, and it required a large deposit, which Sasha wanted her father to approve, but hadn't had time to send to him.

"I'll take care of it," she said meekly. Prunella scared her too.

"I could meet with you again today at four-thirty," the planner said primly.

"I'll be delivering babies until tomorrow. And I need to send the contract to my father for his approval."

"Very well. You have no time to waste," she reminded Sasha again as she arrived at work.

"I'll get back to you soon," Sasha promised, and then forgot about her as soon as she got to labor and delivery. They had four deliveries on hold, a midwife who was driving everyone crazy making demands for her patient, and a set of twins, preemies, coming in by ambulance. "Oh, happy days," she said to Sally at the desk, as she ran to scrub up. "Do we have an anesthesiologist on the floor?"

"Not yet," Sally answered as Sasha ran past her.

"Get two—it sounds like we'll need them." She could hear screaming coming from two of the rooms. **Welcome to my world,** she thought to herself. But this was so much easier than planning a wedding. She knew what to do here. Weddings were a mystery to her, and she had no mother to advise her. Muriel wouldn't even discuss it with her. She walked into the first labor room two minutes later, and was just in time to tell the mother to push after she checked her.

"We're at ten. Let's go," she said to the crying mother as she threw up, and then shouted at her husband and refused to push. "I want to see your little boy, don't you?" Sasha said, smiling calmly at her, as the young woman nodded, and then grudgingly started to push as she screamed. She hadn't wanted an epidural, determined to do it naturally, and now it was too late and she'd have to tough through it, and Sasha could tell it was a big baby. It wasn't going to be easy. "We need another push here . . . again. . . ." she told the struggling woman in labor. "One more . . . another one. You're doing great." She smiled at her as the woman continued to scream, and threw up again. It was a tough delivery that Sasha knew the woman would remember, and it would have been so much better with an epidural, but she had to work with what they had, a big baby, a crying mom, and no drugs. It took another hour of pushing, but the baby finally crowned, and then slid into her hands as she turned it, and then the mother was crying and laughing. The agony was over the minute the baby came out. "Good job, Mom!" Sasha praised her. Sasha was so good at what she did, and loved it so much. It was a great feeling knowing she made a difference to people. She walked out of the delivery room half an hour later, after stitching the woman up, and rushed past the nurses' station, as Sally called out to her.

"You've had three calls from some woman named Prunella," she told her, and Sasha stared at her in disbelief.

"Is she kidding?"

"She told me I had to get you right away, and I said you were in the middle of a delivery. Was it urgent?"

"No, it wasn't. She's my wedding planner. It can wait."

Sally laughed as Sasha disappeared into the next room, just as the woman having twins at thirty-four weeks was brought in on a gurney by paramedics. They had to bring in one of the attendings for her, Sasha couldn't be everywhere at once. The paramedics signed her over and wished her luck.

It was one of those insane days when they delivered babies nonstop all day. She was there till midnight, and Alex was at the apartment when she got home at almost one. He was asleep in her bed, and he rolled over groggily and looked at her when he heard her come in.

"Prunella is mad at you. You didn't call her back," he said sleepily.

"Really? Tough. I was busy." The Elvis Chapel was sounding better every day. She pulled off her scrubs, kicked off her clogs, and climbed into bed with him, and five minutes later, they were both asleep. Prunella could wait.

Chapter 19

Claire and her mother boarded the plane to Milan at JFK on Valentine's Day. It seemed appropriate to Claire to spend it with her mother this year, and they were both excited about the trip. They were flying coach for the sake of their budget, but even that couldn't spoil the fun for them. The plane was full of Italians anxious to get home, and as she listened to the conversations around her, with people next to her, or shouting over them to friends in other rows, Claire couldn't help but remember the exquisite luxury of George's plane and the trips they'd taken together, and the wonderful time they'd had. But now look where he was and who he had turned out to be. It was still hard to believe. First his shocking abandonment of her, and then the discovery of the crimes he had committed. He was clearly a man without a heart or a conscience, a perfect sociopath.

She forced him from her mind and concentrated on what they were doing and where they were going. Claire had brought her computer with her, to show her mother her latest designs. There was so much to do to get their fledgling business off the ground, and her roommates had been patient about deliveries of color swatches, leather and fabric samples, and all the tools and materials they would need to show customers eventually. And they found a lawyer who helped them set up the company. The first trade show they were going to would be in Las Vegas, which sounded like fun to both of them. But not nearly as much as a trip to Milan.

Parabiago was in what was known as the shoe district of Italy, where the finest factories were. They were staying in Milan, less than an hour away, and had located a small hotel near the Via Montenapoleone, where the best shopping was, and where they planned to go after they finished their meetings. Milan was mecca to the fashion world, and Sarah had never been there before. The city was known not only for the important brands located there, like Prada and Gucci, but also for fabulous furs. Claire was aching to shop while they were there, but was trying to save her money for their business. Her mother had been generous, but Claire wanted to make a contribution too. They agreed to one day of shopping in the city before they left.

Sarah loved the designs Claire showed her on her computer. They were sophisticated and sleek, in basic neutral colors that would be solid additions to any wardrobe, and then there were half a dozen more whimsical, frivolous shoes that Claire hoped no woman could resist. There were two basic, very elegant evening shoes, and three pairs of pretty flats. And eventually Claire wanted to add boots. If they produced all of the drawings they had brought with them, there would be twenty different styles in their first line. From the orders they got at the trade show, they would get a good sense of what stores wanted from them that would supplement the brands they already carried. And once they were at the factory, they would have to choose quality of leather and the colors of each style. There was a vast range of quality and possible price points, and they would have a lot to decide on their limited budget. But thanks to her mother, they had a fair amount of leeway to work with, far more than Claire had had when she was designing for Walter Adams, and she was finally getting to design shoes she loved. She was infinitely grateful to her mother for the opportunity she was giving her.

They chatted all through lunch on the flight, and Sarah watched a movie, while Claire caught up on back issues of **Women's Wear Daily.** She had fallen behind recently, while working on the collection, and she wanted to see the fall runway shows from Fashion Week in New York, to make sure she was going in the right direction with the designs for her shoes. There was a lot to incorporate in their plans. And the inner construction of their shoes, and the materials they used, would be important as well. After reading the papers she'd brought with her, Claire fell asleep, and woke up when they were landing in Milan.

Malpensa, the Milan airport, was notorious for chaos, long delays, and an inordinate amount of theft, and it took them an hour to get their bags, and finally get a cab to their hotel, which was small, spare, and clean. It was all they needed, and they went for a walk to take a look around. It wasn't a beautiful city, but it was the center of the fashion world.

They had dinner at a small trattoria, and Claire noticed that the local men were admiring both her and her mother, and assumed they were two friends. Age didn't matter in Italy, her mother was still a beautiful woman, and men looked at her as often as they did at Claire, and Sarah seemed to be enjoying the attention. Even when they didn't try to pursue it, Italian men made it clear when they thought you were attractive. It did a lot for both their egos, and Claire made more of an effort the next day when they got dressed. It made a difference when you knew that someone noticed, even if it was a stranger, and you got a casual eye and a glimmer of a smile as they walked past.

The next day they took a car and driver to the town of Parabiago. There were three factories that Claire had honed in on as good options for them, and one was the factory that Walter Adams used. They had appointments at all three. And by ten o'clock that morning, they had gotten down to business. The first factory they went to was the one she had been to several times with Walter, and they remembered her. She knew it was one of the most reliable and respected factories in Italy, they did solid work, and they did the manufacturing for several important brands in the States, and all over Europe. Claire thought it was a good possibility that they might use them, but she wanted to see the others too to compare them. This was one of the most important decisions they would make.

By eleven o'clock they were at a smaller and more artisanal factory, and many of their shoes were handmade. They fabricated beautiful shoes, with amazing intricacy and delicate detail, but she thought they were too fussy for her designs, and probably not durable enough for their customer. Their strength was evening shoes, the tour of their workrooms was fascinating, and their prices commensurately higher, due to the many hours of craftsmanship they invested in the work. They made the shoes for two haute couture houses in Paris, and the founder of the company, centuries earlier, had made shoes for Marie Antoinette, and all the queens of Italy, and they were extremely proud of it. Claire loved the tour but didn't feel like it was a match for them. They needed something younger and more contemporary and more serviceable for the customer she wanted to target.

The third factory was strikingly modern and had

impressive showrooms to showcase their current and past work. They produced shoes for almost every popular high-end brand, and several secondary lines at their price point. The factory was owned by Biagio Machiolini and his two sons, and like the others had been a family business for generations, and they were cousins of the owners of the second factory they'd seen. Everything about this one was modern, new, and exciting, and the owner's second son, Cesare, was enthusiastic about their new brand and Claire's designs. She showed him everything she'd done, and explained her vision, and the three of them talked for two hours, and then his father and brother, Roberto, joined them and invited Claire and Sarah for lunch and an even more private tour. They left the factory at four o'clock after arriving at noon. They'd been in Parabiago since ten that morning, and the prices they had quoted her, with a reduction for the first year to help them get off the ground, would be very helpful. Claire had a copy of the contract in her briefcase, written in English, so she and her mother could go over the fine print at their hotel, and e-mail it to their lawyer in New York. Claire was familiar with the contracts, as she had handled them for Walter and knew what to expect. And when she read it over carefully in their hotel room, there were no surprises, it was exactly as they had said. All three factories had excellent reputations, and she knew they would be in good hands with any of them. It was a matter of choice and preference, and a certain amount of chemistry, since they would be working together closely, and the factory would have to be responsive to their needs and demands.

"What do you think, Mom?" Claire asked her as she lay on the bed and put the contract down. They had had a great day, and had both learned a lot about the intricacies of the business. It was impossible not to be impressed by the history and skill at each factory they'd seen.

"I think you should make the decision," Sarah said honestly. "You know a lot more about this than I do," she added modestly. She had gained even greater respect for her daughter as she watched her conduct their meetings all day. She knew her stuff, and then some, as well as being a very talented designer.

They went over all three options again, and Claire had wanted to give her a voice in it, since she was their sole investor, but Claire preferred the third factory hands down, and Sarah said she did too.

"And the father is very handsome," Sarah said with a twinkle in her eye.

"So are the sons," Claire added. Cesare and Roberto were both in their early forties, and they'd all had fun at lunch. And the Machiolinis liked the idea that they were a mother-and-daughter team starting a business, in good European tradition, although their business had been in the family for generations.

The two women had dinner at a nearby restaurant again that night, and went back to the factory the next day to go over final details. They had heard from the lawyer, who gave it his approval. And Claire and Sarah signed the contract together, and they all shook hands. Cesare agreed to deliver all twenty prototypes to them on or before April first. It was only six weeks away, but the Machiolinis had a large, efficient operation and assured them they could meet the deadline with ease, and they could make adjustments to the fit later. Claire realized she was going to need a fit model in a European size 37, which was size six and a half to seven in the States. She could use anyone with normal feet, and would need feedback about comfort, and reliability of size. The arches had to fit just right, the heels had to hold the foot properly, and the toebox had to be just high enough for comfort without looking boxy. But with their reliability in production, she didn't expect to have any problems there. The burden was on her now to design shoes that women loved, at the right price point, for the right market, and sell them through the right stores. The trade show in Las Vegas was going to be very important for them, and give them the feedback they needed. They might decide never to produce some of the designs if wholesalers thought they were impractical, too limited in market, or the price too high. Claire was going to try and keep their designs simple so their production costs didn't eat their profit. She had a lot to think about, and she transmitted all her working drawings to the Machiolinis digitally.

They parted friends after a glass of wine, and the two women declined another lunch. They wanted time to shop before they left the next day. They had to get back to New York and get to work on all their future plans. And ironically, Claire got an e-mail from the human resources office at Jimmy Choo that night. They were responding to the résumé she had sent them, and wanted to meet with her. She had sent it to them three months earlier, and now her life had taken a whole new direction. Three months before, she would have jumped at it, but for now it was too late. She thanked them, and said she was already involved with another project. It was funny how life worked.

Claire concentrated on her sketches all the way back to New York. She had also bought a great jacket at Prada, three pairs of shoes at a store she'd never heard of, which were fatally sexy but too extreme for her own line, and a white cotton dress to wear that summer. And Sarah had bought a sweater and beautifully tailored pants and a skirt at Prada. But more important, the trip had been a vast success for their new business. Claire Kelly Designs was off and running, and the Machiolinis were going to turn her dreams into a tangible product. Claire was so excited, she could hardly stand it.

And she noticed that her mother got a text message as soon as they landed at JFK.

"Who was that from?" She wondered if it was from Biagio Machiolini, who had been very taken with her mother and was only slightly older, although he had a wife and six kids, which hadn't stopped him from flirting with her.

"Your father," Sarah said shyly. "He misses me. He was asking how things went in Italy. I told him it went well and we had a lot of fun." He was still shocked that his wife was helping their daughter with her business, and was able to do it. He was beginning to realize that there was a lot about his wife he didn't know. And her absence had shown him how much he missed her and how important she was to him, and demonstrated to him that he had taken her for granted for a long time.

"Is he okay?" Claire asked cautiously. She had very infrequent contact with her father. They had so little to say to each other.

"I hope so," Sarah said quietly, and changed the subject, as they walked to baggage claim to get their bags. Sarah had been as tireless as her daughter on the trip, and as anxious to get to work. In a few months, Claire wanted to hire an assistant, possibly before the Las Vegas trade show, but they didn't need one yet. The two women were more than willing to do all the work, and even some of the heavy lifting, literally, when their samples came in. Both of them were hard workers with a lot of energy. And they chatted animatedly, feeding each other ideas, on the cab ride back to the apartment in

Hell's Kitchen. They had been gone for four days, and it felt like a month, but their business was off to a great start.

At the end of February, on the late-night shift, Lieutenant O'Rourke called Sasha at the hospital. The message said it was urgent, and she was instantly afraid that something had happened to Valentina. They hadn't spoken to each other, or seen each other, in two months by then, for the first time in their life. Even when they traveled, or Sasha had been in medical school, they had never let more than a few days go by without talking. The silence between them had been brutal, and painful for both of them.

She called the lieutenant with a shaking hand and waited with bated breath for what he had to tell her. As always, he was blunt.

"We got him. Apparently Jean-Pierre cheated someone in an arms deal, and shaved off a bigger commission than they'd agreed on, and delivered second-rate goods. Payback time. They had him killed. Thanks to one of our informants, we got the guy who did it, and the French have the man who ordered it. They won't extradite him to us, but they'll try him in France. We have the killer here. He's in custody, and we're keeping him. I don't think they were ever after your sister. But we couldn't know. We had to play it safe, for both of you. We'll release her in the morning, and you can take off your contact lenses and grow your hair." He laughed. More important, they were safe now. "I'll pull my guys off tonight, if you want." Sasha had gotten used to them. There was a rotation of eight men who had been protecting her. They were nice to everyone in the apartment, helped wherever they could, and were friendly to the nurses at work.

"We're going to miss them," Sasha said kindly, and he laughed.

"So will your sister. But that's a whole other story. She's a handful," he commented, and Sasha wondered what she'd been up to. "A handful" was an understatement, as she knew too well. It was her bad behavior and dangerous choices that had gotten them into this mess and put their lives at risk for the past two months. Sasha thanked him and called Alex in neonatal ICU as soon as she hung up.

"They got the killer," she said, exhaling audibly, and Alex closed his eyes. He had never been so stressed in his life, worrying about her. Even the undercover cops with her around the clock didn't completely reassure him.

"Thank God."

Ten minutes later the two men on duty that night came to say goodbye to her. Lieutenant O'Rourke had already called them and relieved them of duty. Sasha thanked and hugged them both, and they left. The nightmare was over, as swiftly as it had begun. And she sent both her parents a text to tell them. After that, it was up to Valentina to contact them, to apologize for what she'd put them all through, but she probably wouldn't, if she knew her sister. Valentina never apologized for anything.

But if she got involved with someone unsavory again, Sasha was going to tell her that she couldn't see her anymore. She had made the decision in the past two months. She couldn't do that to herself, or Alex now. She had seen what a toll it took on him. He had said nothing to his parents, so as not to worry them, but that was hard on him too, since they were very close, and they would have been terrified for him and Sasha, and wondered what he'd gotten himself into. No one in their family had been involved with a nuclear arms dealer, or a hit in an assassination. Valentina had gone way over the line this time—she'd come close to it before, just not to this degree. In this instance, she had inadvertently put her twin at risk too, although Sasha was sure she had never considered the possibility of that when she got involved with Jean-Pierre and closed her eyes to what he was doing. His dangerous lifestyle was written all over him. But Valentina liked all the luxury that went with it. And Sasha found it interesting that the two fabulously rich, lavishly generous men they'd come into contact with recently, Jean-Pierre and George, were high-level criminals. Sasha was grateful and happy with

Alex on a much more human scale. If Valentina wanted a decent life, she'd have to find someone like him, which Sasha knew she'd find boring.

Valentina had developed dangerous tastes and habits and connections with her modeling career. Not everyone used it that way, but Valentina did. It was a high price to pay for expensive thrills. And Jean-Pierre's fleet of bodyguards and armed thugs should have warned her about what he was.

She and Alex went home from the hospital together that night and talked about it. They were both sobered by the experience, and relieved that the drama was over.

When Valentina called her in the morning, tears sprang to Sasha's eyes when she heard her. In spite of the trouble she had caused, for everyone, and for Sasha specifically, they were still twins, with an unseverable bond between them.

"I missed you so much," Sasha breathed into the phone, as tears rolled down her cheeks. "We were all so worried about you."

"So was I," Valentina said flippantly. "Shit, they sent me to a monastery in Arizona. Not even a dude ranch with cute boys, except for the cops they sent with me. A monastery with priests and nuns. I had to wear a habit, and work in the vegetable garden. Some days I was sorry the guy didn't shoot me." As expected, she didn't say a word about Sasha, and the trouble she'd caused her.

"I'd love to see you in a nun's habit." Sasha laughed at her and wiped the tears off her face.

"Don't count on it. Besides, I have to give it back when I leave. They think it's magic or something."

"They probably don't want you turning it into a miniskirt, and wearing it with no underwear and high heels." Her twin was capable of it, as they both knew.

"I wish I'd thought of that. I've been wearing sandals that give me calluses and blisters. My feet are a mess." It was all she could say after two months of hiding from a killer. But she sounded in good spirits, and was thrilled to be coming back to New York. "They're flying me back today," she said nonchalantly, as though she were coming back from a magazine shoot for **Vogue.**

"I can't wait to see you," Sasha said with feeling. "It was hard not being able to call you."

"I know. It was for me too," Valentina admitted. "Are you working today?"

"Not till tonight." They talked for a few more minutes and hung up.

Claire and her mother were going over spreadsheets later that afternoon, sitting on the couch. Abby was packing in her room, which she had been doing for weeks, when she wasn't writing. Charlie was lying in a patch of sunlight near the window, and

Morgan had just come in with groceries, when the doorbell rang, and Sasha opened it, and Valentina was standing there in all her glory, in a short black leather skirt, a red sweater, and thigh-high boots with stiletto heels. The two sisters flew into each other's arms in a crushing embrace, and then Valentina let out a scream, as she looked at her twin.

"What happened to your hair?" It was still short and dark brown.

"You did. They had to change my looks," Sasha said. It was the first day she hadn't worn the blue contact lenses in two months, and she'd thrown them away.

"That **is** a sacrifice. Alex must hate me. You look like shit with dark hair." She grinned.

"Thanks." She noticed that there was a man standing behind her sister then, looking awkward. He was a strong, handsome guy with huge shoulders, and a young face. He was wearing a white T-shirt, jeans, and scuffed cowboy boots, and a windbreaker with an NYPD patch on it, and a suspicious bulge under it, which Sasha recognized now as a shoulder holster, and had hoped never to see again. "Do you still need protection?" she asked her in an undertone. Lieutenant O'Rourke had said it was all over, but Valentina clearly had a cop with her, still.

"A girl always needs protection," Valentina said as she smiled coyly over her shoulder. "This is Bert.

He was on the detail in Arizona, dressed as a priest. We looked pretty cute together, as a priest and a nun." She laughed, and he smiled at her adoringly, and then nodded at Sasha. He looked about six or seven years younger than her sister. And it was suddenly obvious what he was doing there. She had brought him home as the spoils of war. As Sasha looked at him, she remembered the lieutenant's cryptic comment about her sister, that she was a handful. Now she could see why he'd said it. She was involved with one of the cops. Sasha was sure they'd appreciated it at the monastery. Valentina was incurable. There was always a guy, preferably with a gun. But at least this one was on the right side of the law. Sasha wondered what she would do with him now that she was back in her own world. The fast lane would provide its lures very soon, with all the flashy people she knew. Her young cop in the T-shirt would last about five minutes in her world. Sasha invited him to come in and sit down, and he hesitated and then went to pet the dog. Men seemed to love Charlie—every male in the room always gravitated to him.

Abby came out of her room and saw them then, and gave Valentina a hug. And Claire and her mother had done the same. It was always odd seeing her—it was like seeing Sasha, and yet totally different, but you expected them to be the same person. And they were anything but that.

"Welcome back," Abby said warmly, trying not to stare at Bert and wondering who he was. He was actually older than he looked but not by much.

"Do you want me to leave you alone with the girls?" he asked Valentina politely, as they exchanged an intimate look that told the whole story of the past two months and what she had done at the monastery for entertainment. She had switched partners, but not her game.

"Sure," Valentina said easily. "Do you want to come back in half an hour?"

He looked easygoing about it and followed her lead. "Can I take the dog for a walk?" he asked with a grin.

"He'd love it," Abby answered as the dog sat up and gave Bert his paw, who shook it solemnly.

"I worked with a German shepherd for a while," he said seriously, "in narcotics. He was great, but he got shot, and they had to put him down."

"Lucky we didn't do that to you," Sasha said to her twin pointedly as Abby handed Bert the leash, and he and Charlie left. Sasha turned to her twin with a stern expression. "What in hell are you doing? How old is he?"

"Twenty-nine. He just looks like a kid. He's an adult. Very much so." She gave her sister a lascivious look, and Sasha groaned.

"What are you going to do with him now? The poor guy will get eaten alive in your world."

"I've changed," Valentina said demurely. "I don't

want to mess around with bad guys anymore. And how much better does it get than a cop? He's one of the good guys, playing on the right team. And I feel safe with him." Sasha was sorry to hear it, although he was admittedly an improvement over Jean-Pierre, who was as bad as she could have found.

"What about a doctor or a lawyer?"

"Yeah, or that nice guy Morgan worked for, who's going to prison for the next hundred years. Not all the bad ones are so obvious," she told her less-worldly sister. Sasha had led a protected life, by choice. And initially, Valentina had too. She'd gotten lost somewhere along the way, when money and fame and the fast track hit her too soon. "I like Bert. He makes me happy, he's a sweet person. He takes care of me. He's not complicated. He doesn't care who I've been with or why. He lives for today."

"Do you really want to be with a cop? Is he quitting the force for you?" Sasha hoped not, because Valentina would dump him in a hot minute when someone more exciting came along. She was sure her twin was going to break his heart, and possibly destroy his career, and she wouldn't care a whit about it. She did whatever suited her, in the moment, with total disregard for the damage she caused. Sasha loved her sister, but she knew how selfish she was. She was a narcissist through and through.

"I don't care what he does for a living. He's nice to me," she said simply.

"And he's poor," Sasha reminded her. "You don't like poor men." That was part of the problem too. She sold out for money every time, and most of the men whom she met with that kind of money were questionable or dangerous. At least he wasn't.

"I have enough for both of us," Valentina said casually, and then sat down near Claire and her mother. Abby had gone back to her room to continue packing. "What's everyone been up to?"

"We're starting a shoe business," Claire told her. "My mom came to help me, and she's living here now. And Abby is moving to L.A., to work on a movie for a year."

"That's a big change." Valentina looked surprised. The cast of characters at the loft had been stable for years. It was shocking to think of one of them leaving, and then she realized her sister would too when she got married. "How's the wedding coming?" she inquired.

"It's in June. In New York. You're the maid of honor," Sasha informed her. "The girls are my bridesmaids. June fourteenth. You'd better be there," Sasha said seriously.

"Can I bring Bert?" Valentina asked innocently.

"If he's still around by then," which she doubted. It was three and a half months away, a long time for her twin to be with the same guy.

"We'll see," Valentina said vaguely. Bert came back with the dog then, and kissed her lightly when he walked in.

"Great dog! We should get one like that," he told Valentina, and she nodded. She looked like she was ready to do anything for him. Sasha remembered that Patty Hearst had married one of her police bodyguards, so people did sometimes, and got attached to the men who protected them. Maybe it worked. Valentina kissed her and then left with Bert to go to her apartment, in Tribeca. Jean-Pierre had been murdered at his place, not hers, so her apartment was pristine. Bert had brought some things over that afternoon, and she had invited him to move in. The detail was over, but their life together was just beginning. Sasha was still shaking her head when they left, and Claire grinned at her knowingly.

"At least he's gainfully employed and won't go to prison," she commented. It was more than she could say about the man she'd been in love with, who was out on bail, still leading the high life, according to Page Six. He was getting money from somewhere. She went back to work on the spreadsheets then, and Sasha helped Morgan put the groceries away, thinking about Valentina and Bert. It was nice to have her back.

When Abby left at the beginning of March, it was heart-wrenching. They all felt as though they were losing a leg, or an arm, or some essential part of them. Abby was an integral part of their self-made family, and had been there for nine years with Claire. They all cried and were depressed for days afterward. Abby was staying with her parents in L.A. but was planning to get her own apartment. She said she'd move back in a year, but no one believed her. She would get entwined in the life of Hollywood, particularly if Josh's indie film was a success, which sounded likely.

She took Charlie with her, and the house seemed dead. A week later Sasha came home from work and found Morgan crying in the kitchen. And it was hard to guess why Morgan was crying—she had so many reasons to. Her lost job. The fact that she might never find another one as good—a future employer might not trust her, or even hire her. She had been irreversibly tainted by George, maybe forever. And they all missed Abby.

Sasha put her arms around her and gave her a hug. "I miss her too." It was like losing her little sister. Even during her travails with Ivan, she had been a warm, loving presence who brightened their existence. And with Morgan depressed about losing her job, the atmosphere in the apartment had been very subdued. And as Sasha hugged her, she shook her head and sobbed.

"It's not Abby," she managed to choke out the words.

"You'll find another job." She knew Morgan liked working at Max's with him for the time being, but she was worried about the future of her career. Morgan shook her head again, and Sasha looked at her, mystified over why she was sobbing inconsolably.

"I'm pregnant!" Morgan blurted, and collapsed into a kitchen chair with overwhelming grief.

"Oh my God," Sasha said, and sat down next to her. That had never happened to any of them. They were cautious and responsible, and kept an unlimited supply of condoms in both bathrooms for everyone's use. They were grown-ups and took good care. "How did that happen?"

"I don't know. I took an antibiotic for an ear infection—maybe it canceled out my pill, or I missed one. I'm two months pregnant." She looked at Sasha miserably. "I just figured it out, and I took a test. I'm screwed. I missed a period when they closed the office. I thought it was just stress."

"Have you told Max?" Morgan shook her head. She was sure it had happened when George got arrested. They'd had sex more than usual, for comfort. And now her worst nightmare had happened, **and** she was out of a job.

"If I told him, he'd want the baby, and he knows I don't want kids. He'll break up with me if I have an abortion. He's Irish Catholic, and he loves kids. I want an abortion, Sash. I can't even tell him." And then she looked at her friend hopefully. "Would you do it?" Morgan trusted her completely.

"No, but I can refer you to someone who will, if

that's what you want. You should probably tell him, though. He'll get even madder if he finds out later and knows you lied to him."

"I know. I'm screwed either way. And I'm not going to have it. I can't. Children terrify me, they always have. I have no maternal instincts at all."

"You might surprise yourself," Sasha said gently. "You love him, that helps."

All Morgan could do was cry as she sat at the kitchen table with Sasha's arms around her. Morgan said it was the worst thing that had ever happened to her, and Sasha felt sorry for her. Morgan was devastated, and Max figured out for himself that Morgan was pregnant when she threw up three mornings in a row. He asked her, and her face told him the whole story. She didn't want to lie to him and deny it. She burst into tears as soon as he asked.

"Why didn't you tell me?" he asked with a broad smile as he put his arms around her. He was thrilled.

"I don't want it," she said in a deep sorrowful voice. "I always told you that. I don't want kids."

"Planned ones, okay, I get that. But this happened. You can't just brush it away. It's our baby." He had tears in his eyes when he said it, and he was shocked at her expression. She was like a cornered animal, and she would do anything to survive.

"It's not a baby. It's a mistake, an accident. It's a nothing right now," she said, panicked.

"That's bullshit and you know it. How pregnant are you, anyway?" He looked as rattled as she did, but for the opposite reason. He wanted it, she didn't. And he was willing to fight for its survival, she wanted to kill it. It was about to become a huge battle.

"Two months," she answered in a flat tone. "I'm going to have an abortion," she said with an iron will in her eyes.

"When?"

"Soon."

"Over my dead body. Is Sasha doing it?" His eyes were blazing with fury.

"She refused," Morgan said honestly.

"At least there's one decent human being around here. I want you to know that if you have an abortion, I will never forgive you, and it's over with us."

"I know," she said quietly. But it didn't change her mind. She hadn't wanted it to happen this way. She hadn't wanted him to know, because she knew it would end like this, probably forever. She knew it was true when he said that he would never forgive her. It was against everything he believed in, and he wanted their child, he always had. He slammed out of the apartment then, and didn't stay with her that night. She knew the battle they were having over her unwanted pregnancy was the beginning of the end, either way, whoever won.

Chapter 20

The war over the fetus in Morgan's womb raged on for weeks. Max wouldn't sleep at the apartment, and told her not to come to the restaurant until she made a decision. And in his mind there was only one to make, to keep the baby. There was no other acceptable option, to him.

They stopped seeing each other entirely, and Morgan was still sure she wanted an abortion, but hadn't scheduled it yet because she knew that when she did, Max would never see her again. He said it and he meant it, and she believed him. She loved him, but not his baby. And for him they were one and the same—there were no shades of gray, or good reasons for an abortion. It was a yes-or-no decision, to keep it or not. She couldn't have it and send it back. He even asked her to have the baby and let him raise it, and she wouldn't. That sounded twisted to her. She wasn't going to give birth to a child and give it up. It made more sense to put an end to it before it happened and ruined their lives, but it already had.

She tried to explain again how she felt about it, and he wouldn't listen to her. All he wanted to hear was that she had changed her decision. She had made it, but not acted on it yet.

"You have to do something soon," Sasha prodded her, not wanting to influence her. "Either keep it, or terminate. You're getting close to three months, and they won't give you an abortion after that."

"I know. I feel like I'm losing him and the baby at the same time." Sasha didn't disagree. Max had talked to her and he was vehement, not just morally or religiously but because he loved Morgan and had always wanted their child. And he figured this was his only chance—Morgan would never let it happen again. Sasha thought he was right about that. It was a huge trauma to her.

For three weeks, Morgan had sat around the apartment hoping Max would change his mind, but he refused to talk to her. And he had answered none of the e-mails or texts where she had tried to explain her position to him.

"He's being a total asshole," she said to Sasha.

"He's certainly being rigid. Most guys don't want the baby. He does."

"He'd rather lose me than the baby," Morgan added. He had even called a lawyer and had looked into a court order to stop her because it was his child too, but it was her body, and the courts respected that, and wouldn't interfere. It was her right to choose. Max was beside himself over it, and he missed her. But he refused to back down. He had said clearly that if she aborted, they were through.

By now, Morgan was very emotional and cried all the time. She had a few days left to decide, and Sasha went to the doctor with her to support her while she made the final decision. Knowing she would lose Max if she aborted the baby was slowing her down. But she wanted him, not the child.

They did a routine sonogram while she was at the doctor, in Technicolor and 3D, and what they saw was a healthy baby. Its heart was strong, and everything was perfect. She started to cry even more after she saw it, and talked to the doctor about an abortion. She said she would call to set it up the next day, and the doctor didn't push her either way. She said she could fit her in the following afternoon for a termination if that was her decision.

All she did was cry on the way home. She was convinced a baby would destroy her life. She remembered her hideous life as a child, her drunken mother and irresponsible father who cheated on her. The miserable life they had led until they died young, and they had had no pleasure from their children, and had had nothing to give her or her brother. She wanted no part of that nightmare, which was more vivid to her than the baby in 3D.

She went to bed when they got back to the apartment, after she threw up again. She was sick all the time now too, but Sasha thought it was because she wasn't eating and was so upset, which made everything worse. She had been through a lot in the past three months, with the demise of her career, and now an unwanted pregnancy.

Sasha left for work after checking on her, Morgan just lay there crying, and she and Alex talked about it that night.

"Honestly, I don't think she should have the baby," she told Alex. "She's completely traumatized. Anyone who doesn't want kids that badly shouldn't have them."

"So why doesn't she have the abortion?"

"She doesn't want to lose Max, and she will if she does it. He offered to take sole custody if she'll have it and give it to him, and she won't."

"This sounds crazy," Alex said, sorry for both of them.

"It is crazy. For some people, having a baby is not an easy concept. For others, it's an obsession. There are a lot of issues around pregnancy. It's great when it's nice and simple and straightforward, but that's not always the case." And this was one of the most complicated situations she'd seen. Morgan was so desperate, torn between the two options, that Sasha was afraid she'd become suicidal. She was terrified whichever way she turned. Sasha tried to convey that to Max when she stopped by the restaurant to have coffee with him earlier that week, and he didn't want to hear it. For him, it was simple. Have their baby and stay together, or abort it and break up.

"It's not that easy," she told him.

"It is for me." And with that, he ended the conversation.

The absolute deadline for an abortion was the following Monday, and that weekend Sasha and Alex were going to Atlanta, so her parents could meet him. She wasn't looking forward to it, and would have preferred to stay home and keep Morgan company, but they couldn't cancel. They weren't going to have another weekend off for two months, and the wedding was in three, so they flew to Atlanta on Friday night. Her father had invited them to stay with him, but they wanted some time to themselves to decompress between warring parents, so they were staying at a hotel.

They had dinner that night at a restaurant her mother liked. Her mother examined Alex like a piece of property she was buying, and asked him a thousand questions about his parents, and particularly his mother's law practice. She had checked her out on the Internet and was impressed, but didn't admit it.

"You know that I don't believe in marriage, don't you?" she asked him, and he nodded. He was more than a little daunted by her, and he thought she was the toughest human being he'd ever met, male or female.

"Yes, I know that, Mrs. Hartman," he said politely.

"Muriel. Sixty percent of marriages today end in divorce, and the statistics are going up. Why bother? You lose property, you lose income, you pay support. It's a lousy investment. You'll lose less money playing blackjack in Las Vegas. There, at least you have a decent chance if you get a good hand. Even if you get a good hand in marriage, it all blows up in your face sooner or later. One of you cheats, or you both do. They get fat, old, or boring. You can't talk to them. You get to hate them. You stop having sex. It all looks sexy and romantic in the beginning, but it doesn't last. And when it does, you wish it wouldn't. Take my advice—live together, don't commingle your money, and don't waste it on a wedding, or throw your life out the window by getting married. Believe me, you'll thank me one day for the best advice anyone ever gave you. I hear bad stories every day."

"Maybe because the good stories don't wind up in front of a divorce lawyer," Alex said doggedly. "My parents have a good relationship, and they've been married for thirty-eight years."

"That's an accident. Like twins. It doesn't happen often. And maybe you don't know the real story. A lot of parents hide it."

"No, I think they genuinely love each other." And it was what he expected to have with Sasha. Muriel Hartman just shrugged and made it clear she didn't believe it. She was a physically attractive woman in a hard way, but she had the meanest, angriest eyes he'd ever seen and harsh lines on her face.

Sasha tried to get them out of the restaurant as quickly as possible, and she suggested brunch on Sunday before their flight. Her mother said she was playing golf with two women friends who were judges, and couldn't make it.

"I assume you're seeing your father and his air-head wife tomorrow," she said coldly.

"Yes, we are," Sasha said through clenched teeth.

"Enjoy it," she added sarcastically. "See you at the wedding," she said to Alex, hugged her daughter awkwardly without an ounce of warmth, got in her Jaguar, and drove away. Alex looked like he was about to collapse on the sidewalk.

"She is one tough woman," he said looking at Sasha. "How did you grow up with her?"

"She wasn't as bad then, before the divorce. They were unhappy for a long time, but they kept it quiet. Then he left her, and she turned into the witch in **The Wizard of Oz,** with the green face. I was out of the house by then, thank God. She badmouthed my father constantly once he left her. I guess her ego was bruised. But when he met Charlotte, the woman he's married to now, she went insane. She never forgave him for starting a new life and being happy with another woman. And it's worse because Charlotte is so much younger, and beautiful. And she's furious they had more kids. Now she hates everyone. I don't know how her clients stand her.

You have to really hate the man you're divorcing to hire her. She kills them. My sister insists she used to be human once upon a time. I sure don't remember it. She gets along better with Valentina. My mother and I just don't make it anymore." Sasha looked exhausted, and he put an arm around her. "It sure is different than your parents, huh? They're like a family TV show compared to mine, who are like some kind of horror movie. I try not to come home anymore. It's just too hard. And Valentina hates my father. She thinks he turned my mother into this by leaving her, and she says his wife is a ditz. She is, but she loves him, and it's what he wants, and she's really kind of sweet. We're not best friends, but I like her. My father has tried to bury the hatchet with my mother, but she won't let him." Muriel Hartman was angry at the world.

"She makes it very difficult," Alex said as they walked back to their hotel. Atlanta seemed like a nice city, but they hadn't had time to explore it, and all Sasha wanted, whenever she went back to Atlanta now, was to leave town again as soon as she could. She never even called her old friends. Her mother had ruined it for her.

They met her father at his country club for lunch the next day. Steve Hartman was a handsome man, and it was hard to imagine him with Muriel for a day, let alone the twenty-six years they'd been married before he left her. He wasn't an intellectual or an academic, but he was an intelligent businessman who had done extremely well. He wasn't as sharp or astute as Sasha's mother, but he was a kind, warm person, and Alex liked him.

And after lunch they followed him to Buckhead, the very expensive residential part of Atlanta where they lived. They had an enormous house that was more like an estate, with a tennis court and an Olympic-size pool, and beautiful old trees lining the driveway. It was very Southern, and there was a lovely young woman barefoot on the lawn, smiling and waving at them as they drove up, and two beautiful little girls. Steve looked ecstatic as he got out of his car, tossed them in the air, and kissed his wife. As soon as Alex and Sasha got out of their rented car, Sasha saw a problem on the horizon, a big one. Charlotte was pregnant again, which her father hadn't mentioned, and Muriel was going to split a gut at the wedding when she found out. It would be further proof of his happy marriage to someone else. Her mother had never wanted more children after the twins, and her father had always wanted more. Now he had them. And she could never forgive him for moving on without her, and being happy.

"Congratulations," Sasha said after hugging Charlotte, and indicated her round belly in the pretty sundress. "That's exciting."

"Yes, it is," her father acknowledged, beaming at his wife. She was thirty years old, as she had told Alex before, two years younger than Sasha, which hadn't sat well with any of them when he married her at twenty-three, but it no longer mattered to Sasha. Valentina thought it was disgusting, and now she was doing the same thing herself with Bert, who was younger than she was, though not by as many years. Her father and Charlotte were nearly thirty years apart. But so what, if it worked for them?

"When is it due?" Sasha asked, praying it would be before the wedding.

"August," Charlotte said in her Southern drawl that always annoyed Valentina. An August due date meant that she would be seven months pregnant at the wedding—the picture of maternal splendor on her father's arm. Sasha nearly groaned when she said it.

"Will you be up to coming to New York for the wedding?" Sasha asked with a false smile.

"My doctor says I can travel till eight months. Both of the girls were late." Sasha nodded, with a sinking heart. It was one more thing to worry about at the wedding. **Elvis Chapel, here we come,** she thought.

They sat by the pool while a maid in uniform served lemonade and iced tea and lemon cookies, and her dad offered Alex a mint julep or Pimm's Cup, which he declined and stuck with lemonade. It was delicious, and the little girls swam while they chatted, and a nanny came out to dry them off. Their mother had had help for her and Valentina too, while she practiced law, but it was always more haphazard and less formal—local young women, college age babysitters, or foreign au pairs. Steve and Charlotte's nanny was English and formally trained, and extremely polite, as were the children who climbed all over Sasha and called her their big sister, while she teased them and chased them around the lawn. They were cute, and had a wonderful life. Their mother didn't work and hadn't since she gave up modeling to marry Steve, and never looked back. Her days consisted of shopping, manicures, a little charity work, and lunch with her friends.

Her father asked Alex about his residency, and they talked until dinnertime, and then had an early dinner in the gazebo on the lawn. They left by eight o'clock, and all Sasha wanted was to go back to New York. It wasn't anything like their trip to stay with his parents in Chicago, where they actually had fun. With Alex's family, they all had medicine in common, and his mother was the nicest woman she'd ever met, who actually seemed to care how Sasha felt.

"Thank you for being such a good sport. My parents exhaust me." She laid her head back against the seat and looked wiped out as they drove back to the hotel.

"Your father is nice," he said honestly. They were in agreement about her mother and had said it all the night before. Her father and Charlotte were like something in a Southern movie and never seemed real to her. No one was ever tired or dirty or messy or swore, or talked about problems, or things she cared about. It all stayed very superficial.

"My mother is going to have apoplexy when she sees Charlotte pregnant again at the wedding, although she should be used to it by now. And they've been divorced for nearly eight years. I think she'll be pissed till the day she dies, and she wouldn't want to be married to him anyway. They were both unhappy. I think she forgot."

"Pride maybe. It doesn't help that Charlotte's younger than you are, and she's a damn pretty girl," Alex said sensibly.

"Yes, she is." Sasha sighed. It was too late to catch a flight that night, but she switched their flight to an earlier one the next morning, and they left the hotel at eight o'clock, and were back in New York at one. She wanted to kiss the ground.

"Well, that's over with," she said, as they got into a cab at the airport. "We don't have to see them again till the wedding. Are you ready to back out yet?" she asked him, and he laughed.

"Of course not. Just don't ever leave me alone with your mother. She scares me to death."

"Don't worry, I won't. I promise. Don't leave me alone with her either." He agreed.

They went back to the apartment to drop off their

things, and everyone was out, even Morgan, who had hardly left the house recently. Sasha hoped it was a good sign.

At that moment, Morgan was sitting by the river, thinking about her life. She didn't want the baby, but she felt a responsibility to it. It wasn't the baby's fault she had gotten pregnant. She had made her decision. She was going to have it. But she was leaving Max. The fact that he'd been willing to leave her if she didn't have his baby told her what she needed to know. She didn't want to be wanted for their child. And if he wasn't willing to stick by her, whatever decision she made, he didn't really love her. He could have visiting rights to the baby, and even joint custody if he wanted it. But he couldn't have her. He had blown it.

She had written him a letter and dropped it in the mail. She wasn't going back to the restaurant, and didn't want to see him. It was over, and she'd let him know when the baby was born in October, since that was all he cared about. She went for a long walk then, alone.

Chapter 21

Morgan stuck to her decision about Max, and the baby. He groaned when he got the letter at the restaurant, and tried to call her, but she wouldn't take his calls. She had the rest of his clothes dropped off at the restaurant. They hadn't spoken in four weeks since his ultimatum, and now the tables had turned. Morgan wouldn't speak to him. And Max felt helpless to reach her. She had shut the door, and intended to keep it closed. Finally Max called Sasha in desperation.

"You two need to talk to each other," Sasha said sensibly.

"She thinks I don't love her, just the baby." His threat to leave her if she had an abortion had hit her too hard. "I want the baby because I love her, not in lieu of."

"She's very emotional right now," Sasha explained.

"She won't see me."

"And you wouldn't see her for four weeks."

"I wanted to pressure her into keeping it. I wasn't trying to break up with her."

"You said you'd never see her again if she had an abortion. Now she's keeping it and won't see you."

"What can I do, Sash? This is a disaster."

"I know. Maybe give it time."

"I want to be with her, and help her. It's our child, and I love her."

"I think the whole mess with her job and now this was too much for her," Sasha said sadly. Morgan was being very quiet at the apartment, sleeping a lot and going for long walks every day. She was feeling physically better, but Sasha could see she was very depressed. And she was very quiet at their Sunday-night dinners, which Oliver was cooking now. It was strange without Abby and Max.

Morgan decided to tell everyone about the baby later, when it showed. She wasn't happy about the baby and didn't want to pretend she was. The only one she told was her brother, and Oliver and Greg were thrilled and promised not to tell the others. Morgan was in no mood to celebrate it. She was in mourning for her life, Max, and her career. She had called a headhunter for a short-term job for four or five months, but nothing had turned up yet.

She had a lawyer contact Max with an agreement for visitation rights, with an offer to negotiate possible joint custody later. He had thought she was kidding when she said it in her letter. And it almost killed him to hear from her through an attorney.

She wasn't fooling around. The letter said that she didn't know the sex of the baby, and didn't want to, and he would be advised after the baby was born. Tears rolled down his cheeks as he read it. Morgan was out of his life, even if she was going to be the mother of his child.

Max spoke to Oliver too, who said his sister was the most stubborn woman he had ever met. Oliver said she was deeply upset and emphatic that she didn't want to speak to Max. All he could do now was wait till the baby was born, and see if she softened then, but that was more than five months away, an eternity to him. He couldn't even concentrate on his work, was short tempered with his staff, and whenever he cooked, he burned the food. He was obsessed with Morgan and the baby. He still had the key to the apartment, but he didn't dare use it to see her. She'd probably call the police if he did, and have him arrested. He knew now she was capable of it. As far as Morgan was concerned, there was no turning back. Her relationship with Max was over, and Max had gotten the message, loud and clear.

Claire's shoe samples arrived from Italy the first week in April, and they were gorgeous. She screamed when she saw them and danced around the room while her mother laughed. And they had come just in time for the trade show in Las Vegas. She had hired an assistant to go with them, and work for them for a while in New York when they got back. And her roommates were continuing to be patient about the boxes and samples arriving at the apartment. With Sasha and Morgan's permission, she had turned Abby's bedroom into a storeroom, and she and her mother slept in her room. And there were more boxes in the living room. She hired a fit model for an afternoon, and checked the fit. The model said they felt great, and the high heels were at a good pitch. Claire was beside herself with excitement when they got on the plane to Las Vegas.

They stayed at the MGM Grand, and spent most of the day at the convention center, with her mother and Claudia, her new assistant. They set out all their samples in a good-looking display, and a number of retailers wandered by to check them out, including buyers from several big department store chains. They asked her questions about the styles, availability, their price point and delivery capabilities, and quantity, which was an issue for big stores. Claire could satisfy one store, but not ten branches, until they started producing on a bigger scale, and this would only be their first season. But the reaction to their designs was positive from everyone. The buyers loved them.

And on the second day, Claire got the ultimate satisfaction. She spotted Walter from across the room, and he sauntered over to them, trying to be nonchalant, while ogling the shoes on the table. Claire almost laughed and pointed him out to Claudia and her mother. And then he headed straight for her.

"Whose shoes are you selling now?" he said in a cantankerous tone, and she smiled at him and pointed at their sign, with the logo she had designed herself. The sign said clearly Claire Kelly Designs, and his mouth nearly fell open. "Where did you get them made?" he asked her, shocked.

"In Italy" was the only information she gave him and then turned to a buyer who was back for the second time, this time to place an order. And a minute later Walter slunk off.

By the end of the show, they had a stack of very respectable orders, enough to launch their business and support a season. Claire and her mother were beaming and high-fived each other and the young assistant. She had been very helpful during the show, and Claire had decided to keep her. The show had been a wonderful experience. Claire Kelly Designs was up and running, and in the fall would be in some of the best department stores in the country.

"Thanks, Mom," she said as they packed up. "I can never thank you enough." Sarah just smiled at her and gave her a hug. This was why she had come to New York. And she loved that they had started the business together, and so did Claire. She knew she would be forever grateful to her mother for the opportunity she'd given her.

* * *

At the beginning of May, Morgan was four months pregnant, and was having trouble concealing it. She still hadn't told Claire or anyone else yet. Only Sasha knew, and her brother and his partner. And she was embarrassed to have Claire's mother know. They all knew that she and Max had broken up, but she refused to discuss the details, or say why. She and Max hadn't spoken in two months. He finally couldn't stand it, and sat on the front steps of her building one morning, waiting for her to come out. He knew she would sooner or later. She came downstairs an hour after he got there, on the way to a Pilates class for pregnant women. She was looking good, fit, and in shape, and had gained very little weight, except her face was a little fuller.

She was startled when she saw him and tried to go back inside, and he stopped her.

"Morgan, this is insane. Talk to me," he begged her. He looked like a madman as he stood there. He had thought of nothing and no one else for two months.

"Why? We have nothing to say to each other. It's over." She was ice cold.

"No, it's just the beginning," he said, pointing at her stomach. "It doesn't have to be like this. I didn't want you to get an abortion because I love you and wanted our child."

"No, you didn't love me. You told me you'd leave

me if I didn't keep it. You wanted a child. You can have visitation when it's born. Leave me out of it." She sounded strong and angry and very hurt. "You had no respect for what I wanted or for my right to make the decision."

"I was upset. I wouldn't really have left you." He appeared deeply remorseful.

"You didn't talk to me for three weeks, when I needed your support, and you threatened to abandon me."

"I was wrong." And then he asked her what he had been wondering for a month. "Why did you keep it?"

"It felt wrong not to. This was our mistake, not the baby's. I decided to take my responsibilities."

"Are you happy about it at all?" he asked sadly.

"No," she answered honestly. She never lied to him. "Why would I be? I wanted you, not the baby. I was never confused about that. Now I've lost you, and I'm stuck with a child I never wanted." But she would do right by it anyway. She was that kind of person. This wasn't the baby's fault. It was theirs.

"You haven't lost me," he said miserably. "You can't lose me, even if you don't want me anymore." She didn't answer, and he saw tears fill her eyes as she turned away, and he put his arms around her. "I'm sorry I screwed this up so badly." And he realized now that he should probably have let her have the abortion. She had always told him she didn't want children, and she hadn't changed her mind, even pregnant. "I'm sorry. This has all been a terrible mistake. What can I do to make it better?" he said, obviously desperate.

"You can't. It's over for us, and we're stuck with a kid no one wanted and shouldn't have happened."

"I suspect a lot of babies start out that way, and you fall in love with them later."

"Maybe," she said, but she hadn't yet, and didn't expect to. She would do her duty, but no one could force her to want it. He had tried, and it blew up in their faces. But she had made the decision on her own to keep it. She couldn't blame him for that, and she knew it. "Thanks for coming by," she said, and tried to walk past him down the steps, and he wouldn't let her. He looked as stubborn as she did.

"I'm not leaving until you agree to at least try to make this work with me. Let's give it a chance. If you hate me, I'll go away."

"I don't hate you," she said, tired and disappointed. "I don't know what I feel anymore."

"That's a start," he said, holding on to her. "Please, Morgan, please give me another chance." She didn't answer, she just stared at him, and then she felt a strange cramp in the depths of her belly, and she winced.

"What was that?" He had seen it.

"Nothing," she lied to him, and then she had another cramp right after. She hadn't had anything like it during the pregnancy so far. It felt like strong menstrual cramps.

"Is something wrong? Tell me the truth." He held on to her, and she winced again and doubled over.

"I don't know. I'm having bad cramps all of a sudden."

"Like something you ate or the baby?"

"Maybe the baby." She turned to go back upstairs, and he followed her, worried that he had upset her. They hiked up the stairs, and she went to the bathroom in the apartment and came out, looking ashen. "I'm bleeding," she said in a scared voice.

"Let's go to the hospital. I'm not leaving." She didn't want him to, and she didn't argue with him. She thought she might be having a miscarriage, which would be a simple solution to their problems, but suddenly she didn't want that to happen.

They walked down the stairs together to the street, and she stopped twice for cramps again and could feel dampness between her legs. He hailed a cab and helped her in, and he held her hand on the way to the hospital. Morgan called Sasha from the cab. She was on duty and told her where to go and said she'd meet her.

She was waiting for them when they got to the hospital, and took Morgan into an examining room, and asked her if she wanted someone else to examine her, and Morgan said she wanted her to do it. She trusted Sasha more than anyone else, and as Sasha gently examined her, Morgan started crying.

"This is happening because I didn't want it," Morgan said softly. "God is punishing me."

"No, He's not. These things happen." Sasha could see that she was bleeding, but not heavily.

"Let's get a sonogram and see what's going on," she said calmly as she peeled off the glove, and Morgan kept crying. She could feel the baby moving—it had started a few days before—and it felt weird, like real butterflies in her stomach.

Sasha put her in a wheelchair and rolled her down the hall, and Max followed them looking very worried.

"What's happening?" he asked them.

"We don't know yet," Sasha told him.

They took her in for a sonogram right away, while Max waited outside. The technician ran the wand over Morgan's firm belly. They could see the baby on the screen, and it was moving, and seemed peaceful, and then started to suck its thumb. And then the tech commented that it looked like there was a clot, but just a small one.

"That happens sometimes," Sasha explained. "It can cause bleeding. It will probably resorb all by itself. The baby may have bumped it."

"Is it something I did? I've been going to Pilates every day, to stay in shape," Morgan asked, feeling guilty.

"You should cool that for a week or two and take it easy, and give the clot a chance to dissolve. This won't hurt the baby." Morgan closed her eyes then and started to sob.

"I thought I'd killed it because I didn't want it."

"And how do you feel now?" Sasha asked her gently.

"Scared. But I don't want to lose it." Sasha nodded with a smile.

"That sounds about right. Do you want Max to see it?" she asked cautiously. It had surprised her to see them together. Morgan nodded, and Sasha went to get him. They switched to the bigger, brighter screen in 3D so he could get a better look. The baby was still sucking its thumb when Max walked in. He took one glance at the screen and burst into tears, and leaned down to kiss Morgan.

"I love you so much. I'm sorry I've been such a jerk."

"Me too," she said, smiling at him through her own tears. "I don't want to lose the baby." She felt as though she needed to tell everyone now, so it wouldn't happen. And it still might, but Sasha didn't seem worried.

"Do you want to know the sex?" she asked them both, and they nodded in unison and laughed as they held hands. Max had never seen anything so beautiful in his life as the woman he loved and the baby inside her. And as they looked, Sasha pointed at a spot on the screen and smiled. "It's a boy." Max grinned broadly and kissed Morgan again, and she smiled tenderly at him. They seemed like blissful parents, not two people who had broken up and not spoken for two months. And Sasha was pleased too, for them.

Morgan got dressed after that, and Sasha said she could go home, and should take it easy for a week, maybe two. "No Pilates for two weeks. And no make-up sex for two weeks, please, you two." She handed them two copies of the photo of their baby, and they walked out of the hospital in a daze after thanking Sasha.

In a couple of hours, everything had changed and turned around. Max was back, and she had made peace with the trauma and disruption they'd been through. They spent the rest of the day together in the apartment, taking it easy, and then he thought of something.

"Will you come back to work at the restaurant? My books have been a mess since you left." He was grinning and had an arm around her when he asked her, and she laughed.

"Is that all you really wanted?" she teased him.

"Yes, the baby is just a side attraction. I need you to help me with payroll and petty cash."

She laughed at him then, and they kissed. Things were looking up, and then she pulled away from him with a serious expression. "I won't marry you, though. That would ruin everything. We can have the baby, but I don't want to get married."

"You're a damn difficult woman," he said good-humoredly. "Can we live together?"

"Yes. But not married. That would kill the romance in our relationship." To her, marriage was a nightmare, like her parents'.

"You're a nut, but I love you. After the tenth kid, can we get married? I love big Irish families."

"Okay, but not till after the tenth one, then I'll consider it." And as they bantered, she realized that they would have to move. They couldn't live in the loft with a baby. That would leave only Claire at the apartment. Morgan had planned to stay on at the loft alone with the baby, and Claire. They had room now without Abby, and Sasha gone in June. But Max and the baby seemed like too much and not fair to Claire. And as a couple with a child, they needed their own home.

Claire and her mother came in from an appointment at Bergdorf's shortly after, looking pleased. And Claire was as surprised to see Max there as Sasha had been when she saw them together earlier.

"We're having a baby," Morgan blurted out with a grin. Suddenly it was real.

"A boy," Max added.

"But we're not getting married," Morgan said, smiling.

"It would kill the romance in the relationship," he mimicked Morgan's words, and they all laughed.

"Congratulations," Claire said, startled. "When is it due?"

"October." Claire could figure out the rest. They'd have to move, and she and her mother would have the loft to themselves. She could run the business from there. She could afford the rent alone now, but she would miss her friends, and it was shocking and sad how fast things had changed. Maybe Abby would come back in a year, as she said she would, but Claire wasn't counting on that either. And by the summer, she'd be living at the loft alone with her mother.

Chapter 22

As May progressed, Prunella was driving Sasha crazy. The invitations had gone out, engraved by Cartier. They were very simple and elegant. They had chosen the menu, with a tasting at the apartment, and tried five different wedding cakes from three wedding bakers. And Max was giving them the wine as a wedding gift, and the champagne.

Prunella had recommended a photographer and videographer, which she insisted they needed. She had chosen lace tablecloths and linen napkins for them at Sasha's request, and she had her own supply of candelabras, and the caterer was bringing the crystal, silver, and china. They had toured the penthouse on Fifth Avenue, where they were giving the reception, and they had found a small church near the penthouse that was willing to do a six o'clock wedding. The reception was due to start at eight. And Sasha had managed to decide on all of it, in her meager time off from work. They hadn't had a weekend off since they'd gone to Atlanta in March.

And she had found the dress entirely by accident, in a magazine she was reading in the doctors'
lounge. It was a simple white satin dress with a lace
coat over it that she could take off at the reception,
with a lace veil. The coat had a beautiful long train.
She didn't have time to try it on, so Valentina went
to the fitting for her, and Sasha fell in love with it
when she saw it on a cell phone photo her sister sent
her, although Valentina thought it was boring.

"Why don't you get something sexy, with some
cleavage and a low back?" The dress was perfect for
Sasha. And the bridesmaids' dresses were a warm
beige color, simple strapless gowns, which Valentina
said would have looked better in red. Everything
was tasteful and simple. The bridesmaids' bouquets
were going to be small beige orchids, and Sasha's
lily of the valley. She had thought about having her
half-sisters as flower girls, but it would have caused
a war with her mother, which just wasn't worth it
to her.

The men were going to wear black tie, and Alex
was wearing white tie and tails. And Helen Scott
had told her she was wearing navy blue. Muriel
hadn't decided, but had seen an emerald green dress
she liked, or possibly a gold one.

Amazingly, everything was on track, and Prunella
had turned out to be as organized and efficient as
Oliver had been told. Sasha couldn't stand her, but
had to admit she was doing a great job. In spite of
that, Sasha was nervous about all the details com-

ing together on the big day. There was so much
that could go wrong. Helen kept offering to help
her, but Prunella seemed to have it all in control.

A month before the wedding, Sasha's roommates
planned a bachelorette dinner for her. She couldn't
get enough time off for a weekend, but the dinner sounded like fun. Abby had promised to fly
in from L.A., and Claire's mother was invited too.
They were having it at Soho House. And Sasha
even had a dress for that, and a short sexy black one
for the rehearsal dinner Alex's parents were giving
the night before the wedding at the Metropolitan
Club, to which they belonged through their sister
club in Chicago.

Her hair was coming in blond again, although it
was still short, to get rid of the brown dye. She was
going to get it trimmed before the wedding, by a
hairdresser Valentina had recommended. And Alex
was having his bachelor party the same night as
hers, in a private room in a nightclub downtown.

The bachelorette dinner was a big success. Abby
was staying at the apartment with them. Claire had
cleared the shoe boxes off her bed. And Abby confessed during dinner that she was dating Josh, and
she loved his boys. And Morgan talked about the
baby. They were already looking for an apartment,
and she wanted to move that summer before she
got too huge. Sasha and Alex hadn't found one but
were apartment hunting too. And they only wanted
something short term. Sasha was planning to trans-

fer her residency to the University of Chicago when Alex finished his. It appealed to both of them to establish their practices in his native city. And Sasha really liked that idea a lot, and living close to Alex's brother and parents.

Everyone discussed their plans, the wedding, the baby, Abby's movie. There was so much to talk about.

The women were all relaxed and happy when they got back to the apartment, and Claire looked at her mother ruefully.

"I guess it's just going to be you and me here, Mom. Everyone's moving out." It still made Claire sad when she thought about it. Her mother didn't say anything for a minute, and the others had all gone to bed, after a lot of champagne. Only Morgan wasn't drinking, but she had gone to bed too. Sarah took Claire's hand in her own with a sheepish expression, as they sat on the couch at two in the morning.

"I have some plans too. You don't really need me here anymore. The business is taking off. You've got Claudia to help you, and she's very good. And you know how to run this business without me. I've just been along for the fun and the ride, and to support you in the beginning. I'm still going to back you, but I think it's time for me to go home."

"To San Francisco?" Claire looked stunned. "I thought you love it here."

"I do. And it's been a fantastic five months. It's

been the best thing that ever happened to me, other than having you. Your father and I have been talking. He's really been trying. He stopped drinking two months ago, and he wants to start traveling and doing some things together. It may not be perfect, but I love him and we'd both like to try, and see how it goes." Claire looked both happy and sad. She had so loved having her mother there with her. It had filled a huge void for her, and given her an opportunity she would never have had otherwise. She was eternally grateful for that. And now she'd be living in the loft alone. It felt suddenly too grown up.

"When are you going?" Claire looked wistful. Her mother gave her a hug.

"I thought after the wedding might be a good time, in a month." Claire nodded. It was a lot to think about, but she could see that her mother thought it was the right thing to do. And her eyes lit up when she talked about doing things with Jim. And Claire knew she couldn't hang on to her mother forever. The past five months had been a wonderful reprieve from the blows that had come before that.

"You know, you need to think a little more about getting out too." They both knew what she meant, but Claire always said she wasn't ready. It had been six months since George had spun her around and dumped her, and she hadn't recovered yet. Her mother thought she should try. All Claire wanted to do was work, which had been her style before George too, and now even more so. But if her father could change, Claire wondered if she should too. It was a thought.

Claire and Sarah went to bed that night, in the bed that they shared, and it made Claire sad to think about her mother leaving. She turned over on her side in the dark and saw that Sarah was awake. "I'm going to miss you, Mom," she said softly. "Thank you for everything you did. I couldn't have done it without you. Everything had gone so wrong, and then you fixed it with the biggest gift of my life."

"That's what mothers are for," Sarah answered, and kissed her daughter's cheek, and they fell asleep holding hands. It was like being a little girl again, and she felt safe.

Chapter 23

The day of the rehearsal dinner, Sasha and her bridesmaids all went to get manicures and pedicures at a place Valentina recommended. Sasha had gotten her hair cut in a stylish bob for the wedding the day before, and it was all blond now. She couldn't wait to wear her new short sexy black dress that night. The girls were all laughing and talking at the nail salon when her father called her. They had arrived from Atlanta that morning, with the children and their nanny. Muriel was due in that afternoon, and the Scotts had arrived the night before. Alex and Sasha had stopped by the hotel to give them a hug. They were staying at the Plaza, and Ben went out with them afterward, and they stayed out too late, but had fun.

"What's up, Dad?" Sasha saw his name come up on her cell phone. She was off call, and officially on vacation since the day before, and had two weeks off for a honeymoon in Paris. She couldn't think of anything more romantic than Paris in June, with Alex.

"We have a little problem," he said to Sasha in a falsely calm voice.

"What's wrong?" Sasha was instantly on alert.

"Charlotte's having contractions, some pretty strong ones, and she's only seven months pregnant. This shouldn't be happening. She thinks she's in labor."

"Did she call her doctor?" Sasha asked in her professional voice.

"Yes, but she can't evaluate her over the phone. She thinks she should be seen. And to be honest, so do I. The pains are pretty powerful, and they're five minutes apart."

"Do you want me to recommend someone?" Sasha was instantly the doctor, and no longer the daughter.

"Would you take a look at her?"

"Does Charlotte want me to?" Sasha asked fairly.

"Yes, she does. We both do. Are you busy?" Sasha was stunned. **Me? Getting married tomorrow? With a rehearsal dinner for a hundred people tonight? Of course not. Just sitting here eating bonbons waiting for you to call.**

"That's fine. I can meet you at the hospital in twenty minutes," she recovered. Her nails were dry, and she was wearing sandals so she didn't mess up the polish on her toes, which was a pale shell pink, called Ballerina, by Chanel. When she told the others she had to leave, they pleaded with her to stick around—they were going back to the apartment to drink champagne.

"Charlotte has a problem. I promised my father I'd see her." She looked serious as she said it.

"Is she pregnant?" Morgan asked her, surprised.

"Seven months."

Claire rolled her eyes. "Your mother will love that."

"Won't she ever," Sasha agreed with her, and she left the nail salon and found a cab. She was wearing shorts and a T-shirt, and she got to the hospital ten minutes later and put on scrubs. Her father and Charlotte were right behind her. She was in a wheelchair and hunched over in pain. She looked like a woman in labor. At seven months, that was not good.

Sasha took them to an examining room in labor and delivery, and told the nurses she was there.

"Aren't you supposed to be getting married?" one of them asked her.

"Not till tomorrow. I was bored at home. Nothing good on TV," she said, and went to join her father and his wife. Charlotte was crying and scared.

"Were the girls early?" Sasha asked her calmly.

"No, they were late," she answered through another pain.

"What did you do today? Did you lift anything heavy? Your suitcase? The kids?"

"No . . . well . . . kind of. I picked Lizzie up for a

minute, but I've done that before. And she's pretty light." Sasha nodded. Normally that shouldn't have done it, unless she had a predisposition for preterm labor, which she didn't, and she was young.

"Did you have sex? Any fooling around?" she asked them, pretending to herself that he wasn't her father, and he looked sheepish, and Charlotte giggled. **Oh Christ.**

"Could that do it?" Charlotte appeared instantly guilty, and Sasha's father cleared his throat.

"It could. Orgasms can set off labor. Let's check things out." She smiled easily at both of them, as she would any patient, and Steve stood next to his wife's head as Sasha examined Charlotte. There was definitely some bloody show, but her waters were still intact, and her cervix was closed, so nothing major had happened yet. She reported her findings to them, and they were both relieved.

"But we're not in the clear yet. Those contractions will get things going if we don't stop them. If you don't mind, I'd like to give you a shot and see if that will stop the contractions. And I want you on bed rest for a few days."

"But I'll miss the wedding," she said, crushed.

"What would you rather have?" Sasha asked her gently. "Wedding cake and a baby born two months premature tonight or tomorrow, or a nice healthy baby in two months?"

"A baby in two months," Charlotte said sadly, and Steve leaned down and kissed her. "But I bought such a pretty pink dress for tonight, and a gorgeous red one for tomorrow."

"I'd feel a lot safer with you in bed, with no contractions," Sasha said honestly.

"Me too," Steve said in a firm voice as he held his wife's hand. "Can you give her the shot?" he asked, trusting his daughter and grateful for her help. She had been wonderful about it. She went to get it and came back a few minutes later, and Charlotte didn't even feel it. Sasha had a nurse hook up a fetal monitor, and everything was looking good. She noticed that the baby was big, but they said it wasn't twins and it didn't feel like it, just a big baby.

Sasha went back to the nurses' station then to see what was going on.

"You just can't stay away from this place, can you?" the nurses teased her, and Sasha noticed that it was five o'clock, and she called Alex to tell him where she was, and promised she'd make it to the dinner on time. She still had plenty of time to dress. And then she went back to check her stepmother again. The contractions were persistent, but slowing down a little. She waited two hours and gave her another shot, and sedated her, which she thought would help. By then it was seven, and she was going to be late for the dinner. She still had to bathe and dress.

The contractions stopped almost completely at eight after the second shot, and by then Charlotte was dozing, and Sasha told her father she should spend the night at the hospital. She could go back to their hotel the next day, but for now Sasha wanted the nurses to keep an eye on her and the monitor, and her father agreed.

"I think I should stay with her tonight," he said in a whisper, and Sasha nodded. His two daughters were at the hotel with the nanny. He was going to miss the Scotts' rehearsal dinner, but hopefully he'd be there tomorrow to walk her down the aisle, and she said as much to him.

"Of course." It was eight-thirty by then, and there was no way she could go home to dress. Alex had been texting her for the last hour, and she kept promising him she'd be there and not to worry. She couldn't miss her own rehearsal dinner the night before her wedding, and she couldn't get home to change. She only had one choice, to go as she was. It was better than missing it entirely, and she knew they weren't sitting down to dinner till nine.

She took a last look at Charlotte sleeping, and told her father to call if they needed her, and she told the nurses the same thing. And then she flew into the elevator in her scrubs, hailed a cab on the street, gave him the address, and told him she was in a huge hurry. And as they drove there, she realized that Charlotte had just solved a major problem. She couldn't come to the dinner or the wedding, and Muriel would never see that she was pregnant or have to deal with her looking young and beautiful. And her mother would only have to put up with her father for one night, not two, since he was staying with Charlotte tonight. **Yes!** she thought to herself, as they pulled up in front of the Metropolitan Club, and she paid and jumped out, and ran through the door. She was tempted to say to the liveried doorman as she ran by, "Did someone call a doctor?" but she decided to behave, and walked into the beautiful room filled with flowers at the dinner organized by her soon-to-be in-laws, in scrubs and sandals. It was either that, or arrive at ten, when they finished dinner. She saw Alex's look of surprise out of the corner of her eye, and her roommates' as she went to find Helen to apologize.

"I'm so sorry. My father's wife went into preterm labor, and I've been at the hospital with them till now. I couldn't get home to change." Helen smiled broadly, and gave her a warm hug.

"Don't even think about it. You look adorable. I love your hair. How is she?" She was an amazing woman, and Sasha hugged her again as Alex joined them.

"I think she'll be fine. I admitted her for tonight."

"What happened?" Alex asked her, jangled and shocked at what she was wearing.

"It was either this or my cut-off shorts. I went with this. Or come after dinner. Charlotte went into preterm labor."

"And they called you?" He was stunned, although he knew nothing should surprise him anymore— her mother, her sister, bad divorces, or preterm labor.

"Who else would they call in New York?"

"They could have gone to the ER. It's our rehearsal dinner." He seemed a little put out, but his mother was fine about it.

"I know. I'm sorry. I love you. But look at it this way, she's not here tonight, and she can't come tomorrow. I put her on bed rest. And now my mother won't go nuts." He laughed at the silver lining. And then after asking Helen's permission, she went up to the podium, from where Alex's father and some of the guests would be making speeches after dinner. And Sasha picked up the mike and spoke to the room.

"Good evening, everyone. I'm the bride. Until tomorrow, my name is Dr. Hartman. And I wanted you to know that, as my close friends and family know, these are the only clothes I own," she said, pointing to her scrubs, and everyone laughed. "But please don't worry. My sister is lending me a dress for tomorrow. And thank you to the Scotts for this wonderful dinner." She put down the mike then and ran to her table to take her place next to Alex.

"I hope that's not true," he said, serious for a minute.

"What?"

"That your sister is lending you a dress for tomorrow."

She laughed. "Wait and see."

Valentina was wearing a spectacular, very short

gold dress that night, and was there with Bert. He was proud to be at her side.

Helen had done the seating and had put Muriel at their table, and she made a point to spend time talking to her. Muriel looked like she was having a wonderful time. She caught up with Sasha later with a disapproving frown.

"Why didn't you wear a dress?"

"I got stuck at the hospital on an emergency," she said blandly, and her mother walked away shaking her head.

The speeches went smoothly, and were very touching, particularly by her roommates, and Alex's father. Her father was going to speak at the wedding, and Ben, the best man.

She and Alex parted company after the evening, so she wouldn't see him until the wedding. She was spending the night at the loft with the girls. And she called the hospital on the way home to check on Charlotte. They said she was sleeping soundly, the contractions had stopped, and they had rolled a cot in for Sasha's father. All was peaceful.

And Sasha went back to the apartment in Hell's Kitchen for her last night as a single woman, with her best friends.

Chapter 24

The big day dawned blue and gold and sunny on the fourteenth of June. It wasn't too hot or too cool, and Sasha was nervous all day. Her father and Charlotte had gone back to the hotel, and her father said she was resting and propped up in bed.

The hairdresser came at three o'clock to blow-dry Sasha's hair, and do the others. And she got her makeup done at four. She had bathed before they arrived. Sarah had made sandwiches for everyone, and Sasha couldn't eat. She was too excited. Her mother had offered to come downtown to help her, but Sasha didn't need her or want her, and she discouraged her. But Valentina was there, looking fabulous. Bert was going to meet them at the church. Amazingly, she was still seeing him three months after they had gotten back from Arizona, and Valentina insisted it was "the real deal." At least he kept her out of trouble. She'd been taking him to events and parties with her, and he was having fun. He was still with the NYPD, and the talk of his unit, with his supermodel girlfriend, and they were in the press a lot. Valentina seemed a little more normal now, and didn't seem as hell-bent on shocking everyone. He toned her down a little, and she had put some jazz and glamour into Bert's life. They had been mentioned on Page Six several times. They referred to him as supermodel Valentina's drop-dead gorgeous bodyguard. They were a striking pair.

And then the big moment came, and Sasha's friends lifted her wedding dress over her head, with Sarah's help. Abby stood on a chair to assist, and they were careful not to mess up her hair or makeup. The hairdresser attached the long lace veil to her short hair. As soon as Sasha was dressed, Alex called to tell her how much he loved her, and they talked for a few minutes.

The girls had covered the something old, something new department too. She had wrapped a lace handkerchief of her grandmother's around her bouquet, the dress was new, Valentina had given her a pale blue lace thong, and Sarah had lent her a string of pearls. It seemed sad to her for a moment that she had Claire's mother there to help dress her, and not her own, but she didn't want Muriel to spoil it, and she would have. Sasha didn't want to take the chance.

Her father was meeting her at the church, and she rode uptown alone in the limousine he had rented for her. And the girls rode in a second one, right behind her. She could feel them near her, cheering her on. And Prunella was waiting for them at the church in the rectory where they gathered, while Alex's groomsmen ushered people to their seats in the church, which the florist had filled with white flowers. Prunella immediately took charge when they arrived. She lined everyone up, in the proper order, with Valentina last in line, and Sasha's roommates ahead of her in order of height, Abby, Claire, and Morgan. And the moment her mother and the Scotts sat down in their pews, the procession began. There was a brief pause after the girls took their places at the altar with Alex's groomsmen, all friends from medical school, with his brother at his side as best man. And then Sasha and her father came down the aisle in stately elegance, and she could see Alex catch his breath as she walked toward him. It was the most perfect moment of her life.

They exchanged their vows and their rings, were declared husband and wife, Alex kissed her, and everything was a blur after that until the reception and her first dance with Alex and then her father. And then she nearly fainted when she saw her father ask her mother to dance, and Muriel smiled at him, and they danced and actually looked like they were enjoying each other.

Jim had flown in from San Francisco to escort Sarah to the wedding. And Josh was there with Abby in a real tuxedo, not a camouflage jacket, and they were smiling and holding hands. Abby's parents, Joan and Harvey, had flown in. And Max stood proudly beside Morgan. And Bert stood right next to Valentina the entire time and seemed more like a bodyguard than a boyfriend, but there was no denying he was gorgeous, and Sasha noticed later he was a great dancer, and her sister gazed at him adoringly and did nothing scandalous at the wedding or reception, and was surprisingly well behaved.

The penthouse location was perfect, and the night was warm and balmy. Everything was candlelit, and they had seated Ben Scott next to Claire, since they were both alone, and didn't have dates. Sasha wasn't sure she'd like him, but she saw them talking and laughing through most of the evening, and they danced several times.

"So what made you move to Hell's Kitchen?" he asked her when they first sat down, and she laughed.

"It was cheap and I was poor. I'm still poor, but not as poor as I used to be. And I still love it." He asked what she did, and she said she was a shoe designer and had just started her own business. It sounded interesting and fun to him, and she told him about the factory in Italy and the trade show in Las Vegas, and he seemed to enjoy hearing about it.

"It's going to be strange at the apartment now," she said wistfully during dinner. "I've lived there for nine years with roommates. One left in March, and the other two are moving out this summer."

"You're not ready to be alone there?"

"I'm not sure," she said honestly. "I've never tried it. I don't know if I'm that grown-up yet," she said, looking hesitant.

"Have you ever been to Chicago?" he asked her.

"No, I haven't." But she was planning to visit once Sasha and Alex moved there.

"You should come out sometime. Do you like to sail?"

"I love it. I'm from San Francisco. I used to sail on the bay as a kid."

"Have I got a boat for you!" he said, laughing, and they chatted all through the evening, when they weren't dancing, and Sasha elbowed Alex and pointed at them discreetly.

"Maybe we got lucky," she whispered.

"I always thought she'd be great for him," Alex confided to his bride. "I just didn't know how to get them together." The wedding was the perfect occasion.

"Now we just have to get her to Chicago," Sasha said, looking thoughtful.

"He's a big boy—he can afford a ticket to New York. I wonder if he's told her about the boat yet." They both laughed and then went to say hello to his mother and then hers. For once, Muriel had nothing bad to say. Sasha was shocked as she danced away in Alex's arms. "It looks like we have a policeman in the family, by the way," Alex commented. "I know it sounds crazy, but I think he's good for her. Have I told you lately how good you are for me?"

"Not in at least five minutes," she teased him. "Tell me again." And then he kissed her. And out of the corner of her eye, she could see Prunella everywhere, overseeing everything. She was great, wearing a severe black dress that made her look like a member of the Addams Family with her black hair. But she had done her job to perfection.

They went over to talk to Oliver and Greg then. They had been thoroughly enjoying the evening, and Oliver had danced several times with his sister and teased her about the bump. It had really popped in the last month. Morgan was proud of it now, and had adjusted to the idea, with Max's help. And as long as he promised they'd never marry, she agreed to have as many kids as he wanted.

Sasha was standing with all of her roommates later in the evening. They were reminiscing about the early days, and when Morgan and Sasha had moved in, and how well it had worked for so long.

"What are we going to do without each other?" Sasha said sadly.

"Fly around to see each other, I guess," Morgan said.

"Josh and I are moving back in a year," Abby assured them, and they wanted to believe her. And Claire looked at all of them and realized how lucky they were, and somehow remarkably they had found good men as their partners, despite their mistakes along the way. Josh was perfect for Abby and was launching her career, Alex and Sasha were made for each other. Max was the best thing that had ever happened to Morgan. And Claire had survived George's cruel madness, and as they stood together, Sasha could see Ben waiting at a discreet distance to dance with Claire again. And they all agreed that the loft in Hell's Kitchen would be home base to them forever.

"Come and stay with me whenever you want," Claire reminded them, and then Ben got up the courage to sweep her away from her friends and onto the dance floor.

"Now let's talk about your trip to Chicago to see our boat. The Fourth of July would be perfect," he was saying as they danced away.

It was time to cut the cake then. And after that to toss the bouquet, as Prunella handed Sasha the tossing bouquet so she didn't have to give up her real one. And all the single women lined up in orderly fashion under Prunella's direction, as the men stepped aside, and Alex watched his bride adoringly, waiting to take her away.

She stood on a little stool so she could throw the bouquet at them, and her toss was stronger and higher than expected as it sailed over the women's heads, past Claire, where she had aimed it. And without even meaning to, Greg instinctively reached out and caught it, as Oliver looked at him in amazement.

"It's the goalie in me," Greg said apologetically, and everyone laughed, and with a gallant gesture, he handed it to Claire.

Alex and Sasha lingered for a while and finally left the party, as everyone threw rose petals at them on Fifth Avenue, where a white hansom cab pulled by a white horse was waiting to take them to the Plaza for their wedding night before they left for Paris in the morning.

The last faces Sasha saw, as she turned to wave at them, were the three women she had lived with in Hell's Kitchen, standing next to their men. And Ben was with Claire with an arm around her. It was a pretty sight as the white horse clip-clopped them down Fifth Avenue toward the Plaza, and into their future. It was a beautiful night.

And the loft in Hell's Kitchen was in their hearts forever. It had all started there, and the love and bonds it had created would never end.

About the Author

DANIELLE STEEL has been hailed as one of the world's most popular authors, with over 650 million copies of her novels sold. Her many international bestsellers include **Property of a Noblewoman, Blue, Precious Gifts, Undercover, Country, Prodigal Son, Pegasus,** and other highly acclaimed novels. She is also the author of **His Bright Light,** the story of her son Nick Traina's life and death; **A Gift of Hope,** a memoir of her work with the homeless; **Pure Joy,** a tribute to the many dogs her family has loved over the years; and the children's books **Pretty Minnie in Paris** and **Pretty Minnie in Hollywood.**

danielesteel.com
Facebook.com/DanielleSteelOfficial
@daniellesteel

LIKE WHAT YOU'VE READ?

If you enjoyed this large print edition of
THE APARTMENT,
here are a few of Danielle Steel's latest
bestsellers also available in large print.

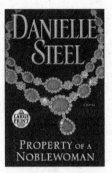

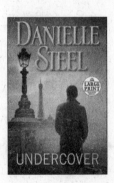